Sculpting Her Heart

Annette Mori

Affinity
Rainbow Publications

2021

ALSO BY ANNETTE MORI

One Shot at Love
Heart Strings Attached with Ali Spooner
The Panty Thief
Pleasure Workers
A Window to Love
The Book Witch
The Book Addict
The Dream Catcher
Free to Love with Ali Spooner
Unconventional Lovers
The Organization with Erin O'Reilly
Captivated
The Termination
The Review
The Ultimate Betrayal
Locked Inside
Out of This World
Asset Management
The Incredibly True Adventure of Two Elves in Love
(Affinity 2014 Christmas Collection)
Love Forever, Live Forever
The True Story of Valentine's Day
Vampire Pussy...Cat
Nicky's Christmas Miracle X3
(It's in Her Kiss, Affinity's Charity Anthology)

Sculpting Her Heart

© 2021 by Annette Mori

Affinity E-Book Press NZ LTD
Canterbury, New Zealand

1st Edition

ISBN: 978-1-99-004909-5

All rights reserved.

Editor: Angela Koenig
Proof Editor: Alexis Smith
Cover Design: Irish Dragon Design
Production Design: Affinity Publication Services

ACKNOWLEDGMENTS

A huge thank you to all of my beta readers who made great suggestions to improve the initial draft: Emily Cubbage, Erin Saluta, Ameliah Faith, Carrie Camp, Dana Holmes, and Danna Micoletti. Special thanks to Ali Spooner who is always my sounding board when I have a difficult issue to resolve. As always, I have to acknowledge Erin O'Reilly who is a constant support and encouragement to me. I am honored to call her a friend and have her support me in my journey. I would also like to express my gratitude to Affinity Rainbow Publications and the wonderful trio—JM Dragon, Erin O'Reilly, and Nancy Kaufman—who continue to provide feedback, to tighten up manuscripts that need assistance, and publish my unconventional work. I am eternally grateful for the opportunities they give me to let my stories see the light of day. I always enjoy working with the beta editor, Nancy Kaufman, who helped tighten my story. Thanks to Angie for her magic as the final editor to tighten the story even further. She is a delight to work with. Inevitably, there are those pesky final errors that slip through and I am thankful that Alexis Smith, the final proof editor, caught those before the book went to print. Thanks to Nancy Kaufman for the final cover. Nancy is also a promoter extraordinaire. A huge thanks to all the other readers and fellow writers who have sent personal emails, written reviews, and posted nice things on Facebook (you know who you are). The Affinity authors are an especially supportive group and often share posts or send words of encouragement. Finally, my wife, Jody, continues her support even when it interferes with our time.

DEDICATION

To all the beautiful men and women on the neurodiverse spectrum who bless us with their gifts, and as always, to my beautiful wife.

TABLE OF CONTENTS

Sculpting Her Heart

Annette Mori

Affinity
Rainbow Publications

2021

PROLOGUE

The fluttering iridescent green wings of the hummingbird temporarily distracted Zari Woods from her current work in progress. The sculpture featured the very distraction hovering in front of her studio. She was frustrated because she couldn't get the wings just right. She didn't know how to create the illusion of those beating wings. Zari thought about the fluttering colors, and then she thought about the fact that she'd never had a fluttering heart like she read might happen to a person in love. She wanted her heart to beat wildly in her chest for someone, but feared that would never happen because she wasn't sure she understood the concept of love.

Her hands stalled over the sculpture, and she felt a sense of loneliness. Achieving celebrity status had allowed Zari the independence she'd yearned for, but love was as elusive as peace on earth. The old adage that money can't buy you love kept running through Zari's head. Jillian, her best friend, had told her as much. Wealth wasn't the answer because interacting with people was tricky. She did okay with her parents and Jillian, but most other human interactions were riddles.

Creating clay models soothed her as much as petting her cat. Her sculpting had started as a way to calm her after one of her epic meltdowns. Allowing her hands to move across the slick texture in methodical repetition, as the sculpture came to life, created the perfect sensation to still the chaos. Once serenity was achieved, she could use the tips of her fingers with absolute precision to refine her art.

The staccato beep, beep, beep that filtered through the open window wasn't enough to detract her, but the pungent odor of diesel exhaust required Zari to seek the source. Her nose wrinkled at the commingling of her honeysuckle plant and diesel exhaust. The two smells did not go well together. She supposed this was a lot like how she never commingled well with anyone else. She hurried to her open window. Two fingers grabbed the edge of the curtain, pushing it aside to take in the sight of a large moving truck that had backed into her neighbor's driveway.

A bright-blue compact car pulled to the curb, and a woman gracefully emerged. Her long, dark hair whipped around her face until she reached into her jacket pocket to retrieve a hair tie. In one fluid motion, she wrapped the flyaway strands into a messy ponytail. While the stranger waited patiently for the two men in the truck to open the back door, Zari got a good look at her profile. Her delicate features came together in perfect symmetry. Zari felt compelled to stop working on the sculpture that had been giving her fits lately to begin one of her new neighbor. Not wanting to finish a project had never crossed her mind before.

Almost as if the woman felt someone staring at her, she cupped her hand over her brow and turned in Zari's direction. Zari didn't believe her new neighbor could see her through the crack in the curtain, but she let the material fall back into place. She wasn't ready to meet her yet.

Zari had heard that art imitates life, but she didn't know what that meant. Admirers of her work had often remarked how lifelike her sculptures were. Was she able to mimic emotion through her art, but never feel it? Zari had no idea that her life would soon take a dramatic turn. One that she'd been hoping for, while never believing it would happen.

CHAPTER ONE

ZARI

I'm twenty-six and still don't have a girlfriend. I've been trying for one since I was eighteen. I've done the research, tried to mimic the faces of those around me that don't fall on the spectrum, gone to the places my only friend recommended, but have not achieved my goal. I don't need to look in the mirror to see a sad face because, when I'm alone, I don't have to mimic anyone.

When I was younger, my mom and dad bought flashcards to help me recognize emotions. I would practice in the mirror to mimic the faces so people would realize when I was sad or angry. I thought it would help others as much as it trained me to know when I frightened a woman. If a potential girlfriend were afraid, that would never work. There isn't a flashcard for love. I asked my mom about that once, and her sad face appeared. I never asked again. But I wonder how I will know if someone loves me. I've learned people don't always tell the truth, and that's not because I take things too literally.

I have a new neighbor. She's pretty. As with every unfamiliar woman, I analyzed her for her potential. It's harder for lesbians because even though the statistics vary, none of the research shows an excess of ten percent of all women would be open to a relationship with another woman.

I like my neighbor's outward appearance, but I haven't introduced myself. I'm waiting to talk to my friend. She always has suggestions for how to approach strangers.

I'll need to practice my smile again. It's been a while. Jillian, my friend, sometimes says my smile is creepy, and I have to *tone that shit down, like a million times*. I didn't understand. So, she showed me by pushing my lips in a little and rearranging them like a glob of clay. I used to work with clay as a medium, but now I work with marble or other stone, except when creating my models. I wish I could sculpt the perfect expressions on my face for every occasion, but sculpting my face is a lot harder than creating my art.

"Not too wide, but show some teeth. Like this," Jillian said and then took a step back with her arms crossed. At first, I thought she was angry because when people cross their arms, it's one of those cues I need to pay attention to. Then Jillian nodded and smiled. I knew that the way she had rearranged my mouth pleased her.

"That's better. You have nice teeth, straight and white, so show them off, but not like a creepy stalker."

"Okay," I responded, but I wasn't sure what the difference was between how she'd rearranged my smile and a creepy stalker. Thankfully, Jillian knows me well.

She pulled out her tablet and began searching for a picture to show me. She pointed to a picture of a man peeking through a door.

"That's Jack Nicholson. Don't you think that's creepy as hell?"

I could see her point about the smile, but I focused on something else. "His eyes are scary."

"Yeah, I guess you're right." She began scrolling some more and pointed to another picture. "Now those are some scary eyes. Charles Manson. He was a serial killer. You don't want to look like a serial killer, that's all I'm saying."

"Ted Bundy was a serial killer. He was handsome, too. Should I avoid smiling like him?"

"Just show a medium number of teeth, and you should be okay." She nodded, and that meant she had finished the conversation.

I wasn't sure what a medium amount meant, but I let it go. Before I got better with people, I would have asked for precise measurements. For example, how many inches across? That can be creepy and annoying, too. I almost asked her about that but stopped myself as Jillian had taught me. If I can't ask questions, how will I know? It's hard having to monitor everything you say.

†

I pushed the curtain aside because I heard my neighbor's car. She was pulling sacks from the backseat and used her hips to close the door. She'd filled her arms with bags. I approved of her efficiency. She could have made several trips instead, and that would have left one arm free to close the door. A lot of other people would have done that. She looked over in my direction, and I hurried to close the curtain. I needed to call Jillian and ask her what to do. I tend to scare strangers, and I didn't want to do that with my new neighbor. I decided she was definitely girlfriend material but only if she was a lesbian or bisexual. Or perhaps gender nonconforming. That was a contemporary option that worked to my advantage.

I pulled my phone from my pocket and called Jillian. "She's home."

"Hi, Zari. Who's home?"

"My neighbor."

"And…"

I've learned from Jillian that when she says *and* without following that one word with more words, she needs additional information.

"I think I'm ready to meet her. She has sufficient attributes to be my girlfriend."

Jillian's laugh came through the tiny speaker too loudly. "First, make sure she's into women. Remember, no going after straight girls. Have you practiced your smile yet?"

"No. Should I do that first?"

"Maybe. But first, I have to ask why you think your neighbor is worthy of being your girlfriend?"

I understood enough that the question pleased me. Jillian's probe had a subtle message, and I rarely pick up on subtle. She was telling me I'm allowed to have a girlfriend, and I don't have to settle for just anyone.

"She's efficient and pretty."

"Well, then go out and buy a ring. You should ask her to marry you."

"It's too soon for that. I need to date her for at least a year before considering that level of commitment."

"Sarcasm, Zari. We've worked on this. I was being sarcastic."

"Oh, right. Sarcasm is hard when I cannot see your face."

"Good point. My bad. Okay, here's what you're going to do. Bake some of those awesome chocolate chip cookies and bring those over to her. You can welcome her to the neighborhood with fresh-baked goods. And don't be weird. No matter what she says, do not cite a bunch of random facts about anything."

"What will I say to her?"

"Keep it simple. Say something like 'welcome to the neighborhood.'"

"Should I tell her my name, or is it too early?"

"Yes, doofus, tell her your name and let her know you live next door. Then offer to help her settle."

"How would I help her settle?"

"I don't know. Maybe something needs fixing, or she needs help to move furniture." Jillian sighed. That was my cue that she'd reached her boiling point of exasperation. I had to get the rest of her advice out quickly—in case she tells me she has to take care of something, when I know she doesn't. I've gotten much better at recognizing untruths.

"I can do that. Especially if I research it."

"Don't tell her you need to research it. You can do that on the sly."

"How?"

"Tell her you need to get your tools or change into work clothes or something. Hey, Zari, I have to go now. Patty needs help with dinner prep."

"Okay." I hung up the phone and made my way to the kitchen to begin baking. I would bring the cookies over after breakfast. Tomorrow is a Saturday, and statistically, more people are home in the mornings on Saturdays. Not Sundays, because twenty-three percent of Americans attend church every week, even though that attendance is not only on Sundays. I'd still have better odds of delivering cookies on Saturday and meeting my pretty new neighbor.

✝

I'm lucky to have Jillian in my life to help me navigate nuances I'm unable to pick up on. When I was an adolescent, I thought I didn't have any interest in boys because that's just what happens when you're neurodiverse or a person with autism. I'm not supposed to say I'm autistic. I still haven't figured that out. My mom says I'm a person first, not a disorder.

Jillian helped me comprehend I'm also a person who is a lesbian. Even though I know lesbianism is not a disorder. I looked that up once. Jillian is also a person who is a lesbian. That's how she knows so much about being a lesbian.

Jillian was the new girl at our school. She arrived when I was thirteen. I think we became friends because we're alike in some ways. Everyone treated Jillian the same as me. They wouldn't talk to her and made the same face when she walked past that they made when they saw me. There isn't a flashcard for that face. One day Jillian made one for me and labeled it *stick up their ass.*

9

When I told her she was my friend only because everyone thought she was weird like me, Jillian said that wasn't true, and she didn't need to be friends with anyone. She was my friend because I was the only interesting person in that crummy school.

I asked my mom about that because I usually require a second confirming source. A third one is even better. But I didn't have a therapy appointment until later that week, and my dad was busy at work that day and didn't come home until late.

"Why is Jillian my friend?" I asked. "She doesn't think it's because nobody likes her either."

My mom's brows furrowed. "What exactly did you say to her?"

"You're my friend because everyone thinks you're weird like me."

"Zari, that isn't a very nice thing to say." She made her disappointed face.

"Should I have said it was because she wears black lipstick?"

"No, Jillian is a nice girl underneath that goth disguise. She's a good friend because you're genuine and truthful. There isn't enough of that in this world, and people like Jillian crave that. Plus, we all need someone in our lives to be there for us, and you are that person for Jillian."

"She says she doesn't need anyone to be her friend, especially a bunch of lame-ass phony Barbie Dolls who'd shit on your face after asking to borrow something from you."

Mom coughed at that. "Remember the rule of not repeating word-for-word everything someone says, particularly if there are swear words involved?"

That wasn't an answer I completely understood, so I looked it up. Science makes sense to me. The Internet helped me comprehend that people with friends live longer. Scientists found that social interaction releases a substance called oxytocin. That helps humans tolerate pain. Then I looked up oxytocin and found out it was the love hormone. So, I asked Jillian if she wanted to be my girlfriend. She didn't. I'm still trying to understand her explanation.

†

Once Jillian told me I was annoying because I cite random facts at inappropriate times. I also have something named hyperthymesia. That means I can remember almost everything in vivid detail. The annoying part presents itself when I share those memories. I've learned that I shouldn't share all my memories in great detail.

I don't understand why Jillian wouldn't want to remember when I asked her to be my girlfriend. Jillian says she doesn't want a replay of the day she hurt me because she loves me. Jillian was quick to add, but not like that. She had to explain what *not like that* meant. Jillian understands that I have feelings, and I'm grateful for that. In high school, I knew when people were treating me poorly, even without seeing Jillian's mad face. Most people don't think I have any feelings at all, but I do.

It was a sunny day, and we were sitting on the hard metal steps. Jillian was smoking a cigarette and blowing the smoke in the other direction because she knew I didn't like smoke in my face. Her eyes transformed into tiny slits, and I turned my head to see where she was looking. I'd learned by now that when something set Jillian off, she would get herself in trouble.

Kirk, the captain of the football team, was kissing his girlfriend, Felicia. He had his hands on her butt.

"Ugh, he looks like he's about to fuck her on the field, and *that's* acceptable behavior, but me wanting to take a girl to the dance isn't?" Jillian smashed her cigarette on the bleacher. I tried not to focus on the dirty cigarette because then I wouldn't get an answer to my next question.

"You want to take a girl to the dance?" I asked.

"Maybe." Her smile sprawled lazily across her face.

"I would go with you."

"I know you would, Zari. That's not exactly how I wanted to stir things up at this stupid, narrow-minded school."

"Why not?"

"Because you're my friend, not my girlfriend. Everyone knows that."

"Will you be my girlfriend, and then we can go to the dance and stir things up? I would like to kiss you and have sex. We can do that if we're girlfriends, right?"

I was proud of myself for asking because I'd thought a lot about Jillian lately. I'd decided she would make an excellent girlfriend. I was already used to her. Her positive traits far outweighed her negative ones. I'd read that opposites attract, and she was very opposite from me. She was messy and loud sometimes. I was neat and mostly quiet unless I had an episode. She had black hair, and I had strawberry blond hair. She wore black all the time, and I liked bright pastels. Plus, she was the only other lesbian in our school. At least that is what I thought until Jillian found the other one.

Jillian laughed. "Zari, you know I love you, but *not like that*."

"Please explain, *not like that*?"

"We're friends without benefits."

"Is friendship like a job where sometimes they offer benefits and other times they don't? I don't need benefits because my mom says Dad's plan covers all my healthcare."

"Not those benefits. I meant sex. Sex is a benefit in a relationship. I'm not the sort of person to have sex with my friends."

"You like girls, and I like girls. I don't understand why we can't be girlfriends."

Jillian sighed and made that face that told me I shouldn't continue to ask questions. "We're not having sex. If you want a girlfriend, I'll help you."

"Getting used to someone new will be hard. Is it because I have autism?"

Jillian pushed against my arm. "Shut up, no, you freak. I already told you. I like that you're more interesting than practically every other person in this school. No more questions."

I wanted to ask what she meant when she said practically every other person. Mari from the track team ended up being Jillian's girlfriend until the other girls on the track team found out. After that, Jillian didn't have a girlfriend anymore. She tried to help me get a girlfriend in high school. I never did.

CHAPTER TWO

FRANKIE

"I'm not mad," I insisted, gritting my teeth. I was. Sam could tell. We'd been together for three years, so the grinding of my teeth was a surefire giveaway. I tossed the remaining knickknacks into the box and used the roll of tape with gusto, closing the box. My actual feelings for the whole situation were showing in how I treated this inanimate object. I didn't have a right to be angry with Sam, but emotions are never rational. They exist without our permission.

"I never wanted you to move." Tears shimmered in the corners of Sam's eyes. "That wasn't why I told you about how I was feeling."

"I know." My throat tightened as I used every bit of strength to keep my tears at bay. Crying would not solve anything.

"A couple of weeks isn't going to make a difference. It'll be the end of the school year, and then I can help you move and settle into your new place."

"It's okay. The movers are doing most of the work. Are you going to be okay with the furniture I've left with you?" My voice softened.

I'd acted rashly as I made the preparations to move out of our cozy two-bedroom house in the questionable neighborhood and into the new gated community. The fact that she couldn't help me move on the day the movers were scheduled was unfair to her. I should not have expected her to take the day off. She was right. I could have organized the move after the school year ended when I didn't have to arrange for a substitute. I could never help her understand the urgency. I needed breathing space.

She reached out and brushed her hand over my cheek. "Yeah, all I really need is a bed, a chair, and a TV. You've left that and more. I have to go now, but let me take this last box out to the car. You've been up since five. It's the least I can do."

"Sorry. I couldn't sleep. I didn't disturb you, did I? You have that big presentation today, right?"

Sam nodded. "Yeah, I do. No, you didn't disturb me. We're going to be okay, right? This won't be for long." Her eyes had that hopeful look I'd learned to recognize when she wanted something badly.

I tried to smile. "One step back does not have to mean we won't take two steps forward given a little time and space."

"That's right. At least your new digs are comfortable. I've always wanted to live in a gated community. I'm kind of jealous about that. But if it means that down the road I get to live there, then I'll suffer alone for as long as it takes." She leaned in and kissed me, and I felt that familiar longing. Picking up the box, she turned away and walked to my car. With the last box neatly settled into the front seat, Sam climbed into her car and waved goodbye, punctuating closure to this chapter in my life. I still had hope that Sam and I would have other chapters, new chapters to look forward to—because this one sucked.

†

I was a glutton for punishment because I returned to the house that evening hoping to make up with Sam after our awkward goodbye. I'd waited for Sam to come home, but it was getting late. I was chopping vegetables for a healthy stir-fry. I cut everything up, and as soon as she came in the door, I would toss the ingredients into the wok. Not that I was a great cook or anything, but stir-fry was an easy dish that wouldn't result in a complaint from Sam.

The laughing I heard as the front door opened surprised me. Sam stumbled into the kitchen with a bottle of wine in her hand. Cori, her work friend, giggled as she held onto Sam's arm. Cori saw me first and took a step away from Sam.

"Oh, hi, um, I thought you moved out?" Cori shifted her feet.

I narrowed my eyes at Cori, then turned my focus to Sam. I couldn't be bothered by Cori's discomfort. Nor should I stoke my little green monster. We'd been over this territory before—ad nauseam. I had no cause to be jealous, but I was.

"I assumed you would be knee deep in unpacking boxes tonight," Sam said before setting the wine on the counter.

I sliced through the awkwardness of the situation. "I thought it would be a nice gesture to make dinner. I know that after a big presentation at work, you either want to celebrate or process what went wrong." I was sending a not-so-subtle message that I knew Sam better than Cori.

"Um, yeah, we were going to celebrate because Cori helped me with the presentation. I offered to buy her dinner as a thank you. We were going to order from that new Thai takeout restaurant," Sam replied.

"I'll just chop a few more vegetables, and Cori can join us for dinner." I glanced over at Cori and painted a fake smile on my face.

Cori volleyed back with her own version of acceptance. Her smile barely resulted in a show of teeth. In fact, she looked constipated.

"Sounds great." Sam's clipped voice revealed how far removed this was from whatever she had envisioned for the evening.

"It looks like the two of you started early. A celebration, I presume." My eyebrow undoubtedly rose to my hairline.

"Uh yeah. We had a couple of drinks at Beau's, then decided to come back here with the wine I bought." Sam pointed unnecessarily to the bottle of wine on the counter. "Would you like a glass? I'll open the bottle while you finish chopping."

"Sure, but make it a small glass. I still have to drive back tonight." I hoped the tinge of sadness did not reach my voice. Initially, I had planned on staying the night. Not living together didn't mean we'd called it quits. We were still together—sort of. It was complicated.

"Okay." Sam had agreed too quickly, which meant I would definitely not be staying the night. My romantic gesture had officially entered the garbage pail.

The evening's painful conversation felt like nails on a chalkboard. The last bite had barely entered my stomach before I made my move to exit. Two is company, and three is a crowd. I hated crowds. My wooden chair scraped against the worn tile of our kitchen floor—correction, Sam's floor. I made quick work on the dishes while Sam and Cori finished the bottle of wine. To be fair, both of them offered to help clean up, but I waved my hand in the air and brushed aside their offer of assistance. Having something to occupy my hands was essential before I acted out my fantasy of pouring the remainder of the red wine into Cori's lap.

Sam walked me to the door and offered me a consolation prize. The kiss was soft and lovely but not full of promise like it might have been if I had stayed.

"Hey, don't forget how much I love you," she whispered. "I'll call you tomorrow, okay?"

I hung onto her promise of love. I needed to believe that eventually, given time and space, we'd work it all out because we loved each other. Didn't love conquer all?

CHAPTER THREE

ZARI

I held the plate of cookies in my left hand and knocked on the front door. My pretty neighbor opened after the fourth knock. I do almost everything in fours. Odd numbers unsettle me.

The corner of her mouth lifted, and she said, "Hello."

I thrust the cookies at her. "Here, I made them today, so they're fresh. I read that there were five ways to give cookies to your neighbor. Even though I like the number four, I chose the visit, which is the fifth way because your car is in the garage, and I couldn't do the car drop with a note. Did you know that twenty-eight percent of Americans don't know the names of their neighbors? I read that in the same article."

She smiled wider, and I decided I liked her smile. It was big, but not scary big like mine could sometimes be.

"Well, I still don't know your name, and you don't know mine. I'd rather be in the majority."

"I'm a lesbian." I thought it was best to get this out right away. I was hoping she would tell me how she identified. Sexual preference was not the right terminology anymore.

She chuckled. "Um, okay. I still want to know your name. I'm Frankie."

"I knew a Frankie once. He worked on my mom's car. You don't look like a Frankie."

She smiled again. "Maybe not, but that's my name. Perhaps you can give me yours now. I assume you're my neighbor."

"Yes, I am. I live next door."

"Ah, yes, the curtain mover. So, is your name a national secret?"

"No."

"Then, can you please tell me your name?"

"Polite manners. That's good." I wanted to pull out my notepad to mark that off as one more trait appealing to me for a potential girlfriend, but she hadn't accepted my cookies yet, so I didn't. She stood there waiting, and I finally understood I still hadn't given her my name. "Zari."

Frankie took the plate of cookies and opened her door wider. "See, now that wasn't so hard. Come in. I have a fresh pot of coffee that would be perfect with your cookies. How decadent to have cookies for breakfast. I say we throw caution to the wind and do just that."

"I had breakfast already. I can't have a snack until two. I can come back then."

"No, no, you don't have to eat a cookie with me, even though eating sweets alone might be the saddest thing." She laughed. "Please come in and tell me more about the other ways to give your neighbor cookies."

I've learned that whenever someone laughs after making a statement, I'm not to take their words literally. Jillian says that's a rule to always follow. Even though there are a lot of regulations in the world, they make things easier for me. I didn't ask why me not having a cookie until two would make her sad.

"Okay. I would like that. Just so you know, I'm neurodiverse, a person with autism," I added. Jillian taught me that not everyone knows what neurodiverse means, but autism is a word most people understand.

She smiled widely again. "I know."

"Jillian says I shouldn't tell prospective girlfriends that until at least the second date. I don't think that's true because they always seem to know, and it explains my odd behavior. How did you know?"

"My sister. She's on the neurodiverse spectrum and one of the coolest people on the planet."

I nodded. "That's good. I haven't been too weird yet, have I? Jillian says I shouldn't talk too much at first because people can only take my weirdness in small quantities. I asked how much specifically, but she never answered. Do you know the answer?"

"I don't think there is a specific rule that applies to everyone. So far, you haven't been too weird with me. Come." Frankie walked farther into her home.

I followed her into the large, open room and waited while she set the cookies on the counter and pulled two cups from a cabinet. I had to get used to coffee at different times of the day because Jillian told me coffee was an excellent first date option. As I looked around her home, I noticed her place was neat except for a few boxes sitting in a corner.

"Do you think opposites always attract? The data seems unclear on this. I like that your home is tidy. I'm very tidy, and that would mean we aren't opposite." I remained standing, waiting for Frankie to answer. I was eager to hear her response because, so far, she met all of my criteria for a girlfriend. Even though I could work with someone messy, I preferred a tidy girlfriend.

"I think love is a lot more complicated than what you may have read in a series of Internet articles." Frankie picked up her pot of coffee and filled both cups, leaving room for cream. "Cream and sugar?"

"Yes, please. Both. Four tablespoons of cream and two teaspoons of sugar are the precise amounts. Or if you have those small containers of non-dairy flavored cream, four, please."

"Thanks for the specific instructions." She opened a drawer and pulled out a set of measuring spoons and followed my directions precisely. I needed to ask Frankie if she was a lesbian before asking her to be my girlfriend because she met all my criteria.

"Are you a lesbian?"

"I am." After putting the correct amount of cream and sugar into my coffee, she pushed the mug in my direction.

"Do you have a girlfriend?"

"Not exactly."

"That's not a very precise answer."

"No, I don't suppose it is, but until I know you a little better, it is the only answer I have to give. It's complicated enough that I wouldn't know how to be precise with an answer."

"I don't like complicated."

"Neither do I." Frankie half smiled, and I recognized a sad face beneath the happy one. Smiles don't always mean someone is happy. "Yet, complicated is what I have. Come on, grab your coffee, and let's go into my living room."

"I like this open space. It's like my house and the home I grew up in. I've been to homes where the kitchen and living room were separate. I don't like those. I could get used to your home more easily because it is so similar."

Frankie chuckled. "My old place was tiny and old, and the kitchen and living room were separate. I like this layout better, too."

"Is that why you moved?"

"No, I moved because my father insisted on helping me buy this house, and I was too tired to argue with him anymore. I also needed to move out of my old house for other reasons. Teachers don't make a lot of money, and my old neighborhood was questionable."

"Questionable?"

"Yeah, it wasn't very nice and a tad dangerous."

"We have a gate. Gates are a barrier to keep out dangerous people."

"Yes, they do. But honestly, access gates are pretentious to me. The heavy-duty security will take a little getting used to. You must have a good job to afford to live in this neighborhood."

"I work at a nursery, but that isn't how I make money. My friend, Jillian, owns the nursery, and I work there because I like plants. Plants are easier to understand than people. I'm good with plants. She lets me grow clover because I'm always looking for a four-leaf clover. It's a mutation, and when you find one, it's easier to find another. I like to dig them up carefully and grow them in separate pots. They're popular at the nursery. The *Oxalis deppei* always has four leaves and looks like a clover, but it's not. It's a wood sorrel. I think that is cheating to grow those and have them in the nursery. They aren't rare."

"I could use a little luck. Maybe I should come by and buy one." Frankie picked up one of the cookies and took a big bite.

"Jillian said I should bring cookies. Maybe I should have brought a four-leaf clover plant."

After she held up one finger and finished chewing, Frankie responded, "No, cookies are better. Jillian was right."

I stood. "I should go. Jillian says that it isn't good to overstay your welcome or spend too much time on a first encounter. She thinks I'm more palatable in smaller doses, especially with new people."

"No, don't go. Unfortunately, Jillian is probably correct with most of the idiots in this world, but I'd like you to stay a little longer, even if you don't eat cookies with me. You haven't even sipped your coffee to tell me if I added the precise amount of cream and sugar that you like."

I sat. "I watched you. I can already tell you were precise, but I'll confirm that for you." I picked up the cup and took a small sip. "There is the correct amount of coffee to cream and sugar ratio. Thank you."

"This is a very spendy neighborhood to live in. You mentioned that working at the nursery isn't how you make a living. What do you do?" Frankie bit into her cookie again.

"I sculpt, and people want to buy what I create. I started sculpting when I was younger to help me focus. It calms me. When one of my teachers noticed my creations, she helped get me a scholarship to attend art school. Now, everyone wants my sculptures, even the ones I did in high school."

Frankie brought her hand to her mouth. "Oh, my God, you're Zari Woods. My father bought one of your sculptures. I've been coveting that piece of art for forever."

"Forever is an impossibility. It's the same as infinite. Everything ends. When did you first see the sculpture?"

"Maybe a year ago." After popping the rest of the cookie in her mouth, she picked up a napkin and wiped both her mouth and fingers. That simple gesture mesmerized me.

"Then you have been coveting the sculpture for one year. I could be more precise if you told me the date and time."

Frankie laughed. "Time sometimes escapes me. I can be precise with many things, but the recollection of specific dates and times always eludes me. History was not a subject I had much of an affinity for."

"You're easy to talk to."

"Thank you, Zari. I enjoy talking with you, too." Frankie picked up a cookie from the plate and held it out to me. "Are you sure you don't want one?"

"No, but eat another one. One cookie missing from the plate will leave things uneven." I had stacked the plate with four cookies to each level, like alternating four-leaf clovers. "Four would be best, but that's a lot of cookies for breakfast."

"That's why I think you should help me. I know new routines are hard, but there has to be a first time for everything, right?" Frankie grabbed another cookie, and that left two cookies on the top layer. It was lopsided, which bothered me

25

because she hadn't picked the second cookie that lay directly across from the first cookie she had selected.

"Good point." I wanted to ensure she removed the entire top level of the stack of cookies. When she handed me two cookies, I put one on the napkin I'd taken from the pile on the coffee table and bit into the one in my hand. Now there were four cookies on top, but only three layers. I shifted uncomfortably in my seat.

Frankie looked at the plate of cookies and then lifted her eyes to mine. "You're uncomfortable because there are three layers of cookies instead of four, right? I don't suppose you'd like to eat another two cookies, would you?"

"No, thank you." I was already doing something outside of my routine. I didn't believe I could eat more without feeling full, and my discomfort was increasing as I looked at the odd number of layers on the plate. "I need to go now."

"Would it help if I removed the plate of cookies? I can't bring myself to throw out four perfectly wonderful chocolate chip cookies. Which, by the way, are my favorite."

"They are?"

"Yes."

Her smile distracted me, and I tried hard to focus on that instead of the cookies. It didn't work because the odd number of layers bothered me too much. I stood.

"I'll bring more tomorrow. Jillian says I make the best cookies."

"Our friendship will result in me gaining one hundred pounds."

"That would be a lot of weight. I suppose if your body distributed the weight in relative proportions, that would be okay. People assume obese women are unhealthy, but that's not always true. A government study revealed that twenty-nine percent of obese people were metabolically healthy. Thirty percent of people with normal weight were metabolically unhealthy. But, if you ever want to get another job, that might pose a problem. In a survey of five hundred hiring professionals, only fifteen-point-six percent would hire a woman who is overweight. I don't think that's fair."

"It's not. I'm not worried."

"Okay." I pivoted toward Frankie's front door. I was already planning my day, and at the top of the list was making more cookies now that I knew they were her favorite. Before I walked out of her front door, I asked, "Do you attend church?"

"Not for a very long time."

"How long?"

One side of her face wrinkled, and she looked at her ceiling. When I was younger, I thought when people did that, they had somehow written the answers to my questions on their walls or ceilings, but Jillian said that's just what people do sometimes when they're thinking.

"At least ten years."

"Okay. I'll come by again tomorrow since you won't be attending church."

Frankie laughed, and then her smile looked more like when Jillian would do something that resulted in detention for her. "Cinnamon rolls are much better breakfast food. They're generally more acceptable, and they're my favorite breakfast. Even better than chocolate chip cookies."

"Would you prefer that over cookies?" I asked.

"Sorry, I shouldn't have done that. I would like you to come again tomorrow and have breakfast with me. I can't promise my rolls will be any good, but I think I should be the one to bake for you after your nice gesture today."

"Are you good at baking?"

She shook her head. "Not even a little bit."

"Don't make the cinnamon rolls, then." I waved goodbye and knew the first thing I planned to do would be to look up how to make cinnamon rolls. YouTube was a better resource than an online recipe.

CHAPTER FOUR

FRANKIE

When the curtain fluttered at my new neighbor's home, I glimpsed the young woman peeking through the drapes. I wondered why such a modern house had curtains instead of blinds. I was already regretting my decision to accept my father's gift. I didn't belong in some hoity-toity gated community. I wasn't sure where I belonged in this town, but I knew they needed me. Resources for special needs kids were usually inadequate in rural communities, but so were potential partners. Not that I was looking for one. I tried to keep some hope that Sam and I would work despite our vastly different perspectives about almost everything. Why I'd agreed to try an open relationship, I'll never know. Sure, I was still young and probably needed to sow my oats, but that was never me. I only ever wanted one special person. For as long as I could remember, one was always enough for me.

The glimpse I caught of the woman made me smile. Blonde. I had a thing for blondes. She was undoubtedly some rich straight girl still living with her parents. Even after hundreds of thousands of dollars spent on a college education, getting a job wasn't always guaranteed, even for wealthy kids from good families. I suppose I wanted to earn my first job. I had a unique way of connecting with the kids. Many of the other teachers didn't have the required patience. I don't know why I still resented my father for pulling a few strings for me. I shouldn't have needed his help, and now I would never know if his meddling or my skills as a teacher was the reason for my current position. Dad seemed to overcompensate with me. I think he thought I was resentful of the amount of attention he paid to my older sister when I was growing up. I wasn't. I loved Penny. She needed his focus. My younger sister had no problem taking his guilt money. She dutifully followed in his footsteps and joined his law firm. Dad had a vision of what I should do with my life, but unfortunately, his vision did not match my own.

I needed to take care of my groceries before the ice cream melted and didn't give my neighbor a second thought as I continued to unpack. The knock on my door the next morning, at what most young people considered an ungodly hour for a Saturday, surprised me.

My beautiful new neighbor stood on my front stoop with a plate of cookies. The sun was reflecting off her strawberry-blonde hair, picking out the red highlights, like ripe fruit. Her deep blue eyes blinked once, and I only caught a glimpse before she looked away. She was beautiful, naturally. Lightly tanned skin revealed the fact that she didn't spend all day inside. I wondered what she did for a living. She looked like she was in great shape.

It might be a gated community, but at least one neighbor was friendly. After she thrust the plate at me, wouldn't meet my eyes, and began spouting facts about the unorthodox ways to give cookies to a new neighbor, I knew. I suppose other people would have judged her behavior as odd. I didn't. I was more comfortable with kids and adults on the spectrum than with my on-again, off-again girlfriend, or my old friends at school who could be cruel and laser-targeted with their taunts. I still beat myself up for how I acted in high school, but I had wanted to fit in rather than be the new kid with the odd older sister.

I didn't know how to answer her question about whether I had a girlfriend. If I didn't quite understand the answer, I knew Zari never would.

For the first time in a very long time, I was looking forward to something—Zari's promise to visit on Sunday, even if it was briefly. I knew she would come around at the same time, so I set my alarm for seven and jumped in the shower. I'd gone back to the store the previous evening to find the small containers of creamer. The big-box store wasn't my favorite place to shop, but I knew they would have the item versus the local grocery store. It would be easier to use them instead of measuring out four tablespoons of creamer. It was a crapshoot whether Zari would notice how I'd gone out of my way to please her. I didn't care. It was enough to know that this insignificant gesture would make her happy. I wanted to see her try to smile again. She had a beautiful mouth with perfect teeth, even if I could practically see every one of them. I was used to seeing my sister smile too widely to find Zari's smile unnerving.

Four crisp knocks on my front door alerted me to Zari's arrival. I was ready for her this morning. She held two square pans stacked on top of one another. Through the plastic wrapping folded carefully on top, I could see four flawlessly situated cinnamon rolls with evenly spread icing on each one.

"I don't normally eat cinnamon rolls for breakfast," she said. That was her morning greeting as she looked anywhere but into my eyes.

"Good morning, Zari. Well, I'd say you were missing out. Let me guess. You have a more traditional breakfast."

"If by traditional you mean oatmeal with fruit, yes I do."

"Did you have your oatmeal already? I hope you didn't because I can't eat all these rolls by myself, and the only food items that go as well with coffee are cookies and scones."

"I'll make scones for you tomorrow, but you probably have to work. What time do you leave?"

"Come in, and we'll talk about that."

I'd already poured her coffee, but I waited to add the cream and sugar. I set both pans on the counter and then added the cream first. She watched me with rabid fascination. I could see her counting the number of creamers. She nodded in satisfaction. I motioned for her to sit on the couch in my living room.

"I'll carry the coffee," she offered.

"Let me dish these up for us, and I'll be right in. They look scrumptious." That earned me one of her too-wide smiles.

Zari placed the two cups on the table with precision. She sat as if someone had strapped an invisible board to her back, with her hands neatly clasped in her lap as she waited for me to finish. I tried to place the two plates next to the coffee cups as if I'd used a tape measure to ensure the correct distance. I knew I'd failed when she readjusted both of them. I wondered if the distance was a multiple of four. That number seemed to have a great deal of meaning for her.

"Homemade cinnamon rolls require advanced preparation. I didn't mind getting up early to bake them this morning. I needed to let them rise overnight." Zari turned her head and glanced in my direction, finding a spot somewhere to the left of my shoulder, but she continued to sit quietly with her hands still resting in her lap.

"Did you learn how to make them by searching the Internet?"

"Yes, there were a lot of recipes to choose from and several YouTube videos. I selected the longest video with an advertisement claiming to explain why dogs eat poop. I don't own a dog, but I listened to the video anyway in case you have a dog."

"I don't have a dog, but I have a cat. Her name is Cleopatra, because she is most definitely a queen. She's a little skittish with new people."

"So am I. New people don't tend to be as nice as you. The video was deceptive. It was an ad for a powder to add to dog food. The ad talked about the different kinds of poop coming out of a dog based on what a dog eats, but I never learned why dogs eat poop."

"Okay, wow. That's a very odd pairing for a video on how to make cinnamon rolls. I know there are usually ads attached to instruction videos because that's how the YouTubers make money, but I would think they'd pick something related to baking. I need to push those pictures out of my head, or I won't be able to enjoy what I assume will be the best cinnamon rolls I've ever tasted."

I dished up the treats. After taking a large bite, I discovered they were amazing. I chewed quickly to let Zari know how much I appreciated her baking them for me. I moaned in delight, and I let the soft, gooey goodness coat my taste buds. "Mmm, these are heavenly," I stated as I swallowed my bite.

"They don't pair ads with a specific topic. Viewer preferences drive the ads. Since I like animals, advertisers assume I will want to watch ads for pet food or nutritional supplements. I had a cat growing up, and she helped to calm me when I became upset. Petting her was the sort of repetitive behavior that allowed me to settle and focus. Jillian said she would come with me to the shelter to pick out a new cat. Ivy was an exceptional companion." Zari gingerly picked up her cinnamon roll and nibbled at the corner.

"Ivy? Tell me why you named her Ivy."

"For the roman numeral IV, which means four. Four is my favorite number."

I laughed. "Ah, that makes perfect sense."

"I have a favorite color, too. Jillian's used to be black, but black isn't a true color. It's the absence of color. Jillian eventually grew *out of that phase*. That's what my mom said. My mom said that Jillian was a nice girl who was covering up her pain with rebellion. Goth is considered rebellious. Jillian loves my mom because she says my mom always sees the good in people, even when it's hard to find. It was easy for me to see the good in Jillian. Do you have a favorite number or color?"

"You won't like my favorite number. It's odd, as in an odd number. My favorite color is blue. The same shade of blue as your eyes. They're extraordinary."

Zari blessed me with direct eye contact for a fraction of a second. "Jillian says my eyes are cerulean like the Caribbean Sea, and she wished she had chick-magnet eyes like mine. Magnets attract metals, not people. That's why I have a hard time finding women to go out with me and become my girlfriend because my eyes aren't really magnets."

"You just haven't met the right ones."

"That's what my mom said. I should go now." Her eyes remained focused on the table. "Overstaying my welcome decreases my chances of establishing a relationship." Setting the remainder of her roll back on the plate exactly in the center, she then turned her wrist to look at her watch. "I only have five more minutes before I have to go to my studio. Should I make scones for tomorrow?"

I was having fun talking with Zari. I'd been around both kids and adults who were on the spectrum, but had never considered dating any of the women I found attractive. Zari had developed adaptive behaviors that I was sure would allow her to find a partner, but that wouldn't be me, because I was still trying to come to terms with my open relationship. Dating Zari while maintaining whatever I had with Sam was a terrible idea. If I didn't understand the rules, I knew Zari never would. That didn't stop me from blurting out an invitation to see her again.

"No, don't bake me anything new. I was serious about not wanting to gain one hundred pounds. How about you come over for dinner tomorrow night? I may not know a lot about baking, but I make a mean lasagna."

Zari tilted her head and glanced fleetingly at me. "I like lasagna. I eat dinner at 5:30."

"Perfect. That should give me plenty of time to put the meal together and pop it into the oven. Should I serve wine with dinner?"

"Jillian gave me alcohol once in high school. She told me I acted more normal after drinking, but I didn't like the taste very much and later got sick. Even though I want to be normal, I decided it wasn't worth the side effects."

"Wish I'd learned that lesson. Although, having only one glass of wine won't normally result in someone getting sick. I think the key is moderation."

"Okay. I will try for moderation. Is this a date?"

"How about we just say I'm enjoying spending time with you and getting to know your likes and dislikes so that I can be a good neighbor."

"Wikipedia isn't always accurate, but I looked up *dating* on Wikipedia, and according to my other research on dating, dinner seems to be an acceptable way to assess my suitability as a prospective partner to have an intimate relationship with. I've already made my decision, so I thought maybe you needed more data."

"Remember when you asked if I have a girlfriend? I didn't give you a very good answer. I can try to explain, but if I don't understand the parameters, I can't expect you to. Sam and I have an open relationship. That means we can date other people. It isn't my choice to be open, but I've accepted this new wrinkle because I'm not quite ready to give up."

"Perseverance. That's a good trait to have. People say I'm persistent, too. I keep trying to find a girlfriend despite the difficulty and how long I've been on this quest. If this open relationship isn't your choice, do you mind if I keep trying with you?"

"I don't mind spending more time with you, but I can't make any promises. Friendship is something I can offer. Frankly, I could use a good friend right about now." All the friends I had were mutual friends with Sam. She'd introduced me to every one. I didn't have my own set of friends separate from Sam. As I thought about my pathetic social life, Zari interrupted my internal pity party without remarking on my offer of friendship. I hoped it was acceptable to her.

"Five minutes have passed. I'll see you tomorrow, Frankie. I hope you have a good day." Zari stood and walked to the front door with her back rigid.

"You, too."

She turned to look at me before stating, "Today is a free day, but I'm going to sculpt today because sometimes an idea gets stuck in my head, and I have to sculpt to set it free." With increasing frequency, Zari honored me with sustained eye contact.

"Will you show me your work someday?"

"Yes, but not on sculpting day." Zari waved and walked out the door.

†

On Monday, I walked into my classroom, and two of my students had a meltdown within five minutes. I knew it was not going to be a stellar day for me. Despite daydreaming about my enjoyable morning with Zari on Sunday, the day kept getting worse until Sam called during my lunch hour. When I saw her name pop up on my screen, I wasn't sure which warring emotion would prevail. On the one hand, I was excited to hear from her after radio silence for two days. She'd offered to help me move in, but after our conversation where she'd laid out her needs to see other people, I wasn't in the mood to have her touching my stuff or deciding where I should put it.

Zari's words snuck into my subconscious about the open relationship not being my choice. I wondered if I was accepting something I shouldn't, hoping that with enough time, Sam would choose me and we'd live happily ever after. Or was I kidding myself that it would all work out?

I excused myself from the teachers' lounge to take the call. Before answering, I breathed in and out to center myself. "Hey, what's up?"

"Hi, gorgeous. I have tickets for Brandi tonight, wanna go?"

Something did not add up about this last-minute invite. I knew that Brandi Carlile tickets were never available at the ninth hour. "How did you manage to get those tickets this late? I heard they sold out in two days. I sure hope you didn't pay an outrageous amount using our joint card. My father is wealthy, not me."

"Of course not. I bought these tickets when they first went on sale. I used my own money."

"So, why the last-minute invite?"

"Cori can't go. She had to go home for a family emergency or something."

Now I was pissed. Not only did Sam buy the tickets for her to take another person, but she had to have known this well before we'd had the conversation about trying to have an open relationship. We hadn't set the rules yet. Plus, she knew how much I loved Brandi.

"I have plans already."

"You do?" She sounded genuinely surprised. "On a Monday night? A school night?"

"Yes, I do. You didn't think I was going to sit at home every evening waiting until you called for us to get together, did you?"

"Honestly, yes. It's what you do. Plus, you never go out on a school night."

She was right. I didn't go out on school nights, except for special occasions. A Brandi Carlile concert certainly fell into the category of a special occasion. She knew I'd have to leave a little earlier from work if we were to make it to the concert in time, and it would be a long night, leaving me exhausted the next day at work.

I preferred staying at home more often than not, even on the weekends. The bar scene had lost its interest for me. I was an old person way before my time. Most women in their twenties were still going out to bars on the weekends. Occasionally I joined Sam when she went to the bars, but I didn't enjoy it as much as she did.

"I have to go, Sam. My kids are waiting for me. Call me when I'm your priority instead of a back-up date."

"You said you'd give this a try. It doesn't sound like you're trying very hard."

"I moved out and accepted my father's guilt house. What more do you want? Never mind. I am not having this conversation with you over the phone on the tail end of my lunch hour. Goodbye, Sam. Have fun at the concert tonight."

I hung up and felt a minuscule amount of satisfaction about having plans and throwing Sam off-kilter for once. I needed to cancel that credit card. Just because she hadn't used it to buy the tickets for Brandi didn't mean she wouldn't for some other purchase unrelated to household goods. We no longer lived together. There was no need for a joint household card.

†

I arrived home in plenty of time to heat my sauce and put together the lasagna. What I didn't anticipate was another phone call from Sam. She knew what time I arrived home after work, so I should have expected another call from her. Sam didn't appreciate it when I blew her off. Ever. When I first met Sam, I thought no one could ever make me feel more alive or worthy of love. Always surrounded by friends, she had an entire entourage around her. A lot of people commanded her attention, but I felt like I was the only one who mattered. She had a way of making a person feel like they were the center of her universe. Until they weren't.

I debated whether to answer my phone. I tossed my keys in the bowl and felt the buzz in my sling pack. She'd keep calling until I answered.

I sighed and removed the phone from my bag. "Hi, Sam. I hope you're on your way to Seattle. You know how traffic can sometimes be a total bitch. And parking."

"I am. I just wanted to check in with you because our conversation was cut short earlier. We should talk about things. I haven't stopped loving you, you know. Come on. You aren't even trying to make it work. So, who is she?"

"Ah, the real purpose for the call. You can't stand not knowing who I have plans with tonight. I thought the rule was, no names. Although, you didn't seem to adhere to that rule when you revealed you had invited Cori to see Brandi Carlile."

"I'm sorry that slipped out. Is it someone we know?"

"I am not having this conversation while you drive to Seattle. I sure hope your date isn't in the passenger seat listening. That's rude, even for you, Sam."

"Of course she's not listening. I'm meeting her there."

"Still not having this conversation over the phone."

"Fine, have dinner with me on Friday. We can go to your favorite place. I'll buy. For the record, I am not using the joint credit card. That was for household expenses. Since we no longer share a household, I have it tucked away. I can't believe you think so little of me. I might not have a rich daddy, but I do have integrity."

"Why even keep the card? Do you think we'll move back in together after this experiment runs its course?"

"Frankie," she began in her patient voice, "we're twenty-seven, not sixty-seven. Making a lifetime commitment this early isn't the smartest idea. And yes, I believe that eventually, we'll both be ready for that level of commitment. Just because I want to explore other people doesn't mean I don't love you or want to spend time with you. Friday?"

"Sure, why not?" I gave in because that is what I always did whenever Sam called.

"So, are we good until Friday?"

"We're good." We weren't. Not by a long shot. But I did still love Sam. I hated that I did. Why couldn't I fall in love with someone sweet like Zari?

I knew Zari would be on time, and serving dinner at close to 5:30 was equally crucial to her routine, so I needed to get a move on to make sure I was ready for her.

CHAPTER FIVE

ZARI

I was pruning the azalea bushes when Jillian strolled into the nursery. At first, Jillian needed me full-time at her nursery, but then the business took hold, and she could afford to hire part-time help. Mondays, Wednesdays, and Fridays were nursery days. I came in on those days because I loved the plants, and because Jillian informed me I needed the practice with people. She warned me not to lock myself away in my studio. She said since more women were gardeners than men, it would be a place to cruise for potential girlfriends. I couldn't find any recent data to support her conclusion, so I've been keeping track on the days I work. Even though she was right, so far, her plan had not worked for me.

"Hey, Zar. Everything looks great. Are you ready to open?"
I nodded. "I started a new sculpture yesterday. It's of Frankie. She has perfect bone structure."

"Whoa. Back the love train up? Who is this Frankie with perfect bone structure, and why haven't I met her?"

"She's the new neighbor that I told you about. I baked her cinnamon rolls yesterday before I started on my sculpture. She's making lasagna tonight. Should I bake dessert? I'm not sure if I will have time before 5:30."

Jillian tapped her chin. "Wow! You sculpted on Sunday. That's your free day. This woman must be something. You could go to the bakery and pick up a pie—Dutch apple or maybe blackberry."

"I should have asked if she likes Dutch apple or blackberry. She likes scones, cookies, and cinnamon rolls. She eats all three for breakfast."

"I was going to suggest you bring a bottle of wine as an alternative to dessert, but now I'm reassessing. It sounds like your girl enjoys sweets. Is this a date?"

"She's in an open relationship with another woman. When I asked if it was a date, she said, 'How about we just say I'm enjoying spending time with you and getting to know your likes and dislikes so I can be a good neighbor.'"

"Oh." Jillian frowned. "Okay, we can work with that. Open relationships rarely work because, deep down, they're usually a one-sided preference. Do you know if she's the one who wanted an open relationship, or was it the other person's idea?"

"It wasn't her choice. She accepted the new wrinkle and wasn't willing to give up. I like that Frankie is persevering."

43

"No, no, no, you don't want her to persevere with this other woman. Okay, we have something to work with. You obviously haven't scared her off yet. Did you do your creepy smile?"

"She has a sister with autism."

"Interesting. Is she hot?"

Before Jillian explained that hot wasn't always literal, like hot to the touch, I touched one of her old girlfriends on the forehead when I first met her and told Jillian that she felt normal to me. That seemed to please her girlfriend after Jillian clarified that she told me Kendra was hot. Then Jillian explained that *hot* was code for exceptional physical attraction. Jillian's been my teacher for slang and odd phrases. Otherwise, I've had to look them up to decipher their meanings. I don't mind looking things up because it provides additional knowledge. Jillian says knowledge is power. I had to look that up, too. Latin is the basis for many sayings. *Ipsa scientia potestas est* means knowledge itself is power. Wikipedia claims the first known use of the phrase was recorded in a tenth-century book.

"She has dark hair and green eyes. She might be Italian because she said she makes a mean lasagna, and that's an Italian dish. Her smile is very nice. She probably had braces when she was younger because her teeth are perfectly straight. She worries about eating too many sweets and gaining one hundred pounds, which would be a lot on her slight frame. I don't think she weighs more than 120 pounds, and she's my height. Her proportions are appropriate. She also has nice-sized breasts. You would say she is hot."

"Please tell me you didn't say she has nice-sized tits yet?"

"No, I didn't. You said I shouldn't compliment a woman on her breasts until we've reached the intimate stage. Then I'm supposed to tell her in a way that shows how much I adore her, but not just for her large breasts."

"Good job. Invite this woman to the nursery. I want to meet her. Then we can start on operation *steal the girlfriend*." Jillian clapped her hands together. Her watch beeped, and she flipped the sign to *OPEN* and unlocked the front door.

I didn't have time to ask if I could get in trouble for stealing a girlfriend. I would ask Jillian about that later. My mom and dad always taught me that stealing was wrong.

†

After Frankie opened her front door, I explained, "I didn't have time to bake a pie because it was a nursery day and pies take a long time. I could have made the pie yesterday, but I was sculpting until dinnertime and then after dinner, too. Jillian said a store-bought pie was just as good, but that's not true. She said if I was worried about bringing a pie I hadn't made myself, I could offer wine, then maybe you wouldn't notice the difference in taste."

"Come in, Zari. I don't plan on getting that drunk. I have to meet Jillian. She sounds fun. Dinner is almost ready. I just have to take it out and let it sit for a minute. Will that be okay? I'll open the bottle of wine for us." She rotated the bottle to read the label. "Very nice. I'm glad you chose local wine."

When Frankie smiled, I knew things were better. I didn't recognize her expression when she first opened the door, and I worried she wasn't happy to see me. It wasn't quite a sad face, nor was it an angry face, but I could see elements of both in her. I worried I'd done the wrong thing again.

"I didn't choose the wine. A nice woman saw me looking at all the labels and asked me what we were having for dinner. I should have thought to look it up on the Internet. She pulled this bottle from the shelf and said it paired well with what we were having. I worried I'd chosen wrong when I first saw your face."

Frankie furrowed her brow. "Why did you think that?"

"I couldn't figure out your expression. It doesn't match the flashcards my mom used to show me, or the faces that I've become accustomed to from my family and Jillian. I know them best. Customers at the nursery still baffle me, and then Jillian slips into the conversation and takes over. She does that when she's afraid I'll do something to make the customer leave without buying anything. That doesn't happen often, especially when I stick to providing useful information about the plants and make recommendations on which items they should purchase to keep them healthy. That means more sales for the nursery when I do that."

"Unfortunately, flashcards don't cover every nuanced emotion. I had a few curve balls thrown at me today." She lifted the bottle of wine. "This will help."

"Did you play baseball with the kids at recess? Were you hurt? I wasn't very good at sports. Neither was Jillian. I've been hit by a softball before. It hurt. A lot. After that, the teacher let me run around the track instead of joining the game."

"I'll tell you all about it when we start dinner. I need to get the lasagna out before it burns. Have a seat at the table." She pointed to a table that was all set with a variety of styles of glasses and a candle in the middle. The candle was off center by an inch, so I moved it. I hoped that was okay. Maybe she didn't like people touching her stuff. I moved it back because I never liked it when Jillian pawed my things and didn't put them back in the same place.

Frankie quirked her eyebrow at me but said nothing. She was busy setting a pan on the hot pad and then opening the bottle of wine I brought. After she poured the wine into two glasses and put them at the table settings, she moved the candle one inch to the right.

"Is the candle in the center now?" she asked.

"Yes, thank you. I'm sorry I moved it."

"You can move anything you want to if you think it's off-kilter. I don't mind. Except for a journal I keep, you can touch anything you want at my place."

"You keep a journal?" That intrigued me.

"I do. Journals don't judge. I can write anything I want in my journal, and it won't show me a disapproving face. Therapists aren't supposed to judge, but they sometimes do that. Unfortunately, I have an uncanny way of picking up on micro-expressions," Frankie said.

"I wish I had that power. I keep a notebook for my observations and sketches. I usually sketch before making a sculpture. The sketch helps me focus."

"I can't wait to see your studio." Frankie picked up the plates sitting on the table, then walked into the kitchen and cut four squares of lasagna. She placed two on each plate.

"I'll show you after I finish the sculpture I'm working on right now." I was glad she'd chosen to serve four squares of lasagna, two each. I wondered if she'd done that specially for me.

"Name the date and time."

"I should be done with the clay model on Friday." I pulled my phone from my pocket to put this in my calendar because

Friday was too far off not to make sure I'd recorded this important date.

Frankie frowned, and I wondered what I'd done wrong.

"I can't see your studio on Friday. Sam called today. She wants to take me to dinner on Friday." When she turned around to pick up the bowl of grated cheese, I couldn't see her expression.

"Sam, your girlfriend, whom you have an open relationship with," I stated. I wanted to call Jillian to find out what I should do with this information. I didn't know how I could steal her away from her girlfriend if she took Frankie to dinner on Friday. Besides, I still hadn't asked about the ethics of stealing her away from Sam. I would do an Internet search on open relationships to supplement whatever advice Jillian would give me.

Frankie offered the bowl of cheese, and I sprinkled it evenly over my two squares. She added a spoonful to the center of each square on her plate, then picked up her glass of wine.

"To new friendships."

I'd watched this ritual on television, so I knew what to do. I picked up my glass and clinked it with hers. After I took a sip of the wine, I had difficulty deciding if I liked the taste. I didn't hate it, but it wasn't as pleasant as the other beverages I chose. I used to drink a lot of soda until I read how unhealthy sugary drinks were. The links to heart disease and diabetes disturbed me.

"You don't like the wine," she stated. "The Zinfandel was a splendid choice. I like a nice Pinot with lasagna, too, but I suppose wine is an acquired taste. If you take a bite of the lasagna and then sip the wine, let me know if that makes a difference for you. Maybe I could see your studio on Saturday," she suggested. "Unless Saturday is a sculpture or nursery day."

"Saturday is a good day to show you my studio. What time will you come to my house?"

"What time would you like me to come?"

I needed to call Jillian to ask her what I should plan for Saturday. I already didn't like Sam, and I hadn't met her yet. I took a chance that Jillian would help me think of something to do after showing her my studio. I wanted to spend more than a few hours with Frankie, but that was a lot of time, and Jillian said I needed to ease a person into getting to know me.

"How about one o'clock? Will that give you enough time to have lunch, or would you like me to make lunch for us? If I make lunch, you should come at noon."

"One sounds perfect. It's a date. Eat, before the lasagna gets cold. Save room for the pie you brought. I'm looking forward to that. I've had a pie from that bakery before, and it's a lot better than mine. But we've already established I'm a shitty baker."

I typed the information into my calendar on my phone. Later, I would transfer the date to my main calendar, where I maintained my various appointments and schedules. I was glad to have plenty of time to prepare for the day.

"I'll bake you a pie on Saturday. What kind is your favorite?"

"You must have some kind of Spidey sense because the Dutch apple pie you brought is one of my favorites. I also like key lime, lemon meringue, blackberry, boysenberry, and the summer strawberry gelatin pie my mother used to make. Honestly, you could have brought any pie, and I would have enjoyed it. By now, you've probably figured out what a sweet tooth I have. Definitely the way to my heart."

I wondered if Sam had courted Frankie with pie, pastry, and cookies. I hoped she hadn't, because then maybe Sam hadn't found the way to her heart yet. Although, it seemed maybe she had.

"Does Sam bring you pies?"

Frankie laughed. "God, no. She's a health nut. Constantly warns me about the evils of processed foods and sugar."

I tucked that piece of information away so I could tell Jillian.

"I believe that life is way too short. Everything in moderation." She lifted her wineglass in the air and then tipped it to take a sip.

After taking a bite of her lasagna, I followed with a sip of my wine. I wanted to test out her suggestion that it would taste better with the meal. It tasted the same to me. "Could I have some water, please?"

"Oh, gosh, yes. I'm sorry. I'm a terrible host. Of course. I guess the wine isn't a big hit. I mean, you don't like the wine, even after tasting it with the lasagna. That's okay. You can be the designated driver."

"I don't drive. My bicycle takes me wherever I need to go. I don't know why I never learned. Mom, Dad, and Jillian offered to teach me. It wasn't important. Should I learn now?"

"Only if you want to. I could teach you. You'd probably make an excellent driver." Frankie slapped her hand against her mouth. "God, I'm sorry. I did not mean to say something that perpetuates stereotypes."

"I don't understand." Frankie looked embarrassed, and I wondered why she was suddenly uncomfortable.

"The movie, *Rainman*."

"I've never seen it."

"It's terrific. Do you like movies?"

"Only when they don't have loud music or sounds. Love stories are good. I learn from them. I don't like movies with explosions or gunfire. I used to like to read comic books, but going to see movies about my favorite comic book characters was out of the question." I wanted to eat more of her lasagna. "Can we talk about movies after dinner? This is good." I sliced off a bite and began chewing as Frankie smiled at me.

"Yeah, we can. I have an idea. Do you trust me?"

I nodded while chewing my food. Then I thought about manners and what I'd learned.

"Jillian always told me I had exceptional manners. Manners are easy because there are specific rules. Always say please and thank you. Open doors for women. Never talk with your mouth full. No elbows on the table. Let other people talk and listen carefully to what they say."

"The only manners that matter to me are treating others with kindness and compassion."

"Do you think it's unkind to be blunt? Jillian says that sometimes a person has to lie because being honest would hurt too much. Do you think she's right?"

"That's a tough one. There is the rule that if you can't say something nice, don't say anything at all. I suppose I adhere to that rule most of the time."

"I don't always know when I'm hurting someone with my honesty. I have learned some rules about being too blunt. Jillian says I should never tell a woman she doesn't look good in an outfit, or that I don't like her new haircut. Women are also particularly sensitive about weight. It's mostly about being out of proportion, except for their breasts. But even if you comment on how large their breasts are, and you like them, you still have to be careful about how you say it and to whom you say it. Giving compliments is a subtlety I'm still working on."

"Aren't we all?"

CHAPTER SIX

FRANKIE

Not that it was surprising, but Zari didn't stay long after dinner. I wasn't sure how I felt about that. I enjoyed my time with Zari. I didn't have to try to be anything for her. I could have two pieces of pie without her giving me a disapproving side glance. I was sure I could say just about anything, and she would unpackage the comment in her logical manner without judgment. Ironically, she was easier to talk with than Sam.

After dinner, when we were having our pie, I told her my idea. It saddened me to think Zari hadn't enjoyed *Wonder Woman* and *Captain Marvel* like every other lesbian I knew on the planet. I was sure she'd read Wonder Woman comics as a kid and probably the last version of Captain Marvel, Carol

Danvers. I'd been a comic book nerd myself. There were so many versions of Captain Marvel, both men and women over the years, and my favorite was Carol Danvers, especially after the movie came out.

"I'd like to share two movies with you that I think you'll like with a few modifications. Remember when I asked you if you trusted me?"

"Yes, you asked before I ate the rest of your wonderful lasagna. Will you show me how to make it? I think I would like to have this as a meal again."

I knew it was a risk to tease her, but I couldn't help myself. "Well, I don't know. It is a secret family recipe. I'm not sure what Mom would say about me giving it out to just anyone. I suppose I could make it again for you or send you home with leftovers."

"I don't understand why people keep secrets. What is the purpose?"

"Now that is an excellent question. Can I get back to you on that when I have a better answer? I'm excited to share my idea."

"Okay."

"I have noise-canceling headphones that I believe will work well to shut out the loud noises in the two movies. I'll turn on the closed captioning, and you can read instead of listening to the dialogue. That way, you can see both *Wonder Woman* and *Captain Marvel*. I'll have to take away your lesbian card until you watch both movies."

"I don't have a lesbian card, but I am a lesbian because I'm attracted to women instead of men. And when I was younger, it was girls versus boys."

I laughed. "That was a lame joke. Sorry. I know you don't have a lesbian card, and I'm glad you're a lesbian."

"You are? Why?"

I shrugged. "For whatever reason, I guess I'm more comfortable hanging around lesbians or queer women."

"Jillian says she's queer and not a lesbian. I don't understand the difference. She tried to explain it to me once. Even after I researched this, I didn't understand. All Jillian says is that lesbian is too restrictive and leaves out bisexuals, non-binary, and the trans community. I would like to try to watch the movies with your headphones. When would you like to do this?"

"How about Saturday after touring your studio?"

"Yes, that would be good. Will I see you before Saturday?"

"Probably. We are neighbors. Maybe I'll stop by the nursery on a day that you work. I think I need to add color to the landscaping. It's too basic right now. You can help me pick out a few plants."

Zari stood, and I knew she was ending the evening. I felt disappointed we wouldn't have more time together. "I work at the nursery on Mondays, Wednesdays, and Fridays. Thank you for dinner. I enjoyed it. It's time for me to go now. Bye, Frankie."

I walked her to the door and debated whether to kiss her on the cheek. In the end, I decided not to startle her. Plus, I didn't know where things were headed, or even where I wanted them to go. I might have more clarity after my dinner date with Sam. The fact that I considered going there with Zari was a testament to how shaky my relationship with Sam was. I'd even had thoughts of ending it with Sam. A clean break for my sanity. At least I wouldn't obsess over the time she spent with other people. I wondered about the concert and if she'd sleep with whomever she ended up taking.

CHAPTER SEVEN

ZARI

I waited until Wednesday to talk with Jillian about my date with Frankie on Saturday. Besides showing her my studio and watching movies, I needed advice on what to plan for the day. The minute Jillian walked through the door, I began following her until she completed her regular morning tasks. I wasn't supposed to start a conversation until she had unlocked the greenhouse, flipped open the sign, added cash to the till, and made sure the front door didn't have the auto-lock engaged. Her routine was just as important as mine, and I respected that.

"I have a date with Frankie on Saturday. She wants to see my studio and watch movies. She says she'll take away my lesbian card until we watch *Wonder Woman* and *Captain Marvel*."

Jillian had her worried face. "Whoa, that's a lot to unpack there. How do you know it's a date for starters?"

"She said it was a date. I've brought treats two days in a row, and then she invited me to her house for dinner. I didn't see her on Tuesday because you said I need to pace myself and not overstay my welcome. I've followed that rule and didn't stay long after pie on Monday."

"Did you kiss her, or did she kiss you on Monday when you left?"

"No."

"Then it might not be a date. Sometimes people use the expression, *it's a date*, but it's not the type of date you think it is. Even I've made that mistake before. I recommend you clarify it's the kind of date you're hoping for. I've seen your studio and watched movies with you, and those weren't dates. Speaking of movies, those are action flicks. What about the loud noises?"

"Frankie said she would turn on the closed captioning and give me noise-canceling headphones to wear."

"Interesting. I'd say curiouser and curiouser, but I don't want to sound like Alice, *Batwoman*'s crazy sister. Which, for the record, is a TV show you should watch with headphones and closed captioning if you're going to earn that lesbian card."

"Okay. What else should I plan for Saturday? She has a date with her girlfriend on Friday, so I will be competing with that. Her girlfriend is taking her to dinner."

"Damn, that's not good. Let me think. How about you prepare a picnic for her? The weather has been nice lately. You can get all the date foods like cheese, wine, fruit. Then add chocolate-covered strawberries. Does she have a bike? You can bike to that park close to you. You should learn to drive and buy a damn car."

"Frankie offered to teach me to drive."

"I offered to teach you to drive." Jillian frowned.

"You are a reckless driver. Why would I learn from you?"

"I am not," Jillian insisted.

"You have three speeding tickets and had to go back to driving school."

"Driving fast is not necessarily reckless. Some people make a living off of driving fast."

"Race drivers are in controlled circumstances, and they drive around a track, not out in traffic with other people that are not professional drivers. You aren't a race driver."

"Fine. Let's get back to the plans for Saturday and this new nugget of information about her offer to teach you to drive. You should take her up on that. Clearly, she isn't turned off by you, or she wouldn't have offered. Yup, a picnic sounds like a good plan." Jillian turned and began stacking the potting soil.

"Aren't picnics for lunch? She isn't coming until after lunch."

Jillian stopped stacking the soil and turned in my direction. "Not necessarily. You could also prepare a picnic dinner. The days are longer now, and it stays warm until late in the evening."

"Okay, that's easier than baking a pie."

"No, you should bake a pie, too. Did you bring her wine for dinner?"

"Yes. The wine didn't taste better with the food, so I still don't like wine."

"You don't have to drink a lot, but you should still have a bottle with your picnic. Wine loosens people up, and you need a little loosening. Not as much loosening as when I introduced you to alcohol in high school. That was too much. No more than two glasses, ever, okay?"

"How will I know when it's okay to kiss her?"

"If she looks at your lips too intently, go for it."

"I look too intently at people sometimes, especially after you tried to teach me how to flirt, but that never earned me a kiss before."

"That's because you never quite mastered flirting. There aren't any flashcards for the face a person makes when they want you to kiss them. Watch that movie, *Desert Hearts,* again, and pay attention to what Vivian looked like when Cay kissed her. I love that scene in the movie. Or, next time Patty comes into the store, we'll show you what it looks like. She still gives me those looks even after two years. I'm a lucky woman, and you will be, too, someday. Let's hope it's with this Frankie person. Hey, do you mind helping me with the potting soil?"

"Okay." I took the other end of the large bag, and we worked together to make neat piles. "Can I get off work early today to purchase the picnic supplies I'll need?"

"Dude, you have until Saturday. But sure, you know you don't have to ask. I appreciate your help with the plants and all, but I can handle my nursery on my own, you know. I do it on Tuesday, Thursday, and Saturday."

"Thanks. I don't have a picnic basket, and if Frankie doesn't have a bike, I'll have to buy one of those for her as well."

"Don't buy anything super expensive, okay? In fact, slow your roll until I meet this woman. I don't want you throwing your money at someone not worthy of you."

"She's worthy. You'll see."

CHAPTER EIGHT

FRANKIE

I'd forgotten to ask Zari at which nursery she worked, but there were only two in town, and one of them was a lot farther away. Since she rode her bike to work, I figured it had to be Growth Spurts. Wednesday was an early release day. I was supposed to collaborate with my fellow teachers on that day to analyze test results to improve the way we presented our lessons. Under an unwritten agreement by all of us, we always left early. Instead, we would accomplish this during our lunch hour. It was the perfect day to visit the nursery.

I nearly ran to my car after leaving my colleagues. I looked forward to seeing Zari and her too-wide smile. Her relationship with Jillian had my curiosity at high speed. Jillian was clearly an influential part of Zari's life, and there was no doubt in my mind that she loved Zari.

When I drove up the gravel path to Growth Spurts, the beauty of the place amazed me. I guessed that the meticulously cared-for garden surrounding a koi pond was a huge draw for customers. The message was simple. Customers would only find top quality plants at this establishment.

Zari had mentioned that Jillian owned the nursery, and it sounded like they were close in age. I wondered how a woman in her twenties could own a business like Growth Spurts. The land alone would have cost a fortune. Maybe she had wealthy parents like me.

I wanted to see more of the nursery. I walked to the back along the stone path that meandered around the plants like a lazy river. More display gardens with an additional pond created a kind of serenity I wanted for my place. The landscaping at my house was rudimentary, and I longed for something that resembled this tranquility. Zari sat on the stone path, doing something I couldn't quite see with her back to me.

A young woman with long black hair emerged from a large greenhouse and greeted me. Her smile was genuine. The intensity of her ice-blue eyes startled me with the contrast to her hair.

"Can I help you find something?" she asked.

"Um, no I..."

Zari turned around and said, "Hi, Frankie."

The beautiful woman looked between Zari and me and quirked her eyebrow at Zari. "Zari, you know this woman?"

"Yes, that's Frankie, my neighbor."

"Oh." The woman smiled at me and held out her hand. "Nice to meet you. I'm Jillian."

Zari scrambled to her feet. "Frankie needs plants and bushes with a lot of color. Her place is very drab, and the weeds are taking over."

"I think we can help her with that. Do you enjoy gardening, Frankie?"

"Not particularly."

"Low maintenance is the way to go, along with blooming ground cover that will help keep the weeds manageable. Zari, you could show her around and make suggestions that will fit what she's looking for. Let me know if you need any help. I'll be in the greenhouse, inspecting my seedlings." Jillian brushed by Zari and whispered something in her ear. Jillian began laughing, and I wondered what she'd said to Zari.

When Zari walked over to me, my curiosity got the best of me, and I asked, "What did Jillian say?"

"She told me to show you the butterfly pea. She said it's colorful. I think she wants me to show you the plant because *Clitoria ternatia* is the proper name. It's a good name because the flower looks a lot like female genitalia. Although, there are a lot of flowers that resemble genitalia. I think that's why Georgia O'Keefe is so popular with lesbians. The plant grows best in zones ten and eleven, but you can always plant it each year as an annual."

"Sounds like a good plan."

"Jillian also said you're hot, and if she weren't already taken, she'd try to steal you away from your girlfriend herself."

I laughed. I liked what I saw regarding how Jillian interacted with Zari. I was sure Zari was asking for advice from Jillian. I would have to be extra careful until I figured my shit out.

†

I was several dollars poorer when I left Growth Spurts with a car full of plants. Jillian assured me they would deliver the rest by the end of business on Thursday. Even though my depleted savings account undoubtedly gave me even less independence from my father, I was looking forward to creating the same tranquility I felt as I sat on the stone bench in front of the koi pond. I didn't know the first thing about ponds. Zari offered to help me, and that created a warm feeling all over. We had a project to work on that would guarantee countless hours of interaction without me having to define our time together.

I could have hired someone to dig the hole, but I needed the physical labor. I wanted to feel the sweat on my brow as I worked to create my special sanctuary. The result would be all the more satisfying.

On the way home, I picked up an order of chicken fajitas at my favorite Mexican restaurant and barely breathed as I wolfed down the food. Late spring meant it was still light out in the evenings. I started digging my hole right away after unloading my car. My problem was that I didn't have the foggiest idea where I wanted to put my new pond.

I was sure I looked like a goofball, staring at my backyard while mumbling to myself. I'd scattered half of the new plants haphazardly around me as I pondered where I would start digging. I didn't hear Zari approach until she interrupted my unintelligible musings.

"Our yards are similar. Would you like to see where I put my pond?"

"You have a pond?" I asked. I'd never been to Zari's house, so I had no idea what it was like. I guessed everything was neat and tidy. Probably perfectly symmetrical.

She nodded. "Would you like to see it tonight or on Saturday after I show you my studio?"

"Good question. I think maybe I should wait. I want this to be something that is all mine, not a copycat of what I would presume is lovely and wonderful, but a reflection of you, not me. My little slice of heaven might be different. Different is good sometimes."

"Okay. Where is your electrical outlet?"

I motioned for her to follow me and pointed to the outdoor outlet covered by a clear plastic box around the corner on the right side of my house.

"Does it make a difference to the placement of the pond?"

"It makes a difference to how long the small trench will need to be where you'll have to run the wires to the outlet."

"Ah, well, in that case…" I pointed to the grassy area on the right side. "I guess this is as good a place as any. I feel bad digging up a patch of this perfectly manicured lawn, especially since it's the only nice part of my back yard. It's like I'm murdering part of my lawn for selfish reasons and covering up my crime with a beautiful pond."

"It would have been better to dig before they put in the grass."

"I suppose it's not the grass's fault that the landscapers were shitty."

"They did a good job with the lawn. It's very healthy and green."

I grabbed one of the new shovels I bought and used my foot to push the blade into the lawn. "Sorry, but this won't be the only patch of grass I dig up. The pitiful number of trees and bushes back here need a lot more friends and family. It's party time."

I only felt slightly ashamed that I'd bought two shovels, believing I might take advantage of Zari's sweet nature, knowing she'd offer to assist me. But Zari didn't grab the other shovel like I thought she would. Instead, she looked on, tilting her head to the side.

"I'll be right back."

Sweat had covered every inch of my body by the time Zari returned with a fist full of small orange flags. I'd only managed a small dent. Digging the hole was going to take a lot of effort.

"I suggest you mark the area with these flags before digging your hole. Do you know how large you want your pond to be? Would you like a round pond or kidney-shaped? Those are the two most popular shapes for a pond. Even square ponds shouldn't have corners. Koi don't do well in square ponds. Corners or complicated shapes impede the flow of water and allow the bad bacteria to colonize. You don't want colonies of bad bacteria."

"That makes sense. Perhaps a kidney shape. Do you think ten to twelve feet long and five to six feet wide is too big?"

"Not if that's what you desire for your new pond. We can mark the area with the flags, and then you can go into your house and look out back to see if you like the shape and size. The pond will need to be at least eighteen inches deep for the fish. Two feet is a better depth to work with. Would you like me to place the flags to your specifications? I have exceptional visuospatial ability."

"I'd love for you to do that because I have no doubt your markings will be perfect. How about if I dish up the pie, and after you finish marking the area, we can look at the size and placement of the pond while having pie and coffee? I assume you already had your dinner since it's now 6:40."

"That would be good."

I watched from my window as Zari methodically placed each flag approximately six inches apart. The kidney quickly took shape, and I waved to her as she squinted in the sunshine. Opening the window, I called out, "Come on in, the pie's ready."

Before entering my house, Zari slipped off her shoes and came inside. "May I wash my hands, please?"

"Sure." I pointed to the kitchen sink and the liquid hand soap I kept there for when I wanted to wash my hands while preparing meals. I sat at the table, waiting for her to join me. "It's a miracle I have anything left of this wonderful pie. I admit to having a piece for breakfast this morning, and of course, I ate a piece last night."

"It is a good pie." Zari picked up her fork and separated a small piece that she promptly put in her mouth. I watched with interest as her mouth gently enveloped the succulent morsel. Zari had a beautiful mouth. I chastised myself for staring at her and having a reaction to something that I was sure she had not intended to be sexual or sensual. But it was for me. I needed to get laid before I did something stupid and made a move to kiss those lush red lips.

"Do I have a crumb on my chin or something? You're staring."

I shook my head and looked down. Now I was the one avoiding direct eye contact. "No, sorry." I broke off a sizeable piece and shoved it into my mouth.

After we finished our pie, Zari stood and walked to the window. "It looks good. A stone patio with a path leading to the pond would look better than the wood deck."

"That would be expensive, huh?"

"At least ten thousand if you hire someone to build it, less if we do it ourselves. The cost of the stone will depend on how large of a patio you wish to build. I would estimate at least three thousand."

"It's going to be a pain in the ass to disassemble this deck, isn't it?"

"Yes, it will be hard work and more likely to be a pain on your lower back. I don't mind hard work, do you?"

I laughed. "Not at all. The exercise will be good for me, especially if you continue to bring me treats."

CHAPTER NINE

_____

ZARI

After Frankie visited Growth Spurts, Jillian and I partially loaded the truck for the delivery Jillian would make after the rest of the trees and bushes came in on Thursday. Brushing her dirty hands on her jeans, Jillian motioned for me to sit on the bench in front of the pond.

"She likes you. I was watching her while you showed her different plants to consider. You know, she's just given you the perfect opportunity to spend more time with her. All the stuff she bought will require a lot of work unless she hires someone to do it for her. She's a teacher, right?"

"Yes."

"How can she afford to live in your prissy community on a teacher's salary?"

"Her father bought the house because the neighborhood she lived in before was questionable."

"Hopefully, Daddy won't offer to have someone do all the work."

"I don't think she will want that. She argued with her father about her house. Do you think he will argue with her again?"

"Probably not. I like her. If I were her girlfriend, there is no way I'd suggest an open relationship. She looks like lesbian royalty. Don't tell Patty I said that, but damn that woman is smokin'. More important, though, is that she's kind. I can tell. I mean, I guessed that when she thought of the headphone thing. A selfish person would not try to accommodate your lovable quirks."

"Not everyone has called them lovable."

"Forget about those asshats. You're smart, kind, and generous. Anyone would be lucky to have you as a girlfriend. The fact that you're also hot is the cherry on the top."

"You didn't think you were lucky when I asked you to be my girlfriend."

"Not true. I knew I was lucky. Sometimes people are meant to be friends and not lovers. There isn't even rhyme or reason for it, so don't ask me why. I don't have an answer for you. Love is a mystery to all of us."

"I don't like mysteries."

"You will when that mysterious love bug bites."

"Will I have to let her bite me before I know?"

"Stop being so literal. Although, light biting can be fun. And no, don't ask about that. Look it up on YouTube. Just type in biting during sex."

†

Jillian was right about offering to help Frankie. After I got a good look at her backyard, and she told me she planned on digging the pond herself, I knew this was a tremendous opportunity to spend a lot of time with her.

While we were taking a break to eat pie, I thought about our upcoming date on Saturday. I needed to know if Frankie had a bike.

"Do you have a bicycle?" I asked.

"That's a pretty random question. I used to, but some jerk stole it before I moved. No gates to protect property that wasn't properly secured. I was surprised since my bike wasn't very special or expensive. Hardly worth stealing."

I looked back at the yard with the flags neatly arranged and knew the work would take a long time to complete. While it was in progress, everything would be so disheveled it would bother me until Frankie finished her project. I could do this. I could help and spend the time with Frankie. Maybe I could work on sculpture days after I finished whatever sculpture I was working on that had inspired me.

"There are still two hours and sixteen minutes of daylight left. If we each dig from opposite ends, we'll be able to avoid running into each other and can more easily spread the mounds of dirt."

Frankie's lips twisted. "I kind of forgot about all the extra dirt. What am I going to do with that?"

"It depends on the soil we turn up. We can use some of it to create raised mounds for your plants and flowerbeds. I recommend putting the dirt on a tarp. It's a lot easier to move to another location. If there are too many rocks, we can separate them before moving the dirt." I evaluated her yard and viable locations for the raised beds when she came very close to me. I could smell her light scent. It wasn't unpleasant, even after starting to dig the hole and loading and unloading her car, which had generated sweat with the exertion. Jillian and I had helped her load, but she had managed to unload and carry everything to her front and back yards.

"I didn't think to buy any tarps, and I wasn't sure where to put all the plants. I sort of arranged them in the approximate locations where I think they might go well together."

Her scent distracted me. "You smell very nice. Don't you stink when you sweat?"

She laughed. "I do, but not as much as a lot of people. Plus, I'm always putting lotion on my skin. It's very dry here. You're probably smelling my lotion."

"Growth Spurts has tarps we can use. I'll call Jillian and have her deliver them with the rest of the plants and trees. It's a good thing you didn't dig up too much grass and dirt already. Even if this soil is salvageable, I recommend adding compost and other clean soil to the beds. It will help the plants flourish."

Frankie's lips turned down again. "I was a bit rash about my purchases today and dipped quite a bit into my meager savings. Do you think the extra compost and dirt will cost a lot? I still have to buy the stone for the patio and for around the pond. Teacher's salary. Remember?"

"Even though doing a project in stages can often leave an unsightly mess, your deck will be okay until you can afford to replace it. I could arrange for the dirt and stones for the pond. It can be my house-warming gift," I offered.

"No, don't do that. Your gift was the treats you've been supplying me with. I'll figure it out. I can always replenish my savings in like the next twenty years." She laughed.

71

I had more money than I knew what to do with because people seemed to like to buy my sculptures. Jillian had warned me about telling random women for two reasons. One, I'd sound like a braggart, and two, I shouldn't reveal how much I was worth lest I attract a gold digger. I told her the Gold Rush was over and had been mostly men, anyway. She had to explain that it was an expression for someone who might be with me because I was well off, which wasn't the right reason to stay with someone. Ever.

"Until we have the tarps, I don't recommend that you continue digging."

"Could you help me place the plants? Your visuospatial abilities will come in handy."

"I can do that. I was hoping you would ask. You've placed some plants in the wrong spots for them to flourish. A balance of color is needed along with the trees and plants yet to arrive. I can envision where they might go as well. I'll get more flags, and we can mark those spots."

"How will you know which plant goes in a particular spot if all the flags are orange?"

I shrugged. "I can see it all in my head, and I'll remember, but if you want, we can use a black magic marker on the flags to write the names of the plants."

"That won't help me because I don't know the names of most of the plants and trees. I'll let you direct me after Jillian delivers them."

"That would be good if you want your landscaping to look professional."

"Wow, I've hit the jackpot with a professional artist and landscaper living next door. You create beauty in more than one way. That's impressive."

"Are you joking or being sarcastic? I have a hard time recognizing that."

"No, not at all. I meant it as a compliment. I am lucky to have you as a neighbor. I won't use sarcasm with you. I promise."

"Thank you. Jillian forgets sometimes. She says sarcasm is her second language."

"It used to be mine, but then I had to temper it when working with the kiddos at my school." Frankie's smile grew wider. It seemed as though talking about her work made her happy.

"You like being a teacher," I stated.

"I love it. I think I was destined to be an exceptional education teacher. The kids are a joy to work with. I'm not sure I would have found my calling if not for my sister."

"The one who is like me?"

"Yeah. I have another sister that I'm not as close to as Penny. She enjoys Father's money way too much. Her pretentiousness has always bothered me. Plus, she's always been a bully and a mean girl."

"There are a lot of those."

"Too many, that's for sure. I wanted to punch all those asshats in the nose when I was in high school. It's a breeding ground for bullies. Sadly, I kept quiet too many times. I didn't want to stick my neck out and feel their wrath. College was a lot better."

"Not for me. Different scares people."

"It does, but it shouldn't."

"Now there are only two hours and three minutes of daylight."

"Okay, okay. I get it. Time to get back to work." Frankie leaned in and kissed me on the cheek. It wasn't a light brush of her lips, but enough pressure to feel nice. "Thanks for helping me."

"Thank you for the kiss with just the right pressure."

"You're welcome."

Frankie's cheeks turned red, and I wondered why she was suddenly flushed. Did I cause her to blush? Jillian told me that a person could have red cheeks for more than one reason. I tried to understand all the different reasons for a person's cheeks to redden. Overexertion or sickness was common. Less typical was embarrassment or a subtle attraction. The last two reasons were more challenging to understand. I didn't ask Frankie about her flush because Jillian said if the glow was one of the latter two reasons, I shouldn't point that out in case it turns their cheeks even redder. She said when a woman blushes, that's a good sign. I couldn't get the word blush out of my mind now.

"I looked up blushing once and learned that when someone experiences emotion, it can trigger a release of adrenaline. When adrenaline is released on a person's nervous system, it causes the capillaries to bring blood closer to the surface of the skin. That's why a person's face turns red."

Frankie smiled and blushed again. "Good to know."

CHAPTER TEN

FRANKIE

I'd kissed Zari on an impulse. Sure, it was only on the cheek, but then she had to point out how it was exactly the right pressure. Of course, it didn't end with that when she explained about blushing as my face turned beet red. *What the hell am I doing?* I needed to be careful. My growing feelings for Zari were expressing themselves in ways I wasn't prepared for. Refocusing on my project had to be the way to change my chaotic emotions. After we'd gone back outside to finish placing the plants around the yard, I could almost see how the balance of color would work. I couldn't wait to see her studio on Saturday. Even though she said it was okay and hadn't revealed that Saturday was a sculpture day, I hadn't wanted to monopolize the entire day because I suspected at least part of Saturday was, in fact, a sculpture day.

When I got home on Thursday, I made a beeline for the backyard, hoping the tarps had been dropped off so I could begin digging inside the perimeter of flags. School would be out soon, and I'd have plenty of time to devote to my new project. I certainly would not spend as much time with Sam, who needed to expand her horizons. The physical exertion wouldn't kill me, and maybe I'd develop a set of muscles that would be hard for Sam to ignore. I knew they wouldn't form in twenty-four hours, but it was nice to dream about having a sculpted body.

Soon I realized something was different. Someone had neatly laid tarps around the future pond and spaced around the yard several additional trees and bushes, filling in some of the bare areas. I ran back to the front yard to find the rest of the plants I'd picked out on Wednesday. I could almost visualize how beautiful everything would look when I finished. As I admired my purchases and stared at my plants, I felt someone approach.

"Jillian delivered the rest of your trees and bushes. She also brought the tarps. I laid them out for you."

"I saw that. Thank you, but you didn't have to do that. I didn't mean to interrupt your sculpture day."

"It's okay. Jillian says a slight change to my routine will help me grow. Besides, Jillian needed to know where to put everything. I told her you didn't have a trained eye, and your knowledge of plants is substandard. You would have killed some of them. She also needed my help to lift the larger trees."

I chuckled after she assessed my insufficient education on plants. "You haven't had dinner yet, have you? I think a pizza will be the right amount of carbs needed to give me the energy to dig. Care to join me?"

"Okay. I enjoy pizza. I should ask about toppings first. I don't like anchovies."

"Who does?"

"My mom and dad."

"Seriously? Ew."

Zari nodded. "Yes, even though anchovies rank last for pizza toppings in the US."

"How about we stick with something basic like tomato and basil? We can get a Margherita."

"Jillian has margaritas with Mexican food. She says it's a rule that she must have one with her fajitas, or else the flavor is totally ruined."

"She has a point, but no, this is different. They sound the same, but one is a yummy type of pizza, and the other is a popular drink with tequila."

"Do you know what kind of basil they use on the pizza? The more common varieties that we have at the nursery are sweet basil, also known as Genovese basil, lemon basil, or Thai basil, but there are sixty different varieties of basil."

I should have known she would know all the details about basil plants. I answered with an educated guess. I hoped she would accept my answer. "I'm relatively certain that most pizzas use the sweet basil, although the other choices might be interesting. I could ask if that's important to you."

"No. I was just curious. I like the taste of all three, but the sweet basil and lemon basil are my favorites. I put them in my salad."

She smiled sweetly at me, and I found it hard not to be charmed by this woman. "Gosh, I never thought to do that. Now that you've suggested it, I'm going to try that the next time I make a salad."

"We should order soon. Pizza takes time to make and deliver."

I wondered how long she would stay after we'd eaten the pizza. Our time together always seemed too short. I'd have to do something to change that. Zari needed to know that I genuinely enjoyed spending time with her, and she didn't need to fear she would overstay her welcome and leave after only a short time. Maybe I could convince her to watch a movie with me, something without loud sounds. That would extend our time together without putting too much pressure on either of us. I enjoyed our conversations more than I had a right to, considering I was having dinner with Sam tomorrow evening. Sam and I had been together for a few years and had lived together for much of that time. Wasn't that worth being patient while she expanded her horizons? After all, she had told me the other night that she saw us having a future together. The problem was that I thought I was starting to have genuine feelings for Zari, and I wasn't sure I knew what I should do with those. I couldn't do an open relationship in the same way as Sam.

†

Sam hadn't seen my new home yet. I gave her the code to the gate and opened the door to let her inside. I glanced over to Zari's and saw the curtain move. There was a car in her driveway, and I wondered who was visiting. I didn't have a right to be jealous, but I was.

Sam whistled. "Wow, this place is huge. Nice neighborhood, too. I feel like I live in the ghetto. But after you moved out, I can't move unless I get another roommate."

I bristled at that comment. "Roommate? Is that all I was to you?"

"Whoa, sorry, babe. I didn't mean it like that. I just meant that losing your contribution to the household income is making it hard. I might have to consider asking someone to move in to share the expenses. The place is too large for one person. I never asked you to move out."

"Well, I wasn't about to sit on the sidelines while you entertained a date in our home. I figured after your promotion that you could afford the place by yourself."

"We could have worked through that, you know. All we had to do was establish a rule that we couldn't bring other women home with us. I would have respected you enough to stick to that rule. Then we could have moved to a better neighborhood."

I lifted my eyebrow. "To rent again, I assume. Buying something together is clearly out of the question. Too much commitment."

"Aw, come on, Frankie, that's not fair. We both agreed it was too early to buy."

"Too early to cohabitate, too, it turns out," I mumbled.

"Hey, I didn't come all the way to fight. I want to take you to a nice dinner. I have something in my car—a housewarming gift. We can drink it later tonight after dinner. I have an overnight bag with me, too." Sam waggled her eyebrows. "You look ravishing tonight."

"That's very presumptuous of you. I'm not sure if that's such a grand idea. I agreed to dinner. I didn't agree to have sex."

"I knew it. You *are* still mad. I assumed you were okay with everything." Sam took hold of my hands and gave me those puppy-dog eyes I had a hard time resisting.

I broke away and put distance between us. "You didn't give me much choice. Maybe I should have ended things when you brought up the notion of having an open relationship. I tried to tell you how much I hated the idea. It's just not me."

Sam looked panicked. "I'm not giving up on us, because you're not willing to try something new. I swear this will only be for a little while. I think it will bring us closer together. You have to admit, things were starting to get a little stale. Before I suggested an open relationship, we hadn't had sex for a month. A whole month. I can't live without sex for a month. You should be happy that I offered this as a solution instead of cheating on you to get my needs met. Lesbian bed death is not a fate I want for us. A lot of couples do this, and it makes them stronger. Please, I love you. I know we can make this work."

Something niggled at me after she'd said she couldn't live without sex. I wondered if she hadn't. Had Sam already been dating others before she had discussed that with me? "I'm not the one who turned away when I would try to initiate."

"I'm not blaming you, hon, just stating a fact." She retook my hands and leaned in for a kiss. It had been a long time, and when her talented lips captured mine, I gave in. Sam was an exceptional kisser and always could get my juices flowing. Yet, something had shifted. While the physical sensation of kissing Sam was pleasant, it lacked the requisite emotion to be amazing. The kiss felt more robotic and technically competent instead of passionate.

She caressed my cheek. "God, I miss you, and I miss this. See, it's already working. I want you so bad right now. It feels like when we first met, and I couldn't keep my hands off of you. We'll get it back, and then I'm sure a commitment will follow. You know that you're the only woman I see in my future."

"Maybe we should try counseling?" I suggested.

The distaste at that suggestion was written all over her face, and I thought of Zari and her flashcards. I assumed they were the same as the ones I used with my neurodiverse kids. I didn't remember a flashcard for the expression on Sam's face, but it was so obvious. I suspected even Zari could decipher Sam's reaction to my suggestion.

"You know how much I hate shrinks. They've never helped me. I'll never forget that loser who tried to therapy me away from my *sinful lifestyle*. Your parents never subjected you to conversion therapy, but trust me, it isn't fun. Therapists are all quacks in my book. I can't believe you suggested this after everything I told you about my childhood." The anger in her voice scared me for a moment. I trusted a therapist would help her work through her issues, but I didn't think Sam would ever believe that.

I sighed. "Therapists aren't all quacks, but I understand. I'm sorry, I won't bring it up again." I pulled away from her, suddenly needing the physical distance.

"Hey, aren't you going to show me the rest of your beautiful mansion? A gorgeous home to match a stunning woman. You will always be the most exquisite woman in the room. You know that none of the women I date are marriage material. They're just fun and games until I'm ready to make you my wife."

Grabbing my hand, she pulled me back into her orbit and kissed me again. I let her hands roam for a smidgeon before that unsettled feeling could take root and ruin the evening. Her last words didn't make me feel better. It reminded me of the men

I'd known who viewed their wives as trophies or possessions. A wife was the final piece—a woman worthy of a man who had finally sowed his oats and needed a family to complete societal expectations of success.

Sam made appreciative noises of each room. When I brought her into the master bedroom, she remarked, "Nice." Then she punctuated her one-word response with a lascivious look. "Hopefully, we'll find our way into this room tonight."

I tamped down my irritation at her assumption that she would stay with me tonight. I wasn't convinced that it was inevitable. As we made our way to the kitchen, her gaze landed on my backyard. Sam's nose scrunched. "What the hell happened back there? Why is there a partially dug hole?"

I proudly responded, "That's where my koi pond will go. I'm creating a space where I can relax and enjoy the soothing sounds of nature. My next-door neighbor, who works at a nursery, is helping. She knows everything about plants, has excellent visuospatial skills, and keeps bringing delectable baked goods."

Sam frowned. "You know sugar is not healthy. It'll just cause unwanted pounds. You tend to pick up extra weight when you've eaten too much."

"Does that mean I won't be wife material if I gain ten pounds?" A full-on hissy fit was moments away.

"No, of course not. You know I'll love you no matter how much weight you gain, but I know you worry about that."

"Obviously, I worry a lot less about it than you. I've very much appreciated her baking and gardening skills," I said, suspecting the praise might get under Sam's skin.

"How is a gardener able to afford to live in this neighborhood? Does she have rich parents, too?"

I barely kept my anger in check. "No, she's a famous artist."

"A gardener and famous artist don't seem to go together. Why does she work at a nursery if she's so famous?" Her nose scrunched in distaste again.

"Don't be pretentious. You know how I hate that. What's wrong with working at a nursery?"

"Nothing. I just think if your neighbor is so famous, she wouldn't need to work at a nursery."

"She doesn't need to work there. She loves working with plants, and her friend owns the place. I think she enjoys helping out."

"How nice of her," Sam said with a hint of sarcasm. "What kind of artist?"

"She sculpts. My father has one of her sculptures. I've coveted that piece ever since he bought it, but I could never afford any of her pieces, even the small ones."

"Why? How much do they go for?"

"Thousands, like many thousands. I believe a few are more than double what I make in a year."

"You'd think she wouldn't waste her time digging holes with you, or working at her friend's place if making her sculptures earns her that much money."

"Not everyone is motivated by money, Sam. We should go now. Don't we have reservations at 6:30?"

"Yeah, right. Are you excited? I got us a table at that new place. It wasn't easy, but you deserve to be spoiled."

"Aren't you taking me to Beau's?"

"Change is good sometimes. I thought you would appreciate the effort to get us reservations at somewhere a lot nicer than Beau's," she responded offhandedly as if my preferences made no difference. She knew better.

"I hope the hype matches the experience."

"Oh, it will. Cori told me it was better than Duke's Seafood in Seattle."

It was typical of Sam to change her mind about where she planned to take me to dinner. My favorite place was no longer on the agenda. I bit my tongue. Cori's name came up way too often for my liking. I was sure Cori was the woman Sam considered her go-to fun-and-games person. Undoubtedly, she wasn't the only one. Sam had mentioned Cori long before I agreed to the open relationship, and I wondered again if they'd slept together before Sam muscled me into accepting the new arrangement. Sam kept insisting she'd never cheated on me, but I had my doubts. The words, *methinks the woman doth protest too much*, kept running through my head.

✝

Against my better judgment, I invited Sam inside after we returned from dinner. Earlier, I'd convinced her to give me the keys to her car and driven us back to my place. I'd stopped at one glass of wine. Sam hadn't. She was already slurring her words and talking too loudly because that's what she did when she was drunk. Sam wasn't a sad drunk or a happy drunk. She was a messy drunk, who thought the world was deaf and couldn't hear her unless she spoke twice as loud.

"Damn, you're so sexy in that dress. I can't wait to take it off you," Sam slurred.

I cringed and hoped that Zari wasn't listening. It was late. I prayed she'd already gone to bed. I didn't dare look lest I see the curtain flutter to confirm Sam's sloppy display was playing before her eyes. Our houses weren't close enough to hear one another, but Sam was so annoyingly loud, she might well be overheard. I couldn't be sure. I knew she was loud enough to wake the dead. Zari would at least hear a commotion, if not the actual words.

Allowing her to lean on me as she held onto the bottle of wine she'd brought as a house-warming gift, I hurried her into the house. "Shh, you'll wake up the neighborhood."

"Do you mean your neighbor? You've been talking a lot about her. She must be hot. I'm not sure I like that you have a hot neighbor. Where's your laptop? I'm going to look her up. Maybe not tonight." She giggled.

"How about coffee?" I held a tiny hope that she would sober up enough to drive home, even though I knew deep inside that ship had sailed. Sending her home drunk was not an option. She'd had most of the bottle of wine we'd had for dinner and two pre-dinner cocktails. As her lips loosened, she let slip how long she'd wanted to try this open relationship but had worried I wouldn't go for it, and she'd lose me. The fact that she'd been thinking about other women, a mere two months after we'd moved in together, sent me into a mini tailspin. As I recalled, in those early days, we still had sex regularly.

I managed to get her inside. Before she plopped onto the couch, she thrust the bottle of wine at me.

"Here, you open this, and we can relax before I ravish your body. Have I mentioned how hot you look tonight? I don't remember you looking this hot before you moved out."

"Sam," I started to say, "I don't think wine is a good idea. You're already going to have a hangover. I know how grumpy you are after a night of drinking, and honestly, I'm not up for entertaining grumpy Sam tomorrow morning."

She set the wine on the coffee table, and I cringed when I heard the loud clang. As I went to inspect the table, hoping she hadn't done any damage, she pulled me onto her lap. "Why have you been so distant tonight?"

Sam's hands began to roam all over my body as I attempted to squirm away and disentangle myself from her. "You're drunk. How about we go to bed? I have a nice guest bedroom all set up."

Her lower lip protruded, and she whined, "You're not going to let me sleep with you?"

"I think both of us will sleep a lot better in separate rooms. I remember how loudly you snore after you've had a few too many."

Her next words took on a hard edge. "And this is why I wanted to explore an open relationship. Why can't you allow yourself to let go once in a while? Would it kill you to share a bottle of wine with me and then make mad, passionate love? If we're supposed to be so in love, isn't that the least I can expect?"

I decided I would not take the bait. I walked out of the room and headed straight for Sam's car. Pulling her overnight bag from the back seat, I slammed her door in frustration. Almost as if it was a well-established habit, I looked toward my neighbor's house and saw the curtain flutter again. There was a soft light coming from the room where I spied the curtain, and I glimpsed Zari's shadow. I wondered if I'd woken her when I slammed the door. Maybe she'd already been disturbed by Sam when I tried to corral her into the house.

"Damn," I muttered.

At least one thing was going right for me because after I entered the house, I found Sam sprawled on the couch with her mouth hanging open unattractively. I said a small prayer of thanks that my bedroom was far from the living room. She'd already started snoring. I would put in my earplugs for good measure.

After grabbing an extra blanket from the hall closet, I tiptoed to Sam and covered her body. I didn't bother giving her a pillow. The throw pillows on the couch would have to suffice. I could lift her head and place a down pillow beneath, but I wasn't about to wake the sleeping beast. The last thing I did before retreating to my bedroom was place a glass of water and two aspirin on the coffee table. Sam never woke in the middle of the night, and that was another blessing. The last thing I wanted was for her to wake in the middle of the night and try to crawl in bed with me. Too bad the bedroom door didn't have a lock, but of course, most contractors didn't put locks on bedroom doors.

†

"Fuck." I heard as I was preparing to brush my teeth. The banging and clanging followed Sam's string of profanity.

She was holding her head and opening cabinets when I walked into the open space of the kitchen. The sun shone brightly, and I smiled, thinking about the time I would spend with Zari today.

"Looking for coffee?" I asked.

She dropped the cup she'd retrieved from the cabinet, and it shattered on the counter. "Shit. Sorry, you startled me. I'm sorry for falling asleep on you last night. It wasn't what I envisioned for our evening. Thanks for the aspirin. They haven't quite kicked in yet. Let me clean up this mess I made. At least it wasn't your favorite cup."

I waved my hand in the air. "Don't worry, I have too many cups, anyway. I needed someone to cull the herd."

Sam laughed. "I always loved your sense of humor."

"Go, sit. I'll clean this up and make coffee. Then after your stomach settles, I'll make breakfast. I'm sure the aspirin will kick in soon."

"So, since I botched last night, how about I take you for breakfast, and then maybe we can spend the day together? I'll think of something fun for us to do after we've had breakfast. The annoying brightness of the sun this morning tells me it will be a pleasant day today." She rubbed her eyes as she made her way gingerly to the couch, pushing the blanket aside.

"Can't. I have plans later on."

Sam quirked her eyebrow. "You do?" she asked. "With who?"

I tamped my frustration as I heard the note of incredulity in her voice.

"Can't say. That would violate our rules. Remember, no names and no talking about dates with other women." Zari didn't really fit into the date category, but Sam didn't know that. Although, if I was brutally honest, something was shifting in the way I viewed Zari, regardless of how I'd tried unsuccessfully to tamp down my feelings. *Would it be so horrible if it was a date?*

Sam opened her mouth to respond, then promptly closed it. The room was eerily quiet as I made the coffee and set the cup in front of Sam, who gulped her first sip.

"Thanks. You remembered how I like it. You do still love me," Sam joked.

I shook my head. "I don't think I've turned feeble in the brief time since I moved out. It's barely been a week."

The knock on the door startled both of us. I didn't wait for Sam to answer as I made my way to the front door.

Zari held a pan covered with aluminum foil in her hands. "I looked on the Internet what breakfast foods are best for hangovers. There's four scooped out bagels with egg, tomato, and avocado. The bagels are whole wheat." Her too-wide smile was plastered on her face, but she avoided looking either of us in the eyes. I stood frozen at the door. I didn't want Zari to get the wrong idea and think that Sam and I had slept together.

Sam stumbled to where I lingered immobile at the door. Her eyes were blinking as she tried to focus. "Hon, who is this?"

Zari remained rigid, still holding our breakfast.

"Oh, um, this is Zari, my next-door neighbor," I answered. "She made us breakfast."

"Wow, really? More baked goods? You know I don't put that sugary crap into my body."

"Oh, but you'll drink an entire bottle of wine," I mumbled.

"It's not baked goods. I looked up the best foods for hangovers. The breakfast is very healthy. You should avoid any acidic drinks like orange juice, but a balance of carbohydrates, protein, and fat will help prevent your blood sugar from dropping or spiking. Plus, breakfast will replenish lost nutrients, electrolytes, and B-vitamins," Zari recited.

"What are you, a walking encyclopedia?" Sam grumbled.

"Don't be rude, Sam. Come on in, Zari. This was very sweet of you. Don't mind the grumpy goose. She's always like this when she has a hangover. By the way, how did you know someone would have a hangover?"

"Alcohol dampens hearing, so when people drink too much, they think they are talking more softly than they are. Sam was loud last night, and she seemed to stumble when you helped her to the door. Jillian always has a hangover the next day when she talks loudly and stumbles."

I waved Zari inside. "Come have coffee with us."

"I can't stay long. I have to prepare for the day. You still want to see the studio?" The hesitation in Zari's voice was heartbreaking. I was glad that Sam had not folded the blanket when Zari's eyes landed on the crumpled fleece. I hoped she would surmise that was where Sam had slept last night. The last thing I wanted her to believe was that Sam and I were back together and completely free of the added complication of an open relationship.

"Of course I do. Nothing has changed."

Sam frowned. "This is who you have plans with today? Figures," she grumbled. "I knew something must be going on after hearing her name a gazillion times."

"A gazillion is not a number, it's a word that means a whole bunch which can't be quantified," Zari offered.

Sam snarled at Zari and then grumbled, "Freak."

I bit my tongue because I wasn't about to get into it with Sam while Zari stood there. I didn't want Zari to feel any worse than she probably already did. Besides, if I let my rage get the best of me, I'd likely raise my voice and make matters worse, although Sam was the recipient of my famous death glare. As soon as Zari left, I knew that Sam and I would have an argument of epic proportions. She knew how I felt about calling people names. That had always hurt my sister, and it was unacceptable to me.

"That's a mad face. I should go." Zari placed the breakfast on the counter, and before she pivoted and walked out the door, she left a parting comment. "I'll see you later today, Frankie. It was nice meeting you, Sam. Although Frankie has told me about you, she hasn't said your name a gazillion times."

I held my laughter back. *Score one for Zari.*

CHAPTER ELEVEN

ZARI

I wasn't asleep when I heard the commotion next door. I was staring at my ceiling, going over my plans for my date with Frankie. Saturdays were usually half sculpture days, but I needed to prepare for our date. I knew that Frankie had gone to dinner with Sam, and curiosity got the best of me. I wanted to see what Sam looked like, so I pushed the curtain aside to get a glimpse of the girlfriend that Jillian said deserves to have Frankie stolen from her. I tried not to think about the stealing part because that wasn't right. She was talking loudly. I estimated her voice at about one hundred decibels. Jillian got like this on occasions when she drank too much. I could barely see a bottle of wine in her hand. I thought that she'd already had too much by the look of her gait and how she leaned against Frankie.

What if Sam stayed the night, and they had sex? Would that diminish my chances with Frankie? I decided I'd get up early the next morning and check things out. If Sam's car was still in the driveway, that would mean she stayed the night. I didn't think Frankie would let Sam drive while under the influence. Frankie seemed too responsible to allow that. Jillian would be mad if I called her tonight while she had her Friday night date with Patty. They'd already stopped by earlier to visit with me before Frankie and Sam had left for their date. I would call first thing in the morning and ask for her advice.

I didn't want Frankie to have sex with Sam. I found myself upset, and even though Friday wasn't a sculpture day, I needed to calm myself. After I saw them enter the house, I went to my studio and began working on the almost-finished sculpture of Frankie. I was supposed to finish the clay model before I showed Frankie my studio, but I kept getting distracted.

It was well after midnight when I completed the model, and I felt calmer, so I headed to bed and fell asleep after setting my alarm for eight.

†

"What the fuck, Zari?" Jillian's gravelly voice came through the phone speaker. "It's before nine. I told you never to call before nine on a Saturday."

"I need some advice."

"Well, I knew that before I answered. This better be a fucking emergency." I heard the rustling of covers.

"I'm not bleeding or at the hospital, but it's important. Sam's car is still in the driveway. She was intoxicated last night. Do you think I still have a date with Frankie today? Should I go there this morning to confirm?"

"I don't think you should worry just yet. Sam probably stayed because she was drunk. Make some hangover food and take it over." Jillian chuckled. "That should really chap her hide. Kindness is hard to fight."

"Chap her hide? That's a new expression you haven't taught me."

"Look it up and let me go back to sleep. You have a plan now. Oh, and call me later to tell me how things work out for you today."

"Thanks, Jillian. I'm sorry for waking you. Tell Patty I said hello."

"She's waving at the phone and grinning at me. Perhaps this isn't the worst thing to happen because she's giving me *the look*. I'm pretty sure I'm getting morning sex. Bye, Zari."

The expression, *chap her hide*, was impeding my Internet search for hangover breakfast foods. I tried to push it away, but when something gets in my head, I have to search for the answers to my questions. It was a quick search, and I wondered why making Sam food to help with a hangover would displease her. I would have to ask Jillian about that later. Much later. I had breakfast to make.

†

My first impression of Sam was that she was pretty, even in her hangover state. Although, her attractiveness diminished the longer I stayed at Frankie's place. Sometimes I had that effect on people. I'd practiced enough with flashcards to understand when someone was angry. I remember when I had too much to drink that one time, and I didn't feel very good the next morning, either. I wondered if I'd had a mad face, too. I'd have to ask Jillian about that later.

I'd already altered my plans for the day, and that upset me a little. Jillian usually had excellent advice, so I hoped my delay to ride to the grocery store and pick up the supplies for the picnic dinner wouldn't throw my whole day off. I had a carefully arranged schedule, and now I was over an hour behind. When I was younger, that would cause an episode, but with years of practice and help from my mom and Jillian, I could handle smaller changes. I'd been doing that successfully for the past two years.

After putting on my bike gear and making sure I'd secured my saddlebags to my bike, I pedaled out of my garage. When I hit the garage door opener I'd installed on my handlebars, I saw Sam's car screech out of Frankie's driveway. I hoped she wasn't still intoxicated. I didn't think she was when I brought breakfast this morning, but Jillian said sometimes people could fool you. She said alcoholics have a particular knack for tricking a person into thinking they were sober when they weren't. Jillian would know. She dated a heavy drinker for a brief time before she met Patty.

I thought about checking on Frankie, but that would have altered my schedule more than I could tolerate. I pushed hard on my pedals to make it to the store in record time.

On my way back, I heard music coming from Frankie's backyard. I was tempted to check it out, but I had groceries to put away and food to prepare. I hurried to make the special picnic dishes I'd researched earlier. Then my curiosity got the best of me. Even though I knew I needed a shower, I hurried to Frankie's after putting in my industrial safety earplugs. I had to figure out why she had music blaring on a Saturday morning. If I could hear the music from far away, I knew it would be loud. I hoped my earplugs would do the trick. I wondered if Frankie's noise-canceling headphones were better.

Sweat poured over her brow, and she looked like she was either singing to the music or muttering. I noticed how the muscles in her arms were more pronounced as she dug. It looked like she was mad at the hole. But how can a person be angry with dirt?

When I got close, she looked up. I couldn't hear what she was saying, but she looked startled. She dropped her shovel and ran to the speaker on her weathered-wood deck. Now I couldn't hear anything at all. The faint sound of music was gone. I pulled out my earplugs and stuffed them in my pocket.

Frankie was breathing hard when she approached. A droplet of sweat made its way down her forehead, and she lifted her tank top to wipe it away. My eyes traveled to her stomach, and I had an insane desire to touch her belly.

"I'm so sorry, Zari. I didn't consider how loud music might disturb you. I'm such an idiot."

"I wasn't disturbed. I don't know if your headphones are better than my earplugs, but these worked fine. I was curious. What are you doing?"

She smiled. "Working out my frustrations with a bit of manual labor. I'm sorry about Sam. She usually has much better manners, especially around beautiful women."

"You think I'm beautiful?" I asked.

"I always say, *beauty is in the eye of the beholder.* However, by all objective standards, I'd bet my house that most people would find you extremely attractive. Unbelievable as it is, Sam was rude because I think she's jealous."

"Did you tell her I was trying to steal you from her?"

Frankie began laughing so hard that she started hiccupping. "No, no, of course not."

"Why not? It's the truth. Although, I haven't quite worked out the ethics of stealing yet. Is this one of those times where being honest could hurt someone?"

"Yeah, something like that. We're still on for today, right? Sam didn't scare you off, did she?"

"Why would Sam scare me off?"

"She was exceptionally rude, and what she said was almost unforgivable. Just because I didn't take her to task while you were standing there doesn't mean she didn't get an earful from me after you left. I was furious with her, and I was afraid I would raise my voice. I didn't want to do that in front of you."

I was getting uncomfortable. I knew Frankie was referring to when Sam called me a freak, but the kids had called me much worse in high school, and I survived. I decided to change the subject. Besides, I wanted to know if Frankie thought Sam was attractive. That might factor into my ability to steal Frankie from Sam. "She's very pretty."

Frankie nodded. "And charming when she wants to be. I could make excuses for her like it was the hangover talking, but I won't. By the way, the breakfast you made for us was divine. Too bad Sam didn't stick around to eat it. She wasn't happy with me after I yelled at her."

I cringed. "Were you as loud as Sam was last night when you yelled? Do you yell a lot?"

Frankie touched my arm. "I didn't raise my voice. It wasn't that kind of yelling. I suppose a more accurate description of what I did was call her out on her bad behavior. I promise not to raise my voice with you. Honestly, I can't think of any reason I would need to."

"I don't understand why people raise their voices. It isn't necessary to hear the words, even when a person is hearing impaired. I read that it was natural to talk louder to a person who is hearing impaired, but all that does is distort the words. It's better to repeat your words."

"Oh, trust me, I repeated a lot of words today. Although she said she heard me the first time, sometimes I think hearing someone and understanding are two completely different concepts. I repeat my arguments if I don't think the other person has heard me. It's a terrible trait."

"I'm not sure if repeating words helps a person who is not hearing impaired understand better. If I don't understand something, Jillian or my mom will use different words to explain it so that I'll understand. Jillian says nuances are lost on me. I had to look up nuances. Sometimes I ask for clarification, and sometimes I do research. Asking too many questions exasperates people. I've learned to listen for the cues. Jillian has a way of sighing, and that tells me she's done answering questions."

"Zari, I hope you never feel you have to stop asking me questions. I'll try not to get irritated with you. There may be times when I don't have a good answer for you, but I'll still attempt to respond to all your questions."

"I'm going to go now because I'm off my schedule. I need to make the dessert and take a shower. I keep my studio clean, but I'll make sure it's tidy enough to show you my work. Dust accumulates in the corners and on my completed work. I don't think there has been enough time for anything to attach itself to my new piece. I think this one is my best model yet."

"Zari, I'm looking forward to spending the day with you and seeing your studio." She brushed her hands on her tank top. "I promise I'll take a shower and won't look like a grubby little boy when I come over."

"I don't think you look like a grubby little boy. You have a lot of dirt on your shirt and face. But that's to be expected when digging a hole. I get dirty when I'm planting trees and shrubs. Everyone gets dirty sometimes. It would be good for you to shower, though. You'd smell a lot better."

Frankie laughed again. "Yes, I would."

CHAPTER TWELVE

FRANKIE

I looked at myself in the mirror and wondered if what I was wearing was okay. Zari didn't seem like the type of person to impress with a slinky dress. Besides, a dress wasn't the right thing to wear to a casual afternoon touring her studio and watching movies. Cargo shorts, a tank top, and an overshirt would have to do. I had finally admitted to myself that this was a date not only in Zari's mind but mine as well. Screw Sam. I would not feel one iota of guilt. Sam had defined the parameters of our relationship. She'd made the bed, so now she'd have to sleep in it. The fact that I was excited about the date only created a slight amount of discomfort. After Sam's reaction to Zari this morning, I was seriously considering whether Sam and I had a future like she had insisted.

I hadn't wanted to come empty-handed to the date, so before my shower, I made a quick trip to the flower shop. Zari didn't like wine and had mentioned preparing dessert. I hoped the flowers were an acceptable offering. She loved plants, but those were live ones.

I was second-guessing my decision to bring flowers as I stood on her doorstep at precisely one. Maybe I should have bought a flowering plant instead, or one of those fruit bouquets.

Zari opened the door and greeted me with her too-wide smile. She'd dressed similarly to me, and I breathed a sigh of relief.

"I hope you like cut flowers, and you don't consider that murder," I said.

"It's okay to cut off the flowers because pruning plants and bushes help them grow stronger. Thank you."

"Whew." I swiped my brow with my free hand.

"It was nice of you to bring flowers. I should bring you flowers. I hope we will have another date, and then I can bring flowers. What are your favorite flowers?"

"Um, I don't know. Nobody's ever given me flowers before. I suppose I like flowers that smell nice—roses, maybe. Or those lilies that are particularly aromatic. I pass by them in the grocery store, and they always seem to catch my nose."

"Orienpet lilies. Those are my favorite. You should come in now. We can go to the studio after I put the flowers in water." Zari accepted the flowers and opened her door wider.

I hadn't expected the cozy living space with colorful artwork and what looked like hand-stitched pillows. Neatly folded, a beautiful quilt sat on top of a comfortable and well-worn sofa in what I assumed was the exact center. For whatever reason, I had envisioned modern furnishings of chrome and muted colors. The tidiness did not surprise me.

Zari opened one of her cherry wood cabinets and retrieved a beautiful crystal vase. She clipped the ends of the flowers and placed them in the vase after filling it with water. Before she added the packet of white powder that came with the flowers, she stuck a thermometer she'd pulled from one of her drawers into the water.

"You're testing the water temperature?" I asked.

"Yes, the water should be around one hundred degrees for the floral preservatives to work best. Cut flowers can't continue to produce the life-sustaining sugars. The preservatives contain sucrose, an acidifier, and a biocide which help preserve the strength and scent of the flower."

"What's a biocide?"

"An antibacterial to kill the microbes that harm cut flowers. One of the biggest risks to cut flowers is bacteria or fungi attacking the open wound at the stem where the flower was cut. Sucrose adds energy to the flower. Tap water is alkaline, which means it has a pH of over seven. The cell sap of flowers should be around three-point-five pH. An acidifier helps the flower take in and transport water more easily by making the water more acidic. A common acidifier is citric acid, like you'll find in lemons and limes. But squeezing lemon or lime juice into the water is not precise. The floral preservatives are easiest."

"Wow, I never knew all that."

"Was that too much information? Jillian says I shouldn't cite information like I'm a walking encyclopedia."

"Not too much information at all. Zari, you know you don't have to change a thing for anyone. If they don't enjoy spending time with you, it's their loss. You should be exactly who you are. You don't need to do anything different to impress me."

"Are you being truthful? I can't always discriminate between truth and lies. Sometimes people will tell little white lies to keep from hurting my feelings."

"I'll always be truthful with you, Zari. I promise."

"Okay. That's good. Jillian and my mom don't lie to me. I appreciate that. You can tell me if I'm acting weird. Jillian does that for me."

I smiled at Zari. It was comforting to know that not only would I trust that everything Zari said to me was truthful, but that I could always be honest with her. As a rule, I tried to use tact when I sensed that others preferred the little white lies to the truth.

I knew Sam had a minimal tolerance for the truth if it was unflattering to her. She needed someone to dote on her and continually stroke her ego. It was exhausting. Maybe that was why she sought affection from others. I had tired of providing the constant praise she needed to keep her mood light. I wondered if her generous compliments to me and others were a subtle fishing expedition for reciprocity. In the beginning, I'd believed I was special, revered by her. Now it felt calculating.

I tried to take in Zari's house with a polite glance here and there, but I was overwhelmed and surprised by the warmth I felt. Her place seemed so unlike her and yet an exact match. Zari was quite the dichotomy—rigid and precise, yet generous and kind. She reminded me of my grandmother, who was nurturing and loving but a stickler for rules. She would envelop us in a hug, and it felt like a warm blanket of comfort and love.

†

103

Zari finished arranging the flowers in a way that seemed to satisfy her need for balance. I'd already selected a multiple of four and had bought eight flowers. She had an eye for color and shape, and arranged the flowers so that color and shape created a spectacular arrangement. I suppose it was the artist living inside Zari that made her so good at this. I was excited to see her studio. I knew she'd blow me away with her finished and unfinished pieces.

As we made our way to the back of the house, she led me into a glass-enclosed addition. The floor of the studio was so clean we could have eaten off of it. There were only a handful of sculptures on display and one off to the side that she'd covered. I wondered if this was the piece she'd been working on.

Walking around, I brushed my fingers over the exquisite detail in each sculpture. The work had a surprising sensuality combined with that same warm feeling I got whenever I was around Zari. It was as if passion and precision slammed together into an explosion of emotion. Most of the sculptures were of women in various poses except for a hummingbird in mid-flight, hovering over a honeysuckle plant. The fine details on his tiny body revealed Zari's remarkable talent. I touched the tip of his wing and told her how impressed I was with her sculptures.

"He is so lifelike. I can almost see his wings beating."

"Thank you. I had a tough time with that sculpture. It was frustrating to try to capture the movement of a hummingbird's wings. It isn't complete. That's the first time I've abandoned a project to start something new." Zari moved to the sculpture that was covered and lifted the cloth.

I gasped. "That's…that's…me."

"You don't like it? It's not the finished product because it's only the clay model. I try to make the clay models as detailed as the final marble sculptures." Zari's head tilted, and the lines in her forehead deepened.

I was naked and stretching. It was like I was reaching for something just out of my grasp. I wondered if Zari intended the sculpture to depict something about me I'd not yet had the chance to figure out.

"I'm naked, and you've captured my body with surprising accuracy. You've even sculpted the places where I prefer to be less squishy. Ugh. I was hoping to tone up a little this summer with all the hole digging and landscaping projects I've decided to tackle. How…how did you do this? I'm fairly certain that if I'd ever been naked around you, I would know."

Zari shrugged. "I have excellent visuospatial ability. It wasn't hard to fill in the places I hadn't exactly seen. With the nice weather this spring, I've seen you in shorts and a tank top. They haven't covered up much of your body. Occasionally, when you sweat a lot, you lift your shirt, and I've studied the parts of your body revealed when you wipe off the moisture. I would still like to see you naked. I could have done a better job with the sculpture."

"Do you have models who sit for you?"

"Sometimes."

"Your sculptures are beautiful. The models must have been…" My voice trailed off as I envisioned eager women sitting in Zari's studio without a stitch of clothing.

"Jillian helps me pick out the models. She interviews them for me. I pay them to sit for me, and they seem pleased by how much I give them for a few hours' work. Jillian said I should never stick the company pen in my pussy. One time I was interested in one of the models as a potential girlfriend. That didn't work out. That's when Jillian gave me that advice. At first, I didn't understand because I don't work for any company but Jillian's. I would never put a pen in my pussy."

I couldn't help myself. I started to laugh. I explained that I wasn't laughing at Zari. "Oh, my goodness, Zari, I promise I am not laughing at you. I'm glad you have someone like Jillian in your life. I don't believe I will ever forget her take on the typically male expression not to get involved with the people you work with."

"Yeah, she said that even though the models were beautiful, none of them were girlfriend material. She feared they would only be after my money. I wanted to sculpt you without entering into a business arrangement. You have perfect bone structure. Is it okay that I didn't ask first?"

"Ask what? To get naked for you?" I winked.

"Are you flirting with me? I can't tell. Jillian says that when a person winks at you, she's flirting."

"Maybe. Let's just say I'm glad you didn't ask me to sit for you while you created this sculpture. Can I ask what you think I'm reaching for?"

"Love and acceptance," she answered matter-of-factly. "If I sculpted myself, I would reach for the same thing. I'm making this sculpture for you. You mentioned you coveted the one your father owns."

"Well, I'm not sure I want to look at my naked body every day, regardless of how amazingly the piece is sculpted. At the same time, I'd also feel squeamish, imagining strangers ogling my squishy butt. Do you ever keep any of your work?"

Zari shook her head. "No, but if you don't want the final marble sculpture, I would be happy to keep it in my house. I think I'd like to look at your squishy butt every day. Should I make you something else?"

I walked to the finished marble sculpture of two women in a passionate embrace, the love written all over the expressions on their finely detailed faces. "How much for this one?"

"I don't know. I don't price my sculptures. The gallery owner does that with Jillian. Jillian says I'm never supposed to price my work because I would give my shit away, and there was no way she was going to let some fucker take advantage of me. But she doesn't have a say in the sculptures I give to family and the ones I gave to her. I'll bring that one over. Do you need a pedestal too?"

"Goodness, no. I feel kind of bad accepting this as a gift. You work hard on your art. Jillian's right about not letting anyone take advantage of your generous nature. I'll talk to Jillian, and maybe we can work out a payment plan."

"Do you mind if I do a little more research on this? I've never had anyone refuse a gift. I don't know how to respond."

I approached Zari and squeezed her arm with just enough pressure to not cause discomfort. "I'm sorry, I don't mean to make you uncomfortable. If accepting the gift is easier, I'll get over my discomfort."

Zari relaxed, and I had an insane desire to take her in my arms and kiss her senseless with just the right amount of pressure to make it enjoyable for her as much as I knew it would be for me. This beautiful, generous, and genuine person was so close I could almost feel her breath against my skin. I pulled away just in time.

"So, what's next on the agenda?"

"I bought you a bike so I could take you to a lake with a walking path. The nature path has various trees, bushes, and other plants beautiful at this time of year. There's also a place where I've found a four-leaf clover before. We can't dig them up, though. I only do that on the property I own. I could take you there another day, but there's only a creek on my property. A lake is better for swimming and boating. We could swim in the lake. It's unseasonably hot today."

"Whoa, I'm still stuck on the bike you bought me. You didn't have to do that."

"I didn't buy the most expensive one. Jillian said I shouldn't buy anything super expensive and to slow my roll. I wanted to take you on a picnic dinner after a bike ride to the lake. I couldn't do that if you didn't have a bike."

"Not that I don't appreciate the gesture. I do. How about if I pay you for the bike because I meant to purchase a new one, anyway? The lake sounds great, but I need to change and put on my bathing suit underneath my clothes."

"Okay. I already have my suit underneath. While you're getting ready, I can roll over your new bike and then get mine from the garage. I also need to pack our dinner and attach the cooler to my bike. I hope you like what I fixed."

"I've no doubt the food will be fabulous."

CHAPTER THIRTEEN

ZARI

I tried not to bother Jillian too much, but I needed to know what to do about Frankie's reluctance to accept my gifts. Did that mean me stealing her away from Sam wasn't a possibility because stealing was wrong? I always thought to give your girlfriend gifts was normal. Then there was the moment where I thought for sure she was going to kiss me. I'd watched *Desert Hearts* again, as Jillian suggested. Then I studied several other romance movies. I felt confident I could decipher the look. She'd glanced at my lips, and her eyes got dark. Maybe I should have tried to kiss her then, but I'd missed an opportunity. It was all so confusing to me.

"Well, at least you waited until a reasonable hour to call. By the way, why are you calling me right now? I thought your date started at one." Jillian hadn't bothered to say hello.

"It did. She's at her house changing. I'm going to take her to the lake. I don't have much time. She doesn't want to accept my gifts. What do I do? Oh, and I think she was going to kiss me."

"As much as I'd like to explore that second part about the kiss, let me just say, good for her. At least you know she isn't after your money."

"I don't think she was very comfortable with the clay model I did of her. She doesn't want the finished sculpture in her house and is fussy about it being displayed somewhere else. She liked the one with the two women that's still in my studio."

"Well, she has good taste. Zari, I wouldn't want to look at myself, either, especially if you sculpted me naked, which I am presuming you did with Frankie. I'm guessing she offered to pay you for the other piece."

"Yes, and the bike, too. Frankie said she wanted to talk with you and work out a payment plan because I told her you set the prices for my work with the gallery owner. Maybe you could make the price affordable to her. She's a teacher and doesn't make a lot."

"Okay, I'll quote her something outrageously low. Will that work for you? Now, tell me about this almost kiss?"

"I think she thought I was upset because she didn't want to accept my gifts. I was confused and told her I needed to do more research to understand why she would refuse my gifts. She squeezed my arm with just the right amount of pressure, and we were so close. I saw her look at my lips, and her eyes got dark. But then she pulled away."

"She already knows you're blunt, and that hasn't scared her. Ask her about it. Tell her you would have welcomed the kiss. Maybe you could ask her if you can kiss her?"

"Okay. I can do that. I really like Frankie. I want this to work out. She isn't happy with Sam, and I know I would be a much better girlfriend. Sam screeched out of her driveway this morning not long after I left."

"Perfect. Keep doing whatever you're doing because it's working, Zari. Now get your ass to her house before she thinks you've abandoned her. Woo the shit out of her."

"Thanks, Jillian."

"You're welcome. What are best buds for? But no more calling early on a Saturday morning." Jillian chuckled and then ended the call.

†

I must have taken too long packing the food and talking with Jillian because Frankie was walking up to my driveway with an enormous smile on her face. She had a bottle of sunscreen in her hand. I was finishing with the cooler and had secured it to my bike. The new bike was leaning on the wall, ready to go. I'd adjusted the seat and handlebars after looking at the length of Frankie's arms and legs. I didn't think I would be off more than an inch.

"Sorry, this has taken so long. I called Jillian to get some advice."

Frankie chuckled. "More advice, huh?"

"Yes, she said I should just ask you if you were about to kiss me earlier. She thinks if I haven't scared you away with how blunt I can be, then asking for clarification is okay."

Frankie turned a deep shade of red. "This is going to be a little new for me—a completely open and honest conversation

111

at all times. Even though the question is a bit unsettling because I didn't think I was that obvious, you deserve an honest answer.

"You weren't obvious, but I've learned to pay close attention to cues. Plus, I recently watched several movies with love stories. Jillian made that suggestion, so I would recognize when you wanted to kiss me."

"Yes, I wanted to kiss you earlier, and then thought I should slow my roll. Things are complicated right now. I haven't ever done an open relationship, and it isn't easy or comfortable for me. The only honorable thing to do would be to figure my shit out first. If I'm going to wait for Sam to get through this phase of hers, I should do that. And if I determine she's not worth waiting for, I should end it. Can you be patient while I figure that out? I think I'm close."

"I'm a very patient person. I should also tell you I would have welcomed the kiss. Should I wait until you figure things out before I ask if it's okay to kiss you?"

"Yeah, I think that would be best because, right now, if you asked, I'd say yes. I don't think that would help unravel things for me. The knots would only get tighter."

"Knots?"

"It's a metaphor for my tangled emotions."

"Metaphors are hard for me because I'm so literal most of the time."

"I know, I'm sorry. I'll try to remember that, but in the meantime, it's always okay to ask. I won't tire of your questions. I promise."

"Okay."

"Hey, I brought sunscreen because I don't know about you, but I tend to burn. Contrary to popular belief, having an olive-hued skin complexion does not guarantee protection from harmful UV rays. Since we'll be outside for a long time, I need to coat my skin with lotion."

"Yes, having darker skin does not safeguard a person from sun damage or skin cancer. I have sunscreen in one of my bags."

Frankie chuckled. "Of course you do. I should have known. Were you ever a girl scout?"

"No. I didn't like joining groups with loud girls."

"That was a joke because girls scouts are always prepared. That's their motto, *Be Prepared*. I was a girl scout, but I can't claim to always be prepared. I certainly was not prepared to meet someone like you at a time in my life when everything else is so chaotic."

"I don't think if I was a girl scout, that would have done much to prepare me. I've had to learn a lot on my own. Jillian and my mom primed me for other people's reactions because that isn't something a person can learn on the Internet. I also had a lot of help from a therapist."

"I should have helped Penny more. Somehow, I get the impression you endured high school a lot better than my sister. She finally joined a support group, but she had it pretty rough there for a while."

I didn't like seeing Frankie's sad face and needed to know if I'd caused that. "Have I made you sad?"

"No, no. I was just thinking of Penny. I have a little regret, that's all."

"Regret?"

"I wasn't there for Penny. If I could do things differently, I would. I had a lot more opportunities to protect her, and I didn't always do that. It wasn't like I was jealous of the attention she received from my parents. It was more about fitting in and how others would judge me. The few times I took a stand didn't end up too well for me. I suppose using my fists versus my words was not the right approach. I deserved the suspension."

I didn't know how to respond to Frankie's confession. I pulled the sunscreen from my bag and offered it to Frankie. "I have thirty sport. It's supposed to stay on better."

"Fifteen should work fine for me. Letting a little vitamin D in will give me a healthy glow."

"We should go now. I propped your bike against the wall and adjusted the seat for you. If it needs further adjusting, I have more tools in my pack."

"How much was the bike? Don't forget; I'm paying you back. Hopefully, this neighborhood is a lot safer than my old one, and I won't have to worry about some jerkwad stealing this new bike. Asshats cut my lock with cable cutters. At least that's what the police said. Apparently, it's a favorite tool for bike thieves."

"I had them install the best u-lock on the market. Although it's heavy, there's a guarantee that comes with the lock."

"You didn't answer how much."

"Eight hundred and nineteen dollars and sixty-six cents with tax." I didn't tell her about the fifty-dollar delivery charge to my house or the cost of the lock because they weren't technically part of the value of the bike. "You don't have to pay me back. I have plenty of money to spend how I wish. Are you refusing because you don't want to appear selfish or because you aren't able to return my romantic intentions? After I talked with Jillian and she didn't answer me about the bike, I did a quick Internet search. Those are two reasons listed."

I was happy to see the tiny smile appear on Frankie's face. "Your gifts are overly generous, and I guess it made me feel uncomfortable. I don't believe you have ulterior motives for the gifts."

"Okay, then I'm supposed to keep offering until you're willing to accept because then you won't appear selfish."

Frankie laughed. "Okay, you win. I would never want to insult you. Can I still pay for the sculpture? How about we settle on that compromise?"

"That works. I already worked that out with Jillian."

"Why do I think I'm going to get the deal of the century?"

"If you mean that Jillian will quote an outrageously low price, then yes."

"I think I'm in real trouble here. You're too hard to argue with because you're so honest and genuine. You never have any ill intent. How can a person compete with that?"

Chapter Fourteen

Frankie

I was definitely out of shape. After only four miles, I began squirming on the seat. She'd chosen an extra cushy saddle for me, but that didn't help. I should have worn bike shorts over my bathing suit and under my cargo shorts. There wasn't enough padding to keep me from chaffing. I could already feel the burn in my legs. Zari glanced in my direction and frowned.

"You haven't been on a bike in a long time," she stated. "We can stop at the park and take a break. The lake is another three miles." She didn't appear winded at all. That should not have surprised me, since a bike was her primary mode of transportation.

"You don't mind?"

"No, I like the park. It's usually quiet enough. There aren't as many varieties of plants there, but they keep the grass mowed, and there are picnic tables spaced out for anyone who doesn't want to sit on the grass."

"I don't mind the grass. It might be cushier than a hard bench."

"I've been looking at recumbent bikes because they're more comfortable on lengthy rides, but now I'm used to my saddle because I've broken it in. I should have bought you a recumbent bike."

"No, this one's great. A lot nicer than my old bike. I'm just being a baby. I need to develop butt calluses. Contrary to how I'm presenting, I do enjoy bike riding."

Zari turned into the small park and glided to a stop at an open picnic table. After she laid her bike against the table, she asked, "I brought apples and cheese for snacks. Are you hungry?"

"I could eat something small. Can I help?" Pulling my water bottle from my bike, I set the bike against the table next to hers, then gulped down the refreshing water, still relatively cold.

"Do you still want to sit on the grass?" she asked.

I rubbed my behind and nodded.

She undid the bungee cord holding the blanket and handed it to me. "You can lay this on the grass over there."

I appreciated the padding to the blanket and smoothed out the wrinkles as best I could. Then I lowered my sore body to the soft material. Leaning back, I lifted my face to the sun.

"This is nice."

Zari laid out the cheese and cut up apples, and I dived right in. She'd also brought my water bottle, which I'd forgotten after setting it on the picnic table.

"I like hard cheese with a nutty flavor. This is my favorite because it's aged just right."

"It's perfect," I responded.

Pushing her hand in her front pocket, she retrieved two small pills. "Here." She held out her hand. "I brought Tylenol. I thought maybe you would be a little sore."

I shook my head. "How is it even possible that you're still single? I don't think I've ever met a more thoughtful person." Accepting the pills, I popped them in my mouth and washed them down with my water.

"Because I ask too many questions, and I'm too blunt."

I chuckled. "You didn't have to answer. That was a rhetorical question."

"Oh. But you should know that sometimes I hurt a person's feelings. I don't mean to. I make most people uncomfortable. Even Jillian tires of me sometimes."

"I can't imagine tiring of you, Zari. I've already learned so much in the limited time I've known you. I suppose being a teacher makes me more receptive to learning uncommon things."

"Can I ask you a personal question?"

I nodded. "Sure."

"How long do you think it will take you to figure your shit out? I would like to move to the kissing stage."

I chuckled. "That's an excellent question. I don't believe I have a precise enough answer for you. At the very least, I'll need to talk things over with Sam, and I don't know when I'll see her again. She left in a huff this morning. Having a meaningful conversation with her when she's still angry isn't the best option. I need to wait for her to cool down. She'll call when she's ready."

"Okay. It helps me to be patient when I have an exact timeframe, and I can put that in my calendar."

"I know, Zari, and I wish I could offer that to you, but I can't."

"Thank you for being honest."

"Always."

"Was this a long enough rest for you?"

I smiled. "Yes, thanks. Three more miles, huh? I think I can manage that. Of course, the way back is a whole new enchilada."

"I didn't make Mexican food. Should I have brought enchiladas?"

"Nope, another combination of expressions. Probably not something anyone else has ever used. Sometimes I dance to the beat of my own drum. I'm going to have fun teaching you new lingo."

†

By the time we arrived at the lake, I was sweaty again. The water looked so refreshing, I locked up my new bike and stripped down to my bathing suit to check out the temperature of the lake.

After jumping in, I sputtered, "Holy shit. This is cold."

Zari folded her shorts and tank top after she'd removed her shoes and socks. She walked to the edge of the water. "It's glacier-fed, so the water is always cold."

"Are you coming in?" I asked.

"Yes." Zari walked into the water as if it was the perfect temperature.

"You don't think it's cold?"

"I don't like loud noises, but extreme cold and hot don't affect me at all. Although, when I was first learning how to swim, I was afraid of the water."

"Good to know."

I was careful not to splash her to play around too much without knowing how she might react. Even though the cold didn't bother her, unexpected splashing might trigger an unpleasant sensory reaction. That didn't stop me from swimming to her and taking her hands.

"I'm used to the cold now. This is nice. I like how clear the water is. I'm accustomed to swimming in slimy lakes filled with algae. I grew up in Moses Lake, which is farther east. The lake would get so grimy. I never wanted to swim anywhere but in our pool."

"Pools are okay. That's where I learned to swim. I prefer this lake because of the walking paths. Would you like me to take you to one of my favorite trails?"

"In a bit. Can we sit in the sun and relax for now?"

"Okay."

Zari seemed restless, and I assumed she was more comfortable walking in nature and pointing out the various plants and shrubs. "Don't worry. I'll let you impress me with your vast knowledge later on."

I shivered as I emerged from the icy lake, but quickly warmed after we laid the blanket on the sand and soaked in the sun's warmth. There was a light breeze that danced across my skin, making the temperature comfortable as I placed my arm behind my head. Unfortunately, it was so comfortable I ended up falling asleep on the blanket and startled awake as I began to snore.

When I opened my eyes, I found Zari studying me as she lay on her side.

"You were snoring."

"Yeah, that's what woke me up." I laughed. "I'm so sorry I fell asleep on you. I'll bet you never had such an electrifying date before," I said.

"That was sarcasm, right? I thought you said you wouldn't use sarcasm with me?"

"I guess it's harder to avoid than I thought. I meant I wouldn't use sarcasm at your expense, to be mean."

"Okay. The noise didn't bother me. It was a soft snoring. Not like my dad. It's been nice to study you. I have an idea for another sculpture."

I flung my arm over my face and groaned. "Ugh, don't waste your materials on another sculpture of me."

"It's not a waste. You are very beautiful," Zari declared.

"I think it's time you showed me those walking trails. I want to know what smells so sweet." I jumped from the blanket and pulled my tank top over my now dry swimsuit, then pulled up my shorts. I found my socks stuffed inside my shoes and put them on to prepare for what I hoped would be a short hike.

Zari led me to the trail and fortunately kept a very reasonable pace. She pointed out the various plants, and I was delighted to discover the elusive huckleberry bush. I wasn't sure if I could find the spot again, but I sure enjoyed popping a few of the sweet and tangy berries into my mouth. I remembered ordering a huckleberry lemon drop one time, and I hoped I could find this spot so that I could make that particular drink. Maybe that would be something Zari would enjoy instead of wine.

†

"Mmm, I don't think anything I could have prepared would have been as lovely as this meal. Even my famed lasagna pales compared to your masterpieces. If you need a back-up occupation, try head chef at any restaurant of your choosing. I'm going to let you cook for me anytime you want." I shoved another bite of the watermelon, tomato, and fresh mozzarella salad into my mouth. "I don't even like watermelon, but this is divine combined with all the other flavors."

"It isn't that hard. I find everything online." She began digging in her cooler. "I hope the chocolate didn't melt."

My ears perked up at her mention of chocolate. "Oooh, I love chocolate."

"I made chocolate-covered strawberries. It's supposed to be a good dessert for a date. I don't have champagne to go with it. I didn't think that was a good idea because we're on bikes. Jillian suggested I bring wine, but I didn't think that was appropriate either. Studies have shown that it is more dangerous to bike while intoxicated than it is to drive while under the influence of alcohol."

"I believe that. I'll have enough trouble pedaling the seven miles completely sober. Adding alcohol would be disastrous. Zari, you know, I don't have to drink to have a good time."

"Why do you think romantic dinners include wine or other alcohol?"

I shrugged. "Alcohol loosens people. I suppose first dates can be hard when you're getting to know someone. It helps make the whole experience a little more comfortable."

"Are you uncomfortable without alcohol?"

"Not at all. If you want to know the truth, I'm more uncomfortable when someone is sloppy drunk."

"Like Sam was last night?"

"Yes, exactly. Sam's only saving grace is that she isn't a mean drunk. She also isn't particularly charming when she gets like that."

"Why?"

"Because she has one thing on her mind, and having a meaningful discussion isn't part of her repertoire when she's intoxicated. Getting me naked is her only goal."

"I can understand why she would want you naked. I'd like to see you naked, too."

I had just taken a sip of water and sputtered. "Oh, uh, well, hopefully, you haven't planned this whole wonderful day so that you can get me naked."

"No, I haven't. I planned this day so I can steal you away from Sam. I know it's wrong to steal because I tried to find instances where stealing is not morally wrong, but I couldn't find any. Even stealing to feed your family was considered wrong. Stealing falls into the category of moral absolutism."

"Stealing me away from Sam is an expression versus the literal meaning of stealing. So, I don't believe that is the same thing. Although, if you were actively trying to be a home wrecker, that would be wrong. I don't believe that applies here. Sam is not my wife or even my exclusive girlfriend anymore."

"That makes me feel better. Although, I should be honest and admit that seeing you naked would be a bonus. I also have a nice feeling whenever I spend time with you, so if you end up being a good friend like Jillian, I'll consider this day a success. I don't want to be friends, though."

"No matter what happens with Sam, I already consider us friends. The 'more' part is still a little fuzzy for me. It's not like I'm not attracted to you or don't think we're compatible. You understand that, right?"

"Yes. You need to figure out your shit first."

"Exactly. Can I have the recipe for your chicken curry salad and that wonderful watermelon dish?"

"Sure, they're easy to make."

"Next time, I'll find the great recipes to surprise you."

"Okay."

CHAPTER FIFTEEN

ZARI

I felt calm on the evening that we watched the superhero movies because Cleopatra had emerged from her hiding place and crawled onto my lap. I was able to pet her the entire time we watched the television. As the credits rolled on *Captain Marvel*, I didn't know what the big deal was. There weren't any kisses between women, and it didn't seem like Captain Marvel or Wonder Woman were lesbians or bi-sexual. I could have done without the love story between Diana Prince and Steve Trevor. I concluded that action films were not my thing, despite the beautiful and powerful women portrayed in the two movies. Strong doesn't have to mean someone who fights villains with their fists. I wanted to talk with Frankie about this because it made little sense to me.

"It looks like Cleo has given you her stamp of approval," Frankie said as she looked at her cat purring in my lap.

"She's a very nice cat. Why do lesbians watch these movies?" I asked.

She looked strangely at me. "Good question. I suppose it's because the movies portray strong women who don't take any crap from men. Plus, they're superheroes who are easy on the eyes."

"There are a lot of pretty women in movies that aren't suggested for lesbians. I liked *Desert Hearts* much better. I learned how to kiss from that movie."

Frankie raised her eyebrow. "That movie certainly had the potential to teach you a lot more than how to kiss."

"Not really. I couldn't quite see what Cay was doing to Vivian under the sheets."

"Well, if you want something more explicit, but honestly I think it pushes the porn envelope, try *Blue is the Warmest Color*. You could also watch the first season of *The L Word*. That has very explicit sex scenes."

"Jillian told me about *The L Word*. Maybe I can order the DVD collection, and you can watch it with me. I don't have to watch *The L Word* for additional education because other movies have taught me quite a lot. I haven't been able to use what I learned yet, but I hope to someday. I think I'm a good kisser, though."

"Good to know," Frankie said, and then laughed. "Okay, next movie night we can watch a lesbian love story, unless you're open to superheroes that are lesbians. I've already seen the first season of *Batwoman*, but I wouldn't mind watching that again."

"Okay. I liked Ruby Rose in *Orange Is the New Black*. Is she as nice to look at in *Batwoman*?"

"Oh yeah. She sure is. I like badass women. *Black Lightning* is also a favorite of mine and has a lesbian superhero. You'll have to wear headphones for both of those."

"I can compromise since you seem to like movies with comic book heroes that feature women. It's important to compromise in a relationship. It can't be all about me and my needs. Mom and Jillian taught me that." I shifted in my seat on the couch and looked at Frankie.

"You're spot on about that."

I wanted to kiss her, but after what I'd just said, I knew I would be kissing her to meet my needs. I didn't think that was what she wanted until she settled things with Sam. I sure wanted her to end her relationship with Sam. It didn't seem like her needs were getting met at all.

"Does Sam meet your needs? It sounds like the open relationship is meeting her needs, but does it meet yours?"

Frankie scrunched her face. "No, it doesn't. Can we talk about something else? I'd rather not be reminded of Sam right now. Besides, I think it's rude to talk about my pseudo-girlfriend while spending time with you."

"Okay. What do you want to talk about? I know a lot about plenty of different topics because I research things whenever something comes up."

"I'm sure you do." Frankie tapped her chin with her index finger. "I should probably decipher where you're at with politics. Did you vote in the last election?"

"I did. It was confusing because the various news stations were reporting different things. I didn't know whom to believe. Finally, I researched the most unbiased news sources and started only watching or reading from those sources. When I heard the candidate talk about a woman's pussy, I decided he would not make a good president. I don't understand how he won."

"You've met my criteria. I know it's narrow-minded of me to limit my friends to those who voted against he-who-should-not-be-named, but that's my stance. I've lost good friends over competing views on that despicable man."

"He isn't very nice. I know that sometimes I say things that hurt people because I'm too honest, but I think he says things that will hurt on purpose."

"Which news sources are the most unbiased from your research."

"The Associated Press, Reuters, the BBC, and The Wall Street Journal. They all seem to stick with the facts. I like Rachel Maddow, but I read that where she works is biased to the left."

"I'm all about the left, so I only watch the news stations that lean left."

"Is it a bad thing that I don't? Jillian watches those same left-leaning stations. Maybe I should, too. If both of you prefer those sources of news, that says a lot."

"No, don't change a thing. I'm sure Jillian has advised you to follow your own path. Becoming a clone of either Jillian or myself won't help you find a girlfriend that is perfect for you."

"I've already found one. I just have to be patient and wait for you to leave Sam."

Frankie smiled at me. "I admire your perseverance."

"Thank you. Are you going to spend the day with Sam tomorrow?"

Sculpting Her Heart

"No, we don't have any plans. I believe I have a date with my backyard tomorrow. That hole is not going to dig itself. Why?"

"I thought that if you spend one day with me and then the next day with Sam, that might help you figure things out. You could use an unbiased approach by giving both of us equal time."

"Wow, that's very magnanimous of you. I doubt Sam would suggest the same thing. But then again, Sam was the one to suggest we have an open relationship, and that I should date others. However, I believe her idea of dates is a little different from mine."

"In what way?"

"It sounds like her dates are all about sex and nothing to do with getting to know the other person."

"Oh. Does Sam want you to have sex with other people?"

"Maybe. I don't know. Perhaps Sam only said I should date others to assuage her own guilt. Or she wants me to pick up a few new techniques. I never know with Sam. She often has ulterior motives. I wouldn't be surprised if she suggested a three-way."

"A three-way is having sex with two people at once, right?"

"Uh-huh."

"Have you done that before?"

Frankie turned away and wouldn't look at me.

"Will you think less of me if I admit that I have once?"

"No. What was it like?"

"Impersonal. I'm not saying there aren't times when people enter into a 'throuple' and emotion accompanies sex, but in my sole experience, that didn't happen."

"I don't think I'd like that either. It might create a sensory overload and then cause a meltdown. It's been a while since I had a meltdown. I only want to have sex with one person."

"Me too. I suppose I'm old-fashioned. I only want to have sex with one person at a time. And I'm not just saying one person in the same room, but one person at a time as in only having a sexual relationship with one person. That's why an open relationship doesn't work for me. Don't even get me started on how awkward it was to insist that Sam get tested regularly."

"Testing is recommended, but the frequency varies. After you told me about your open relationship, I looked it up on the Internet. Testing frequency depends on whether Sam is having sex with men who have sex with other men. Does Sam have sex with men?" I asked.

"Definitely not, which is probably why she bristled at my suggestion, thinking her risk was low. I insisted, and she finally agreed. She didn't make the same request of me. Probably because she didn't believe I would have sex with someone else. She would be right on that account. The question I have to resolve is if I can allow Sam the freedom to explore that without getting upset."

"If you're not spending the day with Sam, would you like help with the hole?"

"Even though I feel like that would be taking advantage of your generosity, I'm going to accept your kind offer. Besides making the job go faster, I get to spend more time with you. Whatever happens, I enjoy our time together."

I wasn't positive, but I thought that maybe whatever I was doing was working. I hoped Frankie would choose me over Sam. Her girlfriend was making mistakes, and so far, it didn't seem like I was pushing Frankie away. She appeared to like my cooking. Even though I usually had breakfast and lunch on Sundays, I thought I would force myself to step out of my comfort zone and make Frankie a nice brunch.

I went to bed happy because Frankie had kissed my cheek again. The kiss delivered a warm feeling throughout my body. I was convinced Frankie would be the one for me like Patty was for Jillian, and Dad was for Mom. Even though I didn't believe in God, I spoke to my ceiling and asked whatever higher power that might exist to make sure Sam kept making mistakes.

†

A few years ago, I'd bought a dolly to help me move sculptures around in my studio and to load into the truck the gallery owner sent before a big show. It made it easier on the guys she always sent to pick up my art. I was glad to have the dolly on Sunday morning because I'd prepared too much food to carry in my arms.

As I reached the front door, I heard the music turn on in her backyard. I rolled the dolly along the grass until I entered her yard. Frankie was stretching, and I must have startled her.

"Zari! I didn't hear you come into the yard. Sorry, is my music too loud?"

"Maybe a little."

She ran to her cell phone, sitting next to the small speaker, and pressed on a button. "Is that better?"

"Yes, thank you."

She glanced at my dolly. "What's that?"

"Brunch."

"Oh, my goodness. That's perfect. I was so eager to get out and begin digging again that I've only had coffee. I suppose that wasn't very smart of me. I will need fuel with what I suspect will be a very long and hard day of manual labor. Do you want to eat on the deck or inside?"

The sun warmed the day, and I thought eating outside would be great. "Outside."

"Sounds wonderful. Let me get the plates."

"I brought plates and utensils."

She laughed. "Of course you did. How silly of me to think you wouldn't have everything we'd need for a fabulous Sunday brunch."

"I didn't bring mimosas because I thought it would not be responsible to drink alcohol before resuming work on the pond. I have a pitcher of orange juice instead."

Frankie walked over and picked up the pitcher of orange juice along with the pan of stuffed French toast. After she set them on the table, I grabbed two of the other items I'd carefully laid inside the aluminum containers. The food covered the small table in no time.

She lifted the pan with the French toast and squealed. "This is one of my all-time favorite breakfast foods. Can I peek at everything else before loading my plate with French toast?"

I pulled off the covers to expose the fruit and cheese platter, various meats and smoked salmon, and eggs Benedict with hollandaise made from scratch. That was a lot harder to prepare than I thought. I'd had to throw away two attempts before I got it right.

"There's a lot here because I didn't know what you liked to eat besides cinnamon rolls and sweet pastries."

"This looks so good. I think there's enough food here to feed the whole gated community."

"Should I call Jillian and Patty? They can help us eat this. I don't know if I want to invite the community."

"You know, that sounds like a great idea. I've met Jillian, but I'd love to meet her partner."

"Her wife."

"Wife? That's great. She looks so young to be already married."

"Jillian said when you know, you know. She told me I would feel it when it happens to me. I should tell her she's right."

Frankie coughed. "You should call before everything gets cold."

"Okay," I said, but I could tell Frankie was uncomfortable.

I decided I needed to talk with Jillian because although I said I would be patient, I desperately wanted to make Frankie my girlfriend. I couldn't ask her to marry me before an appropriate amount of time together. I'd have to research how many months or years we'd have to be in a relationship before I could ask her to marry me. I knew the time frame varied. My dad waited years, but Jillian said she knew right away and had asked Patty six months after their first date.

†

"I waited until ten to call today. Were you having sex this morning?" I asked since they both looked like they had just rolled out of bed.

"Zari! Not a question to ask at brunch," Jillian answered.

"Why not? You haven't showered yet. You tell me when I'm disturbing you during sex, but you didn't grumble at me this morning." I didn't understand why I couldn't ask her that during brunch. I wondered if conversation during brunch differed from other meals. I never got my answer, but it didn't seem essential to pursue.

Frankie chuckled and handed Jillian the pan of French toast. "I recommend the stuffed toast. By the way, it's nice to meet you, Patty."

"You as well. Jillian told me that Zari had a new neighbor she'd been spending time with. When she called with the offer of brunch, we were still lounging in bed. Since Zari never does anything half-assed, I knew the brunch would be delicious." Patty dished her plate and added a piece of toast to Jillian's.

"Looks like your backyard is coming along. I assume where you've placed all the bushes and trees is where you'll plant them." Jillian put a forkful of eggs Benedict in her mouth and moaned. "Fuck me if this isn't the best damn eggs I've ever had. Damn, Zari, you outdid yourself with this brunch." She turned to her wife. "How come you never cook me brunch on Sundays?"

"You know, cooking is not one of my talents. I have other Sunday morning skills." Patty waggled her eyebrows. "I could ask you the same question."

"Touché. Do you guys have plans today?" Jillian asked.

"I feel a little guilty because Zari offered to help me with the hole for the pond and brought brunch. I should have been the one to have a wonderful spread for her. I'll try to make up for it with dinner tonight if she's free." Frankie glanced in my direction. "I feel like I've been monopolizing all her time. She must have better things to do than help me with my massive project."

Jillian said, "She doesn't."

At the same time, I said, "I don't."

Patty looked between the three of us and smiled. "So, Jilly said you're a teacher. Where do you teach?"

"I work in the special education department for the district. I really wish they would change the name to the exceptional education department, but I guess that confuses people. There's only one elementary school here, and I'm the only teacher in the department. I was lucky to have this opportunity. The kids are great, even the ones with emotional challenges. Exceptional education tends to have a hodgepodge of issues. I have to remain adaptive if I'm going to be successful at helping the kids learn."

"I'll bet the kids love you." Jillian scooped up the smoked salmon to add to both plates.

"On most days, they seem to respond well to me, but we all have our moments. Some days are more challenging than others. The trick is to find out what sets a kid off. It's usually something that happened at home. Not every child has supportive or nurturing parents. That's the saddest part of my job, trying to help them when I know the minute they get home, the parents will unravel my work. What about you, Patty? Where do you work?"

"I'm a boring accountant for the local hospital. I help Jillian with her business on the side. She's terrible with numbers."

Jillian nodded and rapidly chewed her food before answering. "I am. That's true. That's how we met. She used to work at a tax office, and I needed someone to do my taxes after the business took off. It was a tangled mess. She set up a simple system that I mostly follow now." Jillian grinned. "When I saw those nerd glasses perched on her nose and her wrinkled brow, I fell in love. She was adorable."

"Right, but I was the one who dared to ask you to dinner." Patty stroked Jillian's arm.

I spent a lot of time around Patty and Jillian but hadn't felt the same longing. I wanted what they had.

"Is that the extent to your falling in love story?" Frankie asked.

Patty laughed. "Not by a long shot. Jilly had a girlfriend when we first met. A shitty one. Nevertheless, she wasn't available. When Jilly kept coming around the office, bringing me more receipts, I started to wonder. I think I even asked her why she didn't keep everything in one place, rather than use the trickle approach. She just shrugged. Then I caught her looking at me. She was just standing with her hip resting against the doorframe. I thought she'd left when I started to dig into her mess of receipts."

"If she had a girlfriend, how did the dinner invitation happen?" Frankie asked.

"I was out one night with friends at this bar that was gay friendly. She was there with her girlfriend, who looked at every other woman in the place but Jilly. I thought she was rude, so the next time she came in to drop off more receipts, I asked why she was with such a douche. I've never been one to hold back my opinions."

Jillian laughed. "She did. I was so flabbergasted. But it was the kick in the ass I needed to send my ex to the curb. The next time I dropped by her office, I found a way to weave into the conversation that I was newly single. She took the bait, and I got a dinner invitation. The rest, they say, is history. We've been inseparable ever since."

"That's a great story," Frankie exclaimed.

I hoped that someday Frankie and I would get to tell our own story.

CHAPTER SIXTEEN

FRANKIE

I had enjoyed my time with Jillian and her wife, Patty. I could tell they had a stable relationship. The comparison between them as a couple and Sam and me was so stark, and I questioned why I had rolled over something so crucial as exclusivity. I did not want an open relationship.

As Zari and I worked side by side, digging the hole, the ring of my cell phone through the Bluetooth speaker interrupted our quiet comfort. I glanced at the phone and saw Sam's name. Sam might continue to call unless I picked up, so I scrambled to answer.

Before I had a chance to disconnect the Bluetooth, "Hey, babe," came through the speaker.

I motioned to Zari that I was going to go inside to take the call. She nodded, and her blank expression was hard to read.

"Are you calling to apologize?" I asked.

"Apologize? For what? You were the one who got angry because I didn't fawn all over your new friend and thank her profusely for being rude."

"And how was she rude? As I recall, you were the surly one calling her a freak. I'm still furious about that. One more step onto that very thin ice, and I guarantee the frigid water won't be pleasant."

Sam's voice rose. "I had a terrible headache, and she was taunting me with her ridiculous, inane chatter. Come on. You had to see what she was doing. She wants you."

"I am not doing this over the phone."

"Fine, then meet me for dinner tonight. I miss you."

"I can't tonight. I have plans."

"With her?"

"None of your business." I sighed. "I can meet you for dinner tomorrow night after you get home from work."

"I can't make it tomorrow. How about if I bring pizza to your place on Tuesday? I can get off a little early from work and be at your place by five."

"Pizza? You never want to get pizza. Why the change?"

"I've been doing some thinking lately. I know I need to pay more attention to your wants and needs. It won't kill me to put crappy food into my body once in a while."

"All right. We do need to talk."

"That sounds ominous. I hope you haven't forgotten what I told you. I still love you. You're my future, Frankie. I promise everything will work out. You can't want to blow what we have to pursue that odd neighbor of yours. Just because you work with special needs kids doesn't mean you have to date someone like that. I could tell right away there was something off about her. She's like your sister, right?"

"You know you're digging yourself into a bigger hole than the one in my backyard. Careful, Sam, you might never crawl out if you keep going."

"I didn't mean anything by it. You know I like your sister. I was just stating a fact. You have to know that your neighbor is autistic. Having a relationship with someone who is autistic is like dating a robot. It would never work. You know that, right?"

"Seriously, Sam, you need to stop talking right now. I'll see you on Tuesday."

The last words I heard were, "I love you," before I ended the call.

†

I couldn't look Zari in the eyes when I came out and turned the music back on. I feared she would somehow know about the horrible things Sam had said, and she'd think I believed them to be true. She didn't say anything to me, so I shattered the unnerving silence as I picked up my shovel.

"That was Sam. We're going to talk on Tuesday. I think that will be a good thing. One way or another, I'll have some kind of resolution."

"Okay." She brushed her damp hair aside and started digging again.

After two straight hours of digging, I began to sway and felt on the verge of passing out. The sweat poured down my face. Zari had been almost religious about drinking cold water every few minutes, but I hadn't been as diligent.

"I need to take a break." On wobbly legs, I made it to the chair on the deck and put my head between my legs. The next thing I knew, I felt a cool rag on my forehead, and I looked into Zari's wide eyes.

"You passed out. It was probably due to dehydration." She held a bottle of water to my lips. "You need to drink. Should I dial 911?"

I grabbed the bottle of water and took a healthy swig. "No, no. I'm embarrassed, but I'll be fine. Just let me sit for a bit."

"I can bike to the store to get you a sports drink. That will help replace your electrolytes."

I chuckled nervously. "No, really, I think the water will be fine."

"Should I have reminded you to drink more water?"

"I'm notorious for not drinking enough water. I shouldn't need a keeper. I'm an adult. Maybe I should take a sip of water every time you drink from your bottle. That'll keep this from happening again."

"I think that is a good plan. Did your phone call with Sam upset you, and that's why you were digging with such fervor that it caused you to forget to drink?"

"Maybe. Sometimes I get too focused on something. In this case, it was finishing this hole. Honestly, I wanted to not think about my upcoming discussion with Sam. I'm not at all looking forward to it."

"You could cancel," she offered.

"I could, but then I'd still be in the uncomfortable limbo state, and I don't want that either."

"Do you want to practice with me? I used to practice with Jillian or my therapist whenever I wanted to talk with someone new. I'm still not very good at it, but I'm better than I was before I would role play with them."

"Nah, I don't think that's a very good idea. I have plenty of time between now and Tuesday to decide what I want to say to her. I'll practice in front of my mirror. That's the way I work out difficult conversations."

"That doesn't work for me. My expressions aren't the same as others. Since I can recognize when people are mad or sad now, Jillian always offered an exaggerated expression as I was trying something out. I've tried to practice my words and expressions in the mirror, but I do better when Jillian helps me. She was even better than my therapist."

"Jillian is a good friend."

"She's the best."

I pinched the bridge of my nose. "I think I'm going to need more than a little water. My head is killing me."

"That's another symptom of dehydration. Are you nauseous, too?"

I chuckled. "Well, I wasn't until you mentioned it, but yeah, I am a little nauseous now. I guess I'm done for the day. That's good because I promised you dinner. I hope you don't mind something light and easy. Would grilled chicken on top of greens work for you? I could add color in the form of blueberries and strawberries."

"That sounds good. I like chicken. Fresh leafy greens have a lot of good vitamins, minerals, and fiber. Some studies indicate a diet rich in leafy greens has a lot of health benefits, including lower risk of obesity, heart disease, and high blood pressure. You were concerned about gaining a hundred pounds with my baked goods, so eating more greens will help."

Unlike Sam, I knew Zari didn't say this with any judgment. She was simply stating a fact. Unfortunately, I worried too much about my weight. I always felt like Sam was scrutinizing every unhealthy morsel I put into my mouth. She wasn't attracted to women with curves or squishy parts. Zari didn't seem to mind.

"Exactly, balance is everything. I'm still going to eat sweets because life is too short to deprive myself."

†

The school year had finished the previous week, but I wanted to organize a few things. I didn't have a chance to do that on Friday. The epic failure of a date with Sam had me leaving before I completed all the end of the school year tasks, and I didn't have my lunch hour to accomplish everything still left undone.

Although I wasn't engaging in the kind of hard manual labor that landscaping required, I didn't want a repeat performance, so I continued to drink from my bottle of water. Before I realized how late it had gotten, I was out of water, and my stomach was growling. I finished packing the rest of my private stash of learning tools to take back to the house and headed to the local bakery and deli for a sandwich. Their homemade bread was to die for. I wondered if I should pick up a loaf for Zari. She always brought me her baked goods. I should return the favor. I wasn't a baker, but I could buy bread from the bakery.

Thinking of Zari made me happy. Whistling, I began to walk up the stairs and into the separate house that was an extension of the bakery where they made the bread and sandwiches. I stopped in my tracks when I saw Sam, sitting across from her co-worker, Cori. They were laughing and looking very cozy. Cori had leaned in to wipe something off of Sam's mouth, and Sam had playfully nipped at her finger. That was demonstration enough for me to pivot and make my way down the stairs.

Unfortunately for me, I tripped on the last stair and fell face-first on the sidewalk. The cement was hard, and when I tried to sit, I saw stars. After the stars floated away, I lifted my hand to my face and felt the sticky substance I knew was blood. I looked around to see if anyone had seen my lack of grace. They had.

"Frankie? Did you follow me?" Sam asked.

I looked at her in disbelief.

The clerk squatted next to me and handed me a napkin. "Here. Are you okay?"

"I think so. I'll just go into your bathroom and clean up if you don't mind. Oh, and as long as I'm here, can you make me a cranberry turkey sandwich?"

Cori wrinkled her nose. "You're going to have a shiner."

I wobbled a bit as the clerk steadied me. With as much grace as I could muster, I climbed the stairs and pushed past Sam. She must have realized what an ass she was to me because she followed me to the bathroom.

Dabbing the small cut on my forehead and the enormous scrape on the entire right side of my face, I took a second to glare at Sam in the mirror. "Contrary to your belief that the world revolves around you, Sam, no, I did not follow you. There's a funny thing that happens when I skip breakfast and my stomach tells me it's time for lunch."

"I'm sorry. Let me help." She pulled a fistful of paper towels from the dispenser.

I pushed her hand away. "No thanks. You should get back to Cori. She'll think you abandoned her."

"Don't be like that. I said I was sorry. We were only having lunch. I jumped to conclusions. I thought maybe you were spying on me or something."

"Now why in the world would I do that? I already told you I didn't want to know about any dates. The last thing I'd want is to see you dating others with my own eyes."

"It's not a date. We work together. We were only having lunch."

"Looked cozy to me. Forget I just said that. I am not having this conversation with you right now. If you don't mind, I'm going to grab my sandwich and go. You can resume your lunch, and I can go home and ice my face."

Sam reached out to touch my cheek. "It looks painful. Maybe I can get off this afternoon and take you home. I can't stay long…" She looked away.

I guessed that she had another date lined up for the evening. "Don't do that. I'm fine. You just got promoted. It wouldn't be great to start taking the afternoons off."

"Okay. If you're sure you don't need me to drive you."

"I'm sure."

"I'll see you tomorrow?" Sam sounded hesitant.

I nodded, then walked out of the bathroom and asked the clerk to add a loaf of fresh bread to my order. I couldn't get out of there fast enough. This time I walked carefully down the stairs with the two bags in my hand. I didn't look back.

CHAPTER SEVENTEEN

ZARI

I kept obsessing about Tuesday because I knew that was the day Frankie would talk with Sam. I felt a little sad we hadn't made any plans for Monday or Wednesday. Jillian told me I needed to give her space.

Tuesday, Tuesday, Tuesday, Tuesday.

I was so focused on thinking about Tuesday that I didn't notice Frankie walking up to my driveway as I was putting away my bike in the garage. Even though my garage was empty because I didn't own a car, I liked hanging my bike and helmet on the wall. That left plenty of room for my mom and dad's car when they came to visit.

"Hey, Zari."

I jumped.

"Sorry, I didn't mean to startle you. I brought you a loaf of bread from the bakery."

I noticed her face first, and then the bag she held in her hands. "What happened to your face?"

"I tripped, and the sidewalk is not a very good kisser." She laughed.

"It looks painful. You should put ice on it. Icing during the first twenty-four to forty-eight hours provides the greatest benefit."

"I have been icing my face. I was waiting for you to return from the nursery because I wanted to bring you the bread I bought. It's not hot out of the oven because I bought it at lunch, but it's still relatively fresh."

"Tonight is taco night. Do you think it will keep until tomorrow? I can make sandwiches for lunch."

"Tacos sound good right now. They're like another kind of comfort food."

"I have enough for two people. Would you like to have tacos with me?"

"I'd love to, but I'm feeling rather guilty. I'm constantly mooching off of you. You're always feeding me. I need to step up my game. Bringing fresh bread was supposed to make a dent in equalizing our friendship."

"You don't want to eat tacos with me?"

"No, I do want to join you for dinner. I'd be crazy to turn down an offer of tacos. Since I can't compete with supplying you with food, how about we start those driving lessons? Remember, I promised to teach you, and we haven't arranged for those lessons yet."

"That will mean a change to my routine. I'll have to adapt to that. How many times a week will I need to schedule?"

"I don't know. I've never taught someone to drive before. How hard can it be?" Frankie smiled.

"You aren't certified to teach?"

Frankie laughed. "I'm certified to teach, just not specifically for driving. Don't you trust me?"

"I'll look on the Internet to find out how many hours of lessons are required."

"I can do research, as well. I'll bet there are lesson plans for driving school. I'll look up the curriculum and follow that. Easy peasy. We'll probably need to schedule two to three times a week. Do you think you can develop a schedule for that? School is out for the summer, so my schedule is wide open. Other than finishing my backyard, I don't have any plans."

"Except for Tuesday," I noted.

Frankie frowned. "Yes, except for Tuesday, but not every Tuesday."

"Okay. I should start the tacos now."

"Can I help?"

"You can grate the cheese."

"I'd love to help you grate the cheese," she said.

Now I had driving lessons on my brain and how I would adapt to a new schedule. I was happy to have a guaranteed time with Frankie. Even though I wanted to go to my laptop and research how many hours were needed to schedule with Frankie, Jillian had warned me that researching the Internet was worse than ignoring your partner while scrolling through your phone. I didn't recognize the difference because I saw plenty of people on dates not paying attention while focusing on their phones. Jillian said I didn't have to understand it wouldn't ever make sense, but I should trust her on this.

†

After we finished eating our tacos and Frankie helped me clean the kitchen, she grinned at me. I thought she might comment on my need to have everything tidy, but she didn't say a thing about how I couldn't have anything sitting on my kitchen counters.

"You want to look up the requirements for driving lessons, don't you?"

"I do."

"Can we look together? I want to see what you find out."

"Okay." I grabbed my laptop and turned it on. Even though my mom had warned me not to let someone see me enter my password, I trusted Frankie. She sat very close to me, and I could smell her sweet scent. It wasn't overpowering. I was grateful for that. When I was younger, I had a meltdown once when an older woman came close, and I wanted to swat away the smell.

"I like the way you smell. I don't need to swat you away."

"Swat me away? Like a fly?" She tilted her head back and laughed, then groaned. "Stop, you're making my face hurt."

"Why would I make your face hurt?"

"Because laughing heightens the pain. Your unique perspective on the world is so refreshing. It brings me joy and makes me laugh."

I found a site after typing, *How many sessions to driving school*. Frankie looked over my shoulder. "It says to schedule two-hour blocks of time for at least fifty hours."

"That sounds about right. Would you mind typing, *driving school curriculum*?" Frankie asked.

I typed her request into the search bar.

While waiting for the search engine to reveal the information Frankie was looking for, I decided to ask about the frequency of our lessons. The first site had talked about sessions once a week, but that would mean twenty-five weeks. That was a long time, nearly six months. "Can we have lessons more than once a week? That would take point-four-eight of a year to complete. I don't think I would like for it to take that long."

"Would two to three times a week work? We could model it after college classes. I suppose it depends on your schedule. Either we could do it on nursery days or sculpting days after you've finished sculpting or working at the nursery."

"It would work best on nursery days because Jillian will allow me to leave early since she said I should take you up on your offer to teach me. Although, she asked why I'd never taken her up on her offer for driving lessons. She thought that since you proposed the lessons, you weren't turned off by me."

"Definitely not. Why haven't you asked Jillian to teach you?" Frankie inquired.

"Because she's a reckless driver. She has three speeding tickets, and the judge sent her back to driving school."

Frankie chuckled. "How do you know I'm not a reckless driver?"

"Are you?"

"No, but you didn't know that when I offered."

I felt my face flush. Frankie was right. I was illogical. "You don't seem reckless or wild like Jillian."

"Looks can sometimes be deceiving."

"Do you have trouble interpreting facial expressions and actions too?"

"Not in the same way, but I think all of us can be fooled by others, no matter how intuitive we are or how well we pay attention to the cues. It's worse when you're in love. Love causes people to go deaf and blind."

I opened my mouth to ask about that. I was very interested in how love might make me deaf and blind.

Before I could ask, she clarified. "Figure of speech, not literally. I'm starting to pick up on things about Sam that I overlooked before because I was so much in love with her."

I felt my heart beat more quickly because she'd said w*as,* as in past tense. I wanted to ask her about that, but she had already focused on the screen after clicking on a site that gave detailed descriptions of their driving school curriculum.

"This is perfect. I should write this down. Better yet, can you email it to me? My email address is Frankieteach@gmail.com."

"Sure." I opened my email account and then composed a message to her with the link embedded into the body. I turned to look at her face. I wanted to know about my suggestion to start on Wednesday. "Is Wednesday too soon to start? I need to mark this on my calendar."

"Not at all. I know there is still daylight well into the evening." She abruptly shifted the conversation. "I should work some more on my backyard, but I'd rather just chill and watch a movie. Besides, I've been neglecting Queen Cleopatra. Maybe she'll bless us with her presence tonight. Are you interested in popcorn and a movie?"

"Will I have to wear headphones?" I wanted to spend more time with Frankie, but I wasn't sure another superhero movie was a good idea. The noise wasn't the only thing that bothered me. Cluttered visuals could also be too much. I didn't enjoy movies with bursts of light or bombs, either.

Laughing, she responded, "No, I won't force my fascination with female superheroes on you. We can either go back to my house and grab the headphones or stay here because there are plenty of romances to choose from. Streaming movies have made things super easy. Your choice."

"Should we watch that movie, *Blue is the Warmest Color*, with the explicit sex?"

Frankie squirmed in her seat. "We can, but I think there are much better movies than that."

"What are your favorites?"

"Well, besides the ultimate classic, *Desert Hearts*, that you've already seen, I would suggest, *Imagine Me and You*, *Carol*, *Saving Face*, and *I Can't Think Straight*. There are so many more, but off the top of my head, those four come to mind."

After watching the trailers for all four, I chose *Saving Face*. Frankie sat next to me on the couch with her thigh touching mine. Even though the pressure was light, I appreciated sitting close to her. I also forgot about Tuesday.

CHAPTER EIGHTEEN

FRANKIE

Not wishing for a repeat of Sunday where I passed out from too little water, I remembered to drink plenty of fluids while making a significant dent into the foundation of my pond. I kept glancing at Zari's house, imagining her working in the studio with her hands caressing her sculptures. I knew I shouldn't be fantasizing about her hands moving across my naked body, but I was.

When I went inside to fill my water bottle, I glanced at the clock and realized it was nearly 4:30. Sam was due any minute, and I needed to jump into the shower. My face was still a little swollen, and it looked like I'd gone a hundred rounds with American Middleweight Gold Medalist, Claressa Shields. I'd never enjoyed watching boxing, and I still didn't. But when I learned women could compete in the 2012 Olympics, I decided to watch those matches at least. I was in my radical feminist phase as a teen and followed everything that spotlighted women breaking into traditionally male-dominated sports.

The hot water felt like a thousand tiny pricks to my face. I soaped up quickly and emerged, gently patting my battered forehead and left cheek. Debating on whether to attempt putting on make-up, I went all natural. It wasn't like I needed to impress Sam. If she didn't like how I looked, to hell with her. I had already decided to be honest and see where the cards would fall. I knew that what I had to say might not go over too well.

The two knocks were brisk and efficient. In some ways, Sam's efficiency reminded me of Zari, but she was nothing like Zari. When I answered the door, Sam leaned in, and then she pursed her lips. That condescending, pitying look made its way to her eyes.

"Aw, hon, that looks terrible." She kissed my right cheek. "I found this amazing fresh pizza place."

Sam strolled into my house like she lived here and set the pizza on the counter. I'd already laid out plates, utensils, and napkins.

I'm sure my smile was tight and forced when I responded. "It smells good."

"They have this roasted chicken, garlic, goat cheese, and arugula pizza that sounded like something you would love. I'm not going to tell you about the crust until you take a bite."

"Why?"

"Because I don't want you to prejudge."

"I'm not exactly the judgmental type. That would be in your wheelhouse," I muttered.

"What?" she asked.

"Never mind. So, how is work going?"

"It's great, but I sort of wish my promotion came with a much bigger raise. Honestly, I'm barely making ends meet. I never thought I'd be one of those people who live from paycheck to paycheck, but that's a distinct possibility unless I figure out a better living arrangement. I sort of wanted to talk with you about that."

"I have wine, cider, and that beer you like," I offered.

"Wine, I think. This pizza is too fancy for beer. Plus, I'm trying to cut down on beer. I'd rather not get a beer belly like my dad. I suppose it's as bad as all that sugar you eat. One of these days, it will affect my body. I might as well nip that in the bud before it's too late." Her eyes roamed across my body. "You must have cut down on the sugar intake. You're looking great."

I glared at her. "I haven't. Probably all the exercise I've been getting." I retrieved the plates from the table and set them next to the box of pizza.

She raised her eyebrow. "About my current situation with money. I figure I have two choices. Cori offered to move in with me, but I'm not sure that's the best idea. She might have the wrong impression about us having an open relationship, and she's getting a little clingy. The better option is for me to move in with you, and we can establish more rules. I won't bring anyone into the house. I promise."

After flipping open the box and putting two pieces on each plate, she brought them to the table while I uncorked the wine and poured each of us a glass.

"Listen, I want to apologize for my reaction to your neighbor. I can't believe I'm going to admit that I was jealous. I have no say in whom you choose to spend time with. After all, I'm the one who wanted to try, uh, this…"

I set the wineglasses on the table and took a seat, sucking in my breath to begin the conversation. Sam had unknowingly provided me with the perfect opening.

"About that. I agreed to an open relationship because I wasn't willing to give up on us, but I don't think I can do it. I never wanted to be in an open relationship. I don't want to date more than one person at a time. That just isn't me."

Sam leaned back in her seat. "I see. So, are you saying that we're done if I can't commit to you forever, right this minute?" Sam's voice rose.

I steeled myself for the answer I knew was the right thing to do, even though a part of me was reluctant to go there. "Yes. I hate to be crude, but it's time you shit or get off the pot, Sam. You might not like sugar, but you sure have finagled a way to have your cake and eat it too. I'm not going to continue to hang around while you sow your oats. You should have done that in your early twenties or teens." I ripped into the pizza and stuffed my mouth before my anger caused me to say anything more. I wished I were in a better mood because the pizza was outstanding. I couldn't even enjoy one of my favorite foods.

"This isn't the 1950s, Frankie. People do not get married right out of high school." Sam sipped her wine first, then bit into her slice.

"I realize that. But solid couples don't go from living together in a committed relationship to casual dating. That's a step back, not a step forward." I set the pizza on my plate. I knew I wasn't going to enjoy this meal until we'd hashed everything out.

"I disagree. All couples go through a stale stage. Wanting something new to shake things up is healthy and necessary. I'll bet half of the divorces in the world could be avoided by adding a bit of excitement and pulling out the societal stick up their ass for a change. The seven-year itch is real," Sam argued.

"We've been together three years, not seven. The other day I spent time with a couple who still look like they're ready to rip off the other's clothes at a moment's notice. I want what they have. They've been together about the same amount of time as us. Something's wrong if you have to sleep with other people to get that spark back with me. Dammit, I deserve to have someone who looks at me like I'm the only woman they'd ever want to spend their life with."

Sam grabbed my hand. "You do, and you know that I love you. This is a minor hiccup."

"No, Sam. This is a tsunami, a seven-point earthquake to me."

"God, you're always so dramatic. How many times do I have to explain that it's just sex with the other women? It has been a little awkward with Cori after I told her I had no intention of breaking up with you."

"You aren't listening. Sam, you are not in a relationship with yourself. There are two of us, and I have a say in this. Ultimatums suck. I know that. I don't know how to make this any clearer. Either we are monogamous, or we are not. If we are not, then we are not a couple, and I'm moving on."

The loud scrape of the chair punctuated the crescendo to our argument. Sam pushed herself from the table and stood.

"I'm going to leave before I say something I'll regret. I've been patient with you because I know that new things throw you for a loop sometimes. I thought with you moving out, it would give you enough space to think things through and adapt. Clearly, I was wrong." She pointed to the slice of pizza on my plate and smirked. "Cauliflower. That's what the crust is made of. Maybe I should have continued to sneak around, because it seems like the only way you can try new things and admit to liking them is when I keep you in the dark."

I was seething now. Sam had lied to me. I should have known that Sam wouldn't bother to ask my permission before doing what she wanted. "Get out. I think we're done."

Sam grabbed the box of pizza and stalked out. "Fine. I'll call you later. Much later, when you've had a chance to cool down."

"Don't. I mean it, Sam. I don't want a future with you. It's one thing to hate the idea of an open relationship, but lying and cheating is a whole new level of something to work through. I will not do that with you. Frankly, I don't have the energy or desire at this point."

The door slammed, and I cringed. How could I have been so blind? The sound of tires squealing roused me from my stupor. I opened my door to see Sam's car fishtail out of my driveway. I wondered how I would remove the black mark she'd left.

"Ouch." I'd forgotten about my face as I put my head in my hand. Then I looked over to Zari's house and saw the flutter of her curtain. I didn't want to run over and cry on her shoulder. Or worse, grab her and kiss her until she turned to rubber in my arms. What kind of person was I to want to run into the arms of another woman two minutes after breaking up with my long-term girlfriend? That would make me as big a shit as Sam.

Dejected, I walked into my house, packed up the one and a half pieces of pizza left on the plate, and curled into a ball on the couch. Crying would only sting my still raw cheek, but I wasn't able to stem the flow. Pain enveloped me in more ways than one.

CHAPTER NINETEEN

ZARI

I closed my curtain and began tugging on my hair. Whenever something upset me, I tugged on my hair. Sometimes I would pull so hard that tiny sections would come out in my hands. I didn't think it was any worse than when a person bit their nails, but Jillian said if it resulted in a bald head, more people would notice my stress habit. She said that even though wigs had come a long way, they still weren't that great, and it was easier to get a manicure and false nails.

I stopped long enough to call Jillian. I wanted to go to Frankie's because I'd heard Sam screech out of the driveway. I didn't need to see Sam's face to know she'd left mad. Really mad.

"You okay, Zari?" Jillian's voice was soft. She already knew that Tuesday was a stressful day because I kept imagining what would happen between Sam and Frankie.

"Sam left mad."

"Okay. How do you know that?"

"The wheels on her car made an awful noise. Should I go to Frankie's to see if she's okay? She has a black eye from yesterday."

"What? You didn't tell me that. If Sam is hitting Frankie, that's a whole new set of facts. Kicking that bitch to the curb won't nearly be enough. I'm going to kick her ass. There is never a reason to hit someone."

"You hit a lot of people in high school," I reminded her.

"I've never hit someone I love. That was different. The popular kids were assholes to you."

"I don't think I could punch someone, even if they were mean to Frankie. I don't think Sam hits her. She just becomes angry and squeals her tires. Frankie has a black eye because she fell yesterday and hurt herself. Last time Sam left mad, Frankie was sad. So, now she might be sad and hurt."

"Hmm, let me think. Sometimes people need space, and sometimes they need a shoulder to cry on. I don't know Frankie well enough to give you advice on whether you should go there. But on the off chance she's the type to want to talk through things with someone, I'd say going over and asking if she wants to talk won't hurt. You said she's honest. She'll tell you if that's not what she needs."

"Okay. Thanks, Jillian."

"No problem. Good luck."

I was still pulling on my hair when I knocked lightly on her door. Frankie's eyes were red and puffy, and it made her black eye stand out even more.

"Your face looks worse. Both eyes are puffy now. Do you have allergies? Maybe that is making it worse."

"Zari?"

"Jillian said I should come on the off chance you're the type of person who wants to talk through things with someone. Are you?"

"Not normally, no. I usually prefer hiding behind closed doors with several pints of ice cream, but you're here, and oddly that's comforting to me right now. Come in."

"Okay."

I followed Frankie into her house as she slumped onto her couch. I stood awkwardly, not knowing whether I should sit beside her or on the chair next to the sofa. I was still tugging on my hair.

"It's Tuesday, and Sam left mad."

She sighed. "Yeah, Sam is not happy with me right now. I'm sorry if it upset you when she screeched out of my driveway." She patted the seat next to her on the couch. "I'm not angry. You can sit next to me."

"I know you're not angry. You're sad." I sat next to her, and she put her hand over mine where I was pulling my hair.

"Seems like we're both upset. I know why I'm upset, but I'm not sure why you were trying to make yourself bald." She pulled her lips in a half-smile.

"It's Tuesday."

"I don't understand. Yes, it's Tuesday."

"Tuesday is the day you were supposed to get a resolution. Sam was mad before, and she was still your girlfriend after that."

"Well, she's not my girlfriend anymore."

"Are you sad because you still want her to be your girlfriend?"

"That would be an oversimplification of how I'm feeling. We've been together for a long time, so yes, I'm disappointed that we couldn't work things out. I also feel guilty about being relieved. I didn't realize how much the whole open relationship was creating angst for me. I had my eyes opened a little wider today."

"Wide eyes mean surprise. Were you surprised?"

"Not exactly. More like I saw the situation with increased clarity. Like when I said love is deaf and blind. I have a greater understanding of our relationship, or rather lack of the kind of relationship I deserve. Wider eyes can also mean a sudden understanding that a person doesn't have until everything clicks in place. Do you remember when you first understood the flashcards your mom showed you, and you could recognize emotions in others?"

I nodded.

"That's sudden understanding, when everything clicks in place like the pieces of a puzzle."

"I'm very good with puzzles, but terrible with people."

"You're perfect just the way you are."

We were so close, and she was looking at me with those beautiful eyes. I thought I recognized the look right before two people kiss, so I leaned in and placed my lips firmly on hers. At first, she kissed me back. I even felt her tongue inside my mouth, and that was nice. Different, but pleasing, like a tingle all over my body, not just inside my mouth. Then she pulled away.

"I...I...shouldn't do this. God, I'm sorry, Zari. My hesitation has nothing to do with you. You're gorgeous and wonderful. I'm not eliminating this as a...um...possibility. It's so wrong to jump out of the arms of one woman and then immediately into the arms of another. Do you understand?"

"No. You had the same look on your face as Vivian right before Cay kissed her."

"Shit, shit, shit. I'm making a mess of things. Okay, how about this? You understand schedules, right?"

I nodded.

"If you see me look like that again in, let's say one month, I won't stop the kiss."

"July fifteenth."

The line in her forehead deepened, and then her mouth formed an o-shape, and she smiled. "That's precisely one month from now."

"Yes. Do you think we can go on dates without kissing in the meantime?"

She laughed, and it didn't seem forced, like sometimes I saw when others would laugh around me.

"I'd like that."

I wanted to ask her how many dates we would need to have before considering her my girlfriend, but I held back. We'd established a timeline for kissing, and that was enough for now.

†

The next day, while I was pulling the weeds in the beds around the front of the nursery, I glanced up to see Jillian's car weave quickly into a parking space.

When she was close enough to hear me, I asked, "Can I leave early today and for the next twenty-four days I work. I came early, so at least the weeding will be done."

She arched her eyebrow. "Yeah, of course, but why?"

"Frankie is going to teach me to drive on nursery days. I don't know if those count as dates or not. We're dating now, but I can't kiss her until July fifteenth, and only if she gives me that same look as Vivian in *Desert Hearts* right before Cay kissed her."

"Whoa, back that train up. What happened last night?"

"I went to her house, and it turns out that she isn't the type to want to talk things over when she's sad. She prefers ice cream. But she said having me there was oddly comforting. Then she said I was perfect just the way I am, and I kissed her. It was nice. She said we couldn't kiss again for another month. Do driving lessons count as dates?"

"Okay, that's a lot to process. Why can't you kiss until July?"

"July fifteenth."

"Whatever, Ms. Precise." Jillian twirled her finger, a gesture that I knew meant to continue talking.

"She said it had nothing to do with me and that she wasn't eliminating that as a possibility, but she thought it was wrong to jump from one woman's arms to another. She offered to establish a schedule because I understand schedules."

"So, I take it she broke up with her douche-bag girlfriend."

I nodded.

"That's good. No, I don't think driving lessons are dates, but that doesn't mean you should squander those opportunities. Frankie obviously enjoys spending time with you. Just continue to be your charming self, and even though they aren't dates, you can still use that time to get to know her more and for her to get to know you. That's what dating is all about."

"A month is a long time to go on dates without kissing her. Should I try to negotiate a different timeframe?"

"No, no, don't do that. You don't want to be a rebound for Frankie. I think it's good that she set that boundary. It means she can see something happening but doesn't want to rush it. Slow isn't always bad. By the time you two kiss again, you could very well be doing the horizontal mambo with all that pent-up sexual energy happening." Jillian grinned. "Look at you. All grown up and ready to have sex."

"I've been ready since I was eighteen."

"Maybe, but this woman could be your Patty. I like her, and I like who you are with her." Jillian patted my shoulder. "I hope things work out for you two."

†

I was sitting outside eating my sandwich when I heard a car spitting gravel on the road leading to the Growth Spurts parking lot. I recognized Sam's car and wondered if she needed plants for the old house that Frankie used to live in with her.

I didn't need to see her face to know she was mad as she stomped in my direction. "What the hell did you do to Frankie? We were fine until you came along." Her voice was loud, and I began tugging on my hair again.

"Tell me what you said, you freak," she yelled.

165

I began rocking. I hadn't done that since I was a child, but I didn't have my earplugs. Jillian never yelled at me.

The door to the store slammed open, and Jillian came barreling out. "What's going on, and why is Zari rocking like that?" Jillian sat next to me, and her voice was soft. "Zari, are you okay? What happened?" Jillian glared at Sam.

"She fucked everything up!" Sam screamed.

"Look. If you want different plants, trees, whatever, we can take care of that without you yelling at Zari. Pick out anything you want, no charge."

"What are you? A moron, like her? She turned my girlfriend against me. I don't need any of your fucking plants."

Jillian jumped from the bench and grabbed Sam's arm. I was afraid she was going to punch her, but she led her away. I could still hear Sam clearly, but Jillian's words were harder to understand because she wasn't yelling.

"Get your fucking hands off of me." Sam twisted her body.

Jillian let go. Then she pulled her phone from her pocket. "Get off my property, and if you so much as take a step closer to Zari, I'll call the police and have you arrested." She held up her phone. "I'm going to say this only once, so listen carefully. If you get anywhere near Zari again, I will make sure your life is miserable. I will hunt you down wherever you work and make a scene of epic proportions."

"You can't keep me from seeing Frankie, and if Zari happens to be around, I can't control that."

"I doubt Frankie will appreciate your bullying Zari any more than I do. Go right ahead. Dig a deeper hole for yourself. I've no doubt whose side Frankie will land on. In fact, from where I'm standing, she's already made her choice. I sure can't blame her. Now get the fuck off my property."

"Fine, but we'll see who Frankie chooses. We have three years together. She isn't about to throw that away for your freaky friend. Don't confuse her pity, or maybe guilt over not being there for her sister, for genuine feelings. She's nice because that's who Frankie is."

After Sam left, Jillian sat next to me until I stopped rocking. I was still upset, but now I was distressed for a whole different reason. Nobody was yelling anymore, yet Sam's words worried me.

"Do you think Sam is right? Frankie is nice. Did she tell me I needed to wait until July fifteenth because she pities me or is guilty?"

"No way. She broke up with that piece of shit before you tried to kiss her. I haven't spent as much time around Frankie as you have, but I've seen how she looks at you and how the two of you interact. Somehow you click."

"Frankie said something about having wide eyes now and a sudden understanding when all the pieces click into place like a puzzle. Do you think she meant we fit together like a puzzle?"

"I'm not sure, but I think you do. You know how I'm always right about these things."

"No, you aren't."

"Okay, mostly right." She slung her arm around my shoulder. "Listen, you call me or the police if she ever comes to your house. Don't let her inside, either. Promise?"

I nodded. "Sam's tires are loud. I usually know when she leaves, but not always when she arrives."

"Use that peephole in your door. Talk to Frankie. Maybe she won't want her coming around either and you can have them change the gate code."

"Okay."

"I'm glad you live in a community with a gate."

CHAPTER TWENTY

FRANKIE

I made sure I stopped working on my yard in enough time to take a shower and be ready for Zari's first driving lesson. When Zari rode her bike up the driveway, her head was bent, and she didn't glance in my direction. Something was off. I could tell.

I walked to her garage and greeted her. "Hey, Zari. Are you ready for your first driving lesson?"

She didn't look in my direction or bless me with her too-wide smile as she answered, "Yes."

Cautiously, I stepped closer and firmly touched her arm. "Did something happen today to upset you?"

"If I have them change the gate code, will you give the new code to Sam?"

I was confused. Zari still wasn't looking at me. Not that she ever maintained eye contact for long, but she had significantly improved as we got to know each other better. "Zari, will you look at me, please?"

Zari glanced at me for a second and then began tugging her hair.

"You know, not telling me about something is like a lie. A lie by omission. I can tell something's up."

"Sam came to Growth Spurts today. She was loud. Jillian told her to get the fuck off her property after she threatened to hunt her down at work and make a scene of epic proportions." Her words came tumbling out.

"What?" I screeched, and Zari tugged harder on her hair.

"Are you going to yell at me, too?"

I pulled Zari into a very firm hug and stroked her back. "No, no, I'm so sorry. We'll go together to ask them to change the gate code." I let my arms drop, took a step back, then pointed to the winding road that led to the other properties. "The president of the association lives down that road, right?"

Zari nodded.

"How about we do that right now, and then we can have our driving lesson if you're still up for it? Unless you want to cancel and do something else. Can I ask what helps you settle when you get upset?"

"Sculpting. But today is not a sculpting day. So, digging in the dirt to plant trees and shrubs, or looking for four-leaf clovers helps."

I made myself smile, even though I was so angry about how Sam had frightened Zari. "Well, I have a lot of dirt to dig in. Maybe we can dig together for a bit, and if you're still up for it, have a shorter driving lesson. Or I could go over the schedule for your lessons and tell you what we're going to cover at each lesson. That way, you'll know what to expect."

I hoped this would help Zari. Knowing what I planned to cover would help her adjust to the schedule. That was something that had always worked for me before. Zari could do outside research to prepare for each lesson, and that would give her a modicum of control.

"We have enough time before dinner to plant the lilac bushes," she stated.

"Any chance I can talk you into joining me for takeout?" I wanted to spend more time with Zari to make sure she settled.

"What kind of takeout?"

"There's this little Vietnamese restaurant that opened a short while ago. I've wanted to try that." That wasn't a lie. I had planned on asking her to try the food with me.

"I haven't had Vietnamese food before."

"Do you trust me?"

"Yes."

"Okay, I'll order for us. And, Zari, don't worry about Sam. I'm going to talk to her and make this right."

"Will you start being her girlfriend again? I think that's what she wants."

It took every ounce of effort not to show my anger, but I was sure my eyes narrowed as I gritted my teeth. "No, because it's not about what Sam wants anymore. It's about what I want."

"Frankie, can I ask another question?" This time she looked directly at me. I could spot how she tried to size me up for the truth. Having to adapt to people around you who would tell a lie effortlessly probably made Zari good at reading people.

"You can always ask me anything." Zari didn't break eye contact with me, and that was almost a first.

"Did you say I can't kiss you until July fifteenth because you pity me or feel guilty about not being there for your sister?" she asked.

"Absolutely not." My eyes were steady. I hoped she believed me.

"That's what Jillian said. She told me you broke up with that piece of shit before the kiss and that she thought we clicked."

Zari's parroting of what Jillian said caused me to break out in laughter. "I like Jillian. She's right."

"Jillian says she's always right, but she's not. I'm glad she was right this time."

†

Changing the code to the gate was incredibly easy. The homeowners' association had little tolerance for drama. By the time we finished planting the lilac bushes, going over the curriculum for the driving lessons, and had eaten dinner, Zari seemed to return to her usual self. I was glad she enjoyed the Vietnamese food because that was a risk, especially in her fragile state. I didn't have to be there to know that Sam was a total ass.

I watched Zari go to her house and close the door before I let my anger take hold. I was fuming. Grabbing my phone, I punched in Sam's number.

"Hey, I'm so glad you called," she answered. Her voice was almost chipper.

"This isn't a social call, Sam. I want to know what gives you the right to harass Zari at her work? What the hell were you thinking?"

"We were fine until she came along," she whined. "I'm not giving up on us just because Zari put stupid ideas in your head. What happened? Did she spout a few facts about how couples who are in open relationships don't last?"

"Stop being an ignorant ass. I held hope we could eventually have a friendship again, but you've completely blown that notion right out the door. I'm so angry with you. I'm tempted to take a restraining order out on you so that you stay far away from Zari and me. I've no doubt Jillian will have you arrested if you set foot on her property."

"Okay, okay, I'll admit, I should not have gone to that damn nursery. That was wrong, but I was so scared. I'm still scared, Frankie. I can't lose you. We can forget the whole open relationship thing. Just please tell me we aren't over," Sam begged. "You mean more to me than anyone."

I could hear Sam sniff, and I knew she was crying. I wavered for a second, but then I gathered my strength as I remembered that she had lied to me. I could not trust a word that came out of her mouth. "I'm sorry, Sam. I can't forget the breach of trust. We want different things."

"Please don't do this. I'll do anything. Name it."

"I don't—"

"How about if we take a short break," Sam interrupted. "A little space for both of us, and then we'll talk again. I know you'll end up missing me as much as I'm going to miss you. Please, just consider this as an option."

She wore me down, and I stupidly let her push the door open an inch. "I need a lot more than a day or two to think things through. In the meantime, don't call me and don't drop by. I'll call you when I'm ready to talk. I mean it, Sam. If you so much as place a single toe over the boundary I just set, I will get that restraining order."

I ended the call and sighed. How would I tell Zari about what I'd agreed to? When she'd kissed me yesterday, it took all my willpower to establish an arbitrary timeline. Her lips felt as soft as I thought they would. Although I'd told Sam I'd consider getting back together with her, I was still technically single. Wasn't I? I'd told her we were through. Besides, I shouldn't feel one bit guilty. Before the break, Sam had set the rules. We could see other people. So why was I feeling like I'd done something wrong by kissing Zari back and slipping my tongue inside her mouth? I groaned. Complicated did not begin to describe my love life. Two women, and I wasn't having sex with either of them.

It was a good thing Thursday was a sculpture day. I needed a day to myself. I was also glad for summer break because I wasn't getting any sleep as I worried the hours away.

†

I stood in my backyard, looking at the hole that was now two-feet deep. I hadn't the foggiest idea what to do next. I wasn't sure how to arrange the thick black liner I'd bought. I was sure there was some trick. Zari would know what to do, but I couldn't bother her while she was working. I'd already injected chaos into her life and schedule. I wasn't sure how much more she could handle. Order and precision were necessary for her, and right now, I was anything but ordered and precise. It seemed like everything was in flux. How could I drag her into the drama?

Grabbing my silver insulated water bottle, I gulped down nearly half of the cold liquid. Buying the expensive thermos was one of my better purchases. There was still ice in the bottle after several hours in the blistering sun. I smiled, feeling very accomplished. The pond hole was done. I had at least eight more holes to dig so that we could plant the trees and bushes. That would take several more days to accomplish, but I had visions of sitting next to my gurgling pond watching the fish lazily swim beneath the surface. It should have been revealing that the person I envisioned seated next to me while I relaxed in the evening was Zari and not Sam.

It hadn't even been twenty-four hours, and already I missed Zari. I missed her telling me about the latest advice she'd received from Jillian. Or the obscure facts about a particular plant or other topics of conversation.

I glanced at her house, longing to see her peek through her curtains. Maybe she would notice I was alone and pining for her company. I wiped the sweat from my brow. I decided to head to the store and buy ice cream. That would cool me down.

I ran inside and slapped a baseball cap on my head before climbing into my car. I figured when I returned, it would only be polite to offer to share my refreshingly sweet treat with Zari. After all the times she brought me food, I rationalized she would enjoy taking a break on such a scorcher of a day. Undoubtedly, her studio was air-conditioned, but that tiny fact did not matter in my scheme to see Zari before our Friday lesson.

I'd barely parked my car before heading to Zari's with two pints of ice cream tucked away in the paper bag I had in my hands.

Zari answered after a few moments. Wisps of hair had escaped her messy ponytail. I licked my lips as I noticed her defined arms on display from her loose-fitting tank top. My eyes fell briefly to her perfect clavicle and then traveled to her mouth. Her cheeks were flushed, as if she'd run to the door.

Holding out my bag, I tentatively asked, "Ice cream break?"

"Won't we spoil our dinner?"

"Maybe, but it's way too hot to turn down a cool treat in the middle of the day when the sun is at its hottest."

"That's sort of logical." She pivoted to the side, and I followed her.

I began to second guess my selfish need to see Zari. "Did I disturb you at an important point in your work?"

"No, I was cleaning up. The faces are giving me problems. I can't yet see their expressions. I know what I want them to look like, but I haven't gotten it right yet. I usually pencil things out first."

"You draw, too?"

"Yes. Can I put away the rest of my tools and sweep before ice cream?"

"Of course. I'm sorry. Should I come back a little later?"

"No. I think maybe you came here for another reason than eating ice cream. It seems important."

I chuckled nervously. "Busted. I was feeling a little lost. First, I wasn't sure how to put the black liner into the pond after finishing the hole. Then, honestly, I was missing you. We've spent so much time together, it felt like there was another hole I didn't know what to do with."

"Another hole?"

"Yeah, sometimes people talk about holes in their emotions like something is missing that needs to be filled."

"I think I understand. Like the hole I feel because I don't have a girlfriend. At first, I thought I would be perfectly fine by myself, but then I met Jillian. I like myself better when I'm around others that I care for. I can help you with the liner."

I smiled at Zari. "Yeah, I know, but that isn't why I came over. I wasn't angling for your help. I loathe feeling like I'm taking advantage of you."

"You think I'm naïve. That isn't true. Everybody can be vulnerable and taken advantage of. Sam took advantage of you. I want to spend time with you as much as you want to spend time with me. That means neither of us is taking advantage of the other. I find reasons to come and see you, too. Can I clean the studio now?"

"Let me put the ice cream in your freezer, and I can help. The job will get done quicker, and that will get us to the ice cream sooner." I grinned at her.

"Okay, but I can't show you my latest piece. It isn't finished yet. I never show anyone my sculptures until I've completed the clay model."

"I wouldn't dream of crossing any boundaries you've set."

Zari began walking, and I followed her. "I know you wouldn't, even though I think maybe you let Sam violate your rules when you agreed to an open relationship because you didn't want that. Why?"

"That is an excellent question. Can I think about that a little bit and get back to you with an answer? I'm not sure I've figured it out yet."

Although Zari's studio appeared clean to me, I noticed the thin layer of dust with a few large chunks around the covered piece. I wasn't sure what kind of chisel tools she used to create her masterpieces. I would ask her about that later. She was efficient as she put on booties before entering her studio, then wiped the tools on her bench with careful exactness, before placing them inside her cabinet. I grabbed another pair of boots to put on. Finding the broom and dustpan, I began sweeping up dust and pieces of clay. The only thing left in the room were her sculptures, a shop vac, and a small silver trash can. I dumped the debris into the trash. Zari rolled her small shop vac to the area around the hidden sculpture and sucked up the remainder of invisible dust. She covered every inch of the floor with absolute focus.

"It's good now, except for our booties. I usually take them off at the door and then run the vacuum over them. I don't like tracking dust in my house."

I took her cue and removed my booties, placing them in the basket next to a tall cabinet. After she vacuumed her shoe coverings and then mine, she put the basket inside the cabinet along with the shop vac, broom, and dustpan.

"Ice cream time?" I asked.

"Okay."

I was happy to see her pull out an ice cream scoop because that meant she enjoyed ice cream. But I shook my head and said, "You don't need that. It's why I buy ice cream in pints. All you need is a spoon. Fewer dishes to wash." I winked at her.

She pulled two spoons from a drawer and smiled. "That is better. More efficient."

"Either you can put the lids to the pint containers in the refrigerator so the residual doesn't melt too much, or toss them in the garbage if you think we'll completely demolish our dinner appetites. I vote for the latter, but it's your call."

"I think I should start small." She pulled off the lid and put hers in the refrigerator. I sighed but followed suit. I was too settled now that I was eating ice cream with Zari to let her know about my conversation with Sam, but somehow, she pulled it out of me with ease. It was hard not to squeal like a pig around Zari. She was so open and honest that she made me want to emulate her in every way.

CHAPTER TWENTY-ONE

ZARI

Sometimes I'm more observant than people who aren't on the spectrum. I've had to learn that so I wouldn't communicate as badly with others. I could tell that Frankie was anxious. At least my mind focused on something other than July fifteenth.

"Did something happen to you today? You don't seem like yourself."

Her spoon made a squelching, popping noise as she removed it from her mouth and swallowed her bite of ice cream. "What?"

"You're kind of fidgety. You get that way when you're not happy."

"I wasn't going to tell you about it yet."

"Why?"

"I don't know. I guess I feel weak and don't want you to get the wrong impression."

"Weak? I don't think you're weak, and not just physically because you dug a lot of the hole by yourself."

"I talked to Sam yesterday and agreed to think more about our relationship. I may have given her false hope that we'd get back together," she blurted out.

"Oh. Does that mean I won't get to kiss you on July fifteenth?" I'm not very expressive, so I was sure my face didn't show disappointment, but I think Frankie could tell this did not make me happy. At all.

"I don't know. I was so angry at Sam. Then I heard her cry on the other end of the phone. It softened me. Sam hardly ever cries. She told me she would do anything, including give up on the notion of an open relationship. But, here's the thing, I think I took the easy path by agreeing to think about it. It wasn't the path I wanted to take, and I don't believe things will work out for us in the long run." Frankie rambled and frowned at the same time.

"I don't think being kind is a weakness, but it also doesn't allow you to find the right path." I was proud of myself for understanding her decision-making process.

She looked at me and smiled. "You are amazing." Shaking her head, she put a little more physical distance between us and muttered, "Rules are good."

I saw the look again, and that meant I thought she might want to kiss me. "I like rules."

"I know you do. Usually, I stick to the rules, especially if I'm the one who established them, but sometimes it's so tempting to break them."

"I don't break rules. Are you talking about July fifteenth? Was that a rule? I thought it was a schedule," I said.

"It's perhaps a schedule and a rule. Is it acceptable to change a rule or a schedule?"

"Yes. Sometimes I've had to rearrange my schedule, and over the years, a few rules have changed. But I need to know when the rules change."

"That's fair. Would it be okay to change the July fifteenth date?"

"Yes. I would like to reschedule that date. It's a long way away."

"How does June sixteenth sound?" Her eyes half-closed, and the slightest hint of a smile appeared on her face.

"Today is June sixteenth."

"Yes, it is," she answered.

"I'd like that schedule change."

Frankie set her spoon on the counter and pressed her lips to mine. I wrapped my arms securely around her waist as she brought our bodies together. When she sucked my bottom lip, it felt so good I never wanted the kiss to end. I was happy when I heard her groan because I'd watched enough movies that the noise did not alarm me. Although, for a second, I thought her injured cheek and forehead were the cause. Maybe I'd brushed the raw skin unintentionally. The vibration was a new sensation that wasn't at all unpleasant.

After she ended the kiss, I asked, "Can we do that some more?"

"Definitely."

"Your face doesn't hurt? What about Sam? Will you tell her about the kiss? I don't want her to come to Growth Spurts and yell again."

"I'm not sure what I'll say to Sam, but you don't have to worry about her coming to the nursery. I made it clear if she approached you again, I'd take out a restraining order. And no, my lips are just fine, no pain there." She grinned.

"Okay. Can I kiss you now?"

"Please do."

We spent the rest of the evening kissing on the couch. A few times, Frankie's hands traveled up the sides of my breasts, and that was another feeling I liked very much, even though I felt an odd sensation in my panties. After that, I understood when someone talked about how wet someone had made them.

†

We were back to an established schedule on Friday. I was both nervous and excited for my first driving lesson. I wondered if I could kiss her again or if there were days for kissing and days for driving lessons, and it wasn't in the rules to combine the two. That would be my first question to Frankie.

As I rolled up my driveway, I craned my neck to see if Frankie was outside waiting for me. I couldn't see well into her backyard until I made the final turn into my garage. I was so focused on looking for Frankie that I slammed into the edge of the garage and toppled over.

As I was dusting off, Frankie came barreling up the driveway. "Zari, are you hurt? Do I need to get the first aid kit? God, we're a pair."

I shook my head to let her know I was okay. "A pair of what? Does one night of kissing mean you're my girlfriend now?"

183

Frankie frowned. "No, I meant that we both might look like we'd been boxing with each other instead of kissing." She ended her explanation with a smile.

"So, I can't call you my girlfriend?" I asked in confusion.

"Maybe we can avoid labeling it, okay? Labels are for cans and jars."

"Yes, they help people know what's inside when you can't see through the glass or can. Sometimes, even if the glass is clear, it could be any number of things, so a label helps."

Frankie frowned again. "I suppose you need a tidy label. I'm being unfair to you. Let me think about this, and I'll get back to you on that."

"Okay." I lifted my shirt and noticed the black and blue marks already appearing on my side.

"How about we ice that before starting our lesson?" she suggested. "Let me go back to my place and get the books I bought for you. We can flip through the books while you're icing your side. Does that sound like a good plan?"

"Yes. Can I kiss you on driving days, or is that only acceptable on days we don't have driving lessons?"

Frankie blushed. "I think maybe that would be okay on driving days, even though I'll probably revert to teacher mode the minute I go through our lessons and show you the pages of the book I want you to read after each lesson." She stepped closer and gave me a quick kiss. It wasn't like yesterday, but it was nice. "I'll see you back at your place in a few minutes. Then after we've gone over the book, we'll head to my car to finish the hands-on part of the lesson."

†

Not only did I leave the door unlocked, but I'd cracked it open, so I wouldn't have to get up off the couch and answer the door while icing my side. Frankie slipped next to me on the couch, and I didn't feel crowded or over stimulated by her proximity. It felt nice.

Frankie made learning to drive easy. She broke everything down to a set of rules to follow. She bought me three books to learn the rules and to help me pass the written test. I watched Frankie as she transformed into teacher mode. At first, she was a little tentative. She began shuffling the three books until she apparently found the one she wanted.

Holding onto the first book, she explained, "I wasn't sure which books to purchase when I did my search on Amazon, so I got all three. I know you like to be thorough in your research. This one has 250 questions, which will help you prepare for the written test. The others are supplemental reading to help with the driving part."

"How much do I owe you for the books? I could have gotten them, like in college, when our professors would give us a reading list."

Frankie waved her hand. "It's a gift, like the bike you bought me."

"Okay. Thank you."

"Today will be pretty basic. I'm going to orient you to my car, even though every car is a little different. When you buy your own, you'll need to locate everything I'm going to show you today. It shouldn't be too hard. Cars come with owner's manuals that you can read from cover to cover."

"I suppose after I get my license, shopping for a car would be the next step, but I enjoy biking to the nursery."

"You don't have to change anything. Having a driver's license or a car gives you more options and the ability to travel farther to places you might like to see."

"That makes sense. There are so many choices for cars. Is there a book to help me choose?"

"We can cross that bridge when we get to it. I'd love to go car shopping with you." Frankie's voice lifted, and I could tell she was excited. "After I show you all the safety features on the car and how to adjust the seat and mirrors specifically for you, we'll practice starts and stops, turning a little with proper steering techniques, and where you should hold your hands on the steering wheel."

"Eight o'clock and four o'clock."

Frankie smiled. "Yeah, that's right. Have you already done advanced research?"

"No, my mom always reminds my dad when he gets lazy and drops one of his hands from the steering wheel. She also tells him, *eyes straight ahead*. My dad is not a skillful driver. When he offered to teach me in high school, I told him if I wanted to learn, I'd ask Mom."

"I'm honored that you're letting me teach you."

"Although I haven't had a need yet, I like the idea of traveling a little farther from home, even if it's scary."

"New things are scary to most people. They don't always admit that as readily as you. After our lesson today, do you want to join me for dinner? I bought a beautiful piece of wild-caught salmon. I don't know if you like fish or not, but salmon is one of my favorites. Healthy and tasty."

"I like fish. I've only had cod when I order fish and chips, or salmon and halibut at nice restaurants."

"You don't seem the type of person who frequents nice restaurants."

"I'm not, but the food was good. There were several gallery owners interested in my sculptures. A few of them lived in Seattle. One was in New York, but I didn't want to fly there, so I told her I didn't want to put my sculptures in a gallery that was so far away."

"You've never been on an airplane?"

I shook my head. "One time I tried to research which country has the most four-leaf clovers, but it doesn't seem like there is any consensus on that. Some people might think it's Ireland because of the widely used shamrock on St. Patrick's Day. The shamrock always has three leaves, so there is a big difference between a shamrock and a four-leaf clover. Although shamrock comes from the Irish word *seamrog*, which loosely translates to little clover, there isn't any agreement about which specific variety of clover is the true shamrock. I would have gotten on an airplane to travel to Ireland if they had the most four-leaf clovers."

Frankie got a dreamy look on her face. "I'd love to go to Ireland someday. It's beautiful there. Or at least the pictures I've seen have tempted me. There are a lot of places I'd like to travel to."

"I get offers to travel all over the world and show my art. I should accept some of them and take you, even if it's scary." I wanted Frankie to know that I would compromise because I read it was important in a relationship.

Frankie tilted her head and looked at me. "I think you are the sweetest woman I've ever known."

CHAPTER TWENTY-TWO

FRANKIE

Without a lot of fanfare, Zari and I fell into a comfortable rhythm. On driving lesson days, I would plan enough food for two people and offer to share my food with Zari. She never turned me down. It was challenging to ensure dinner was ready as close to 5:30 as humanly possible, but I knew how important that was to Zari, so I made an effort. On sculpture days, she would cook. That first weekend after her driving lesson, she helped me lay down the liner and plant several trees and bushes. I didn't want shale for the waterfall, so I dragged Zari to two different places that stocked the specific flagstone I was looking for.

We acted more like an established couple than I ever had with Sam. There was one tiny exception. We hadn't ventured much further than kissing. There was a part of me that thought I shouldn't have that level of intimacy with Zari until I had a final resolution with Sam, even though I'd tried and been unsuccessful.

I almost hated myself for wondering if sex with Zari would ever be as good as sex with Sam. When Sam and I first met, we couldn't keep our hands off one another. It was hot and frequent, unlike the last six months of our tumultuous relationship. That was such a shitty thing to hold me back from calling up Sam to end things once and for all. I needed to stop wavering on my decision.

Zari hadn't asked about Sam, and I hadn't offered. I cared so much for Zari, and she needed to know where she stood. I knew I was falling for her. It was well past the time that I should call Sam and invite her for the talk. Although inviting Sam for dinner might give her the wrong idea, she deserved a face-to-face discussion in a comfortable setting. Regardless of how shitty she'd been lately, three years was nothing to sneeze at, and it hadn't always been terrible. Before I made those arrangements, Zari needed to know we wouldn't be having dinner together like usual, and I was dreading telling her that more than calling Sam.

The quarry delivered the flagstone late on Friday. Zari and I had plans to lay it out and build the waterfall around the piping and electrical set-up she'd already laid out for me. I was expecting her and her latest baked goods any minute.

As I sat on the deck drinking coffee, I paused mid-sip and took a minute to marvel at her beauty as she walked toward me. She wore a light sweatshirt that I knew would come off before noon. Her khaki shorts were always pristine in the mornings until we began our work. I admired how she got them so clean after a day of digging in the dirt. She carried a bouquet of lilies, a large pan, and wore her too-wide smile that I'd come to love.

"You brought flowers. Thank you." I leaned in to smell the fragrant lilies and then took them from her. "God, I love how they smell."

"I remember when you said that nobody had ever brought you flowers, and you liked the smell when you passed them in the grocery store."

"You're spoiling me. I should be the one to bring you flowers every day since you keep me stocked with home-baked goods. What's for breakfast this morning?" I asked.

"Blueberry scones with a cinnamon crunch topping."

"Mmm, that sounds so good. I'm starved."

"Would you like beef or chicken today?"

She already knew my expressions, and I'm sure the loss of my smile was a major clue before I even said that I planned to call Sam.

"Come, sit. Your coffee with four creamers is on the table here."

"Something is wrong," she stated. "I've done something wrong."

"No, you haven't." After she set down the pan, I grabbed her hand. "I need to talk with Sam tonight. I was going to call her to see if she would come over."

"Will you tell her we've been kissing?"

I scrunched my face. "I don't think so. It's none of Sam's business."

"She wouldn't be happy."

"No, she wouldn't."

"Are you embarrassed about kissing me because I'm not your girlfriend yet?"

I squeezed her hand. "No, I am not at all embarrassed. We should talk about the whole label thing again after I've spoken with Sam."

"Okay. Will you give Sam the new gate code?"

"No, I'll meet her at the gate. Are you free tomorrow? I want to take you for a drive."

Her brow furrowed. "Sunday is not a driving lesson day."

"I know. You took me to one of your favorite places by the lake, now I want to take you to my favorite place. I'll drive. Are you up for a new adventure?"

"We've been having a lot of those."

"We have. Too much? I'm so impressed with your willingness to step out of your comfort zone and establish new schedules."

"Not too much. Jillian and all the websites talk about how important compromise is to a relationship."

"Damn. I've been selfish. What would you like to do tomorrow?"

Her wide smile reappeared. "I'd like to go on a drive to see your favorite place."

At that moment, I knew. I wasn't falling in love anymore. I'd already landed, although it took me a while longer to admit that to anyone else but myself. Side note—admitting that to myself wasn't exactly a conscious thought.

†

"Can you give me a few moments? I'll wash the dishes, and then I need to make the call."

Zari nodded and pulled on her hair. I took her hand and kissed her. "Don't be nervous. I promise it will all be okay."

191

After I'd washed our cups and wrapped the remaining scones in plastic wrap, I breathed in a mouthful of air and then punched in Sam's number.

Her groggy voice was a dead giveaway that I'd woken her. "Hello."

"Hi, it's me."

I heard the rustling of bed sheets. "Give me a minute. I just woke up." After more rustling of bed linen, I heard her close the door. "I'm so happy to hear from you, Frankie. I've missed you." Her voice was low, almost as if she was trying to keep someone else from hearing her.

"I'm sorry. Did I wake you up?"

"Um, yeah. I had a late night."

"Listen, the reason I'm calling is that I'm ready to talk tonight."

"Oh, uh, yeah, sure. I had plans, but I'll cancel them. You're more important."

I sighed. "Come by around six, and I'll have dinner for us. Nothing fancy. Maybe grilled chicken over greens. That should be healthy enough for you. Um, I'll meet you at the gate."

I heard the hesitation on the other end of the phone. Probably because I'd said I would meet her at the gate. "That's wonderful. I'll bring the wine. And Frankie, I'm so glad you called. I can't wait to see you. I love you."

"Yeah, I'll see you tonight. Bye, Sam." I did not want to get into anything over the phone to correct whatever misunderstanding she might have for the purpose of the evening. Apparently, mentioning the dinner was nothing fancy was not direct enough to let her know I was not planning a romantic dinner for two.

192

I didn't wait to hear her say goodbye as I ended the call. I'd bet my house she was in bed with another woman, but it didn't matter anymore. Strangely, knowing this didn't hurt. I was moving on. I had moved on. She just didn't know that yet. Even though the hard part wasn't over, I bounced into the backyard, feeling like a weight had lifted from my shoulders.

Zari was stacking the flagstone into piles separated by size. That would make it easier to find the right piece of stone. I would have left them, and the job would have been infinitely more difficult. Zari was so perfect for me. But was I perfect for her?

I walked over and placed my hand on her shoulder. She remained squatting, focused on her task. "All done," she announced.

"You are such a blessing. I'm so happy you're in my life," I said to her, and I meant every word.

†

I didn't bother to put on anything fancy after I'd taken my shower. What was the point? I didn't need to impress Sam. I was planning on sticking to my guns and ending things. Sam, however, had different ideas. After my phone buzzed to let me know she'd arrived, I met her at the gate and punched in the code. When I saw what she was wearing, I knew we weren't on the same page. We weren't even in the same book. She had on her crisp turquoise shirt and form-fitting pants—the ones that hugged her hips and showed off her ass. The outfit used to be a sure-fire way to the bedroom before our sex life had become beyond anemic. *Damn, why hadn't I said something more when I had the chance?* The simple answer was that I wasn't prepared

193

to get into it over the phone. I believed hard conversations should always occur face-to-face.

She rolled down her window, and I responded mechanically, the way I should to her appearance. "You look nice. I'm afraid I expected a more casual evening." I gestured to my baggy T-shirt and shorts.

I climbed in her car, and she drove to my house. Before she followed me to my front door, she reached into the back seat and retrieved her gifts for the evening. We walked silently to the door, and I waved her inside.

She held out a dozen red roses and a bottle of wine. I winced at the hopeful look she gave me. "I brought you flowers. These had the sweetest smell. They're your favorite, right? Roses?"

They weren't, at least not anymore, after Zari had given me a bouquet of Orienpet lilies. In all the years Sam and I had been together, she'd never brought me flowers. I wondered how she even knew which ones I liked. She probably went with an old standard because roses were often the flower chosen for romance. I didn't challenge or acknowledge her guess, and simply said, "Thanks."

Zari's lilies were prominently displayed on the center island in my kitchen, still permeating the air with their sweet scent. Sam narrowed her eyes at the lilies. "I see you already have flowers."

"I'm sure I'll be able to find something else to put the roses in." I needed to interrupt the awkwardness of the moment. "Are you hungry?" I didn't give her a chance to answer. "I'll put the chicken on the grill."

Sam set the wine and flowers on the counter and grabbed my wrist. She tried to pull me into an embrace, but I placed my hands on her chest to keep her from trying to kiss me hello.

"Don't."

"But...I thought we were going to talk and work through everything," Sam sputtered.

"If I don't start dinner, we'll be eating at nine."

"Would that be so bad? I seem to remember in our first year together, dinner was often interrupted. We couldn't keep our hands off of each other or our clothes on our bodies. I want that back. You're still a beautiful woman that I'm wildly attracted to." Sam's brows lifted in confusion and hurt.

"Why don't you open the wine for us? The wine opener is in the top drawer to the right of the stove."

Sam sighed. "Sure, I can do that. I could use a glass of wine right now."

I busied myself with the chicken and finding something to put her roses in. I'd used the only vase I owned for Zari's flowers.

An uneasy silence fell between us as I struggled to think of small talk that would fill the void until I delivered my carefully prepared speech. Sam had already finished her first glass of wine and was pouring another. I hadn't even taken a sip of mine yet.

I set the salad on the table and then went to the kitchen to retrieve two different dressings. Sam was now pouring her third glass and had emptied the bottle, setting it on the table with a loud thud.

"Maybe you should slow down."

She glared at me and growled. "I don't need a mother. I need a lover."

I bit my tongue to keep from spitting out the retort that naturally flowed to my brain. *I doubt you have any trouble finding lovers, and therein lies the problem.* I wasn't ready for battle. Instead, I asked, "How's the new job?"

She half-smiled. "Same shit, different day. Although, my new boss is cool. I think they realized that giving me a new title, a shit ton of extra assignments, but only a tiny raise is not enough of an incentive to keep me happy. She allows me to work from home when I'm not needed in the office."

I nodded. "That's good." I figured if I started eating, that would give us both a break at trying to keep the conversation going when it was so painfully awkward for both of us. I felt like we were on a first date where we didn't know a single thing about the other person rather than knowing everything and anticipating the terrible trajectory of the evening.

She attempted to keep things on the surface. "How's your backyard project going?"

"I'll show it to you after we eat. We can sit on the deck after dinner."

"I thought you might set things up outside. It's a little windy but still nice."

I shrugged. "I didn't even think of that until you mentioned my project."

"It's okay. Your house is comfortable. Eating inside is fine. It beats our shabby place. My shabby place," she corrected. "You've traded up."

"Sorry, I was trying to help when I finally accepted my father's offer. We both needed space and distance. For different reasons, but still…"

†

With the dishes put away, there was nothing left to do but have the conversation. I steeled myself for what would undoubtedly be a tough discussion. My only saving grace was that Sam seemed to have mellowed, almost as if she knew what was coming and would ultimately accept the finality of our relationship. Maybe it was the wine or something else that brought her to this place.

As we stepped onto the back deck and took our seats, the sun was setting. Any other time, this would have been a flawless end to a romantic evening. Maybe this would be the picture-perfect alternative for us.

"I've practiced what I need to say, so can you let me get it all out before you respond?"

"I can do that." Her words were quiet. Subdued.

"First, I wanted to say I'm sorry if you got the wrong impression about tonight. I just didn't want to talk over the phone. A public place didn't seem right, either." I paused before launching into the speech I had mulled over in my head. "Maybe if we had met at another time in our lives, we would have worked out, but that didn't happen. We want different things at this particular moment. And neither of us will do what is needed to stay together. If we were meant to be, we'd fight harder for us. I know you were in bed with someone else this morning…"

Sam opened her mouth to speak, but I held up my hand.

"It doesn't bother me. Honest. I understand that's what you need right now. In some ways, you're right. We are young. But here's the thing. If we were madly in love with one another and our needs were met, neither of us would find comfort with another."

"Have you slept with her yet?"

"Who? Zari?"

"Yeah."

"No, but I won't lie and say I don't have feelings for her, because I do."

"Do you love her?"

"I could."

"And it's not because you feel guilty about not being fully there for your sister?"

"No, that's not what's happening," I assured her. "I do still love you, but if it takes an ultimatum to keep us together, that will never do. Relationships are hard work, especially after that initial honeymoon stage."

"I should have made more of an effort." Tears appeared at the corner of her eyes.

"Maybe. You certainly used to, but then so did I. I don't think you're the only one who should have made that effort. Zari isn't shy about letting me know she wants me in her own sweet and quirky way. She's driven and precise. It feels good to be the focus of her attention. I get the feeling that even if the way she goes about dating differs vastly from what I'm used to, she'll never stop trying to please me or work at keeping us together. She's funny and kind and honest to a fault. Trust will never be an issue."

The words had slipped out of my mouth before I censored myself. I didn't want to be that person who rubbed salt in a wound. I didn't intend to be cruel. Fortunately, Sam didn't seem to notice my gaffe. I got the sense she was trying to understand my connection to Zari.

"What about passion? We had passion and electrifying chemistry in the beginning."

"If you're talking about great sex, you're right. We had that. You used to make me feel like I was the center of your universe. I miss that. But, I'm just not sure that for the long-haul, great sex is as important to me as it is to you. I want that, sure, but I want other things even more."

"How about we leave the door open a slight crack? If things don't work out with Zari, you'll call, and maybe I'll be at a different place. I can't see myself dating several people at once in my forties. That might be exhausting." She laughed. "Frankie, you were my first love. People never forget their first love. I know I won't ever forget you. I'll probably kick myself in the ass for being such an idiot and letting you go so easily."

I was surprised at how well she was taking things. "Damn straight, you will." I let a ghost of a smile appear on my face. "Can I ask a favor of you?"

"Of course."

"If we run into each other when we're out and about town, can you be less of an ass to Zari? You can be very charming when you want to be. I'd prefer you to show her that side of yourself. Otherwise, she'll wonder what I ever saw in you." I grinned.

"Sure, as long as you're less of an ass to Cori when you see us out and about. Or anyone else I hang with."

"Cori, huh? I thought she was too clingy."

"She's not as bad as I thought. Probably a bigger proponent of multiple partners than I am."

"Thanks for taking this so well. You made this conversation a lot easier on me than I thought you would."

"Yeah, well. I guess I'm not as thick-headed as you believed. Besides, you made some excellent points, that if I'm honest, I've already considered before you brought them up.

I'm thankful you aren't trashing my needs and wants, or judging the fact that we want different things."

"I'm not. I promise. And, for what it's worth, I boxed you into a corner where you thought you couldn't be honest with me. I knew you were restless."

"That didn't give me the right to go there before talking with you about it. I'm sorry."

"Apology accepted. It might be difficult to be friends right off the bat, but hopefully, we'll get there."

"Count on it. Will you tell Zari I'm sorry for being an asshat? I promise not to scream at her again. I felt bad when she started rocking. I should know better. I understand why you had the gate code changed and wouldn't give it to me."

"I'll tell her. I've no doubt she is a very forgiving person. Perhaps someday I'll be able to share the code with you. By the way, you don't need a code when exiting the community."

"Well, I better go before it hits me how much I'm giving up. I'll always love you."

"Me too."

Slowly, she stood and silently walked into the house. "I guess it's time to exit while I'm still behaving myself."

"Are you okay to drive?"

"Yeah, our discussion was sobering in more ways than one. I'm fine, really. I didn't finish the third glass. I know I need to cut down."

I chuckled nervously. "You said it, not me. I was wondering how that fits in with your whole my-body-is-a-temple belief system."

"We must have been out of sync for me to consume so much lately to calm my nerves. That's telling right there." She reached for the front door.

"It is," I agreed.

With the door open, she turned around, appearing almost to delay her departure. "By the way, sorry about that long black mark in your driveway."

I waved my hand in the air. "Meh, it's okay. I'm sure there are special chemicals to remove it. I'll ask Zari. Her specialty is researching obscure facts or, in this case, remedies to common household issues."

"That doesn't bother you? How she spouts off facts at odd moments?"

"No. I find it charming."

Nodding, she tentatively reached for me, and I let her hug me goodbye. "Thanks for dinner." I could see how hard she was trying to keep the tears from escaping.

I watched her walk to her car, shoulders drooping, and waved as she gently rolled down the road. I glanced toward Zari's house, hoping she was still awake, but I didn't see any lights or fluttering curtains. I kept wavering over whether I should disturb her. After arguing with myself over the right thing to do, I finally decided it was selfish to wake her. Neither of us was going anywhere, and I'd already told her not to worry.

CHAPTER TWENTY-THREE

ZARI

I hadn't wanted to jinx things with Frankie, so I didn't tell Jillian about all the kissing or the flowers I brought her on sculpting day. Jillian would have been proud of me for interrupting my schedule to strap the cooler on my bike and make the trip to the flower shop. It was worth it when I saw Frankie smile and bend to smell the lilies. I recognized the radiant look on her face.

Sam hadn't screeched off last night, and that had me worried. I wondered if the kissing would stop now. I began tugging my hair again. When I'd pulled several strands out, I decided to call Jillian and confess about not sticking to the original July fifteenth schedule for kissing.

"It's Sunday and early again. I thought we established the rule already, Zari. No phone calls before ten."

"Don't be mean." I heard Patty say in the background.

"I have an emergency. We didn't stick to the July fifteenth schedule, and Sam didn't screech out of the driveway yesterday."

"Well, I'm not sure how those two things are linked. Can you give me a little more information to go on?"

"We started kissing again on June sixteenth. We've been kissing every day since, and one time she touched the side of my breast. Yesterday we didn't have dinner together like normal because she made dinner for Sam. Sam brought her roses. She's never done that before."

"I can't believe I'm leading with this question, because we will loop back to the kissing and touching of breasts, but how do you know she's never brought her flowers?"

"Because Frankie told me that no one has ever brought her flowers before. I bought her lilies on a sculpting day. I had to put them in a cooler, so I wouldn't ruin them. Knowing how to drive and having a car would have been better, but I kept them fresh in the cooler on my bike."

"Okay, too much extraneous information that I don't need. Let's get back to the kissing and other stuff. Who broke the rule first?"

"She did."

"Tell me exactly what happened."

"She came to my house with ice cream the Thursday before last. I think she felt guilty and was trying to tell me she had talked to Sam and reopened a door or something. Then she told me I was amazing. We talked about rules and schedules. She thought the no kissing until July fifteenth was a rule, and I considered it a schedule. So, I guess she reassessed that and said it was maybe a rule and a schedule. She asked if I ever changed my schedule or established new rules. Sometimes I make changes. So, she changed it to June sixteenth and kissed me."

"Was there tongue action?"

"Jillian!" Patty yelled in the background.

"What? It's a legit question. I should be mad at Zari for not saying a single word about all the kissing this past week and a half."

"Yes, she put her tongue in my mouth and sucked my bottom lip. I liked that."

Jillian chuckled. "I'll bet you did. What's not to like? I hope you returned the favor and didn't kiss her back like a wooden doll."

"Do you mean did I put my tongue inside her mouth?"

"Yes, doofus."

"I did. What about Sam not leaving mad? Do you think that means she got what she wants, and Frankie agreed to get back together with her?"

"I don't know. You've never been shy about asking direct questions. Do your fancy baking thing and go there and ask Frankie. Even if she got back with Sam, I don't think you have to worry. She doesn't want what Sam is offering. You are a perfect contrast to a woman who doesn't know how great she has it and risks it all by wanting to date others. Feel free to remind her that you're not only willing to be monogamous, but that's what you're looking for. That is what you want with Frankie, right?"

"Yes. I love her. I want to have sex with her. Should I ask her when we can schedule sex for the first time?"

"If you can avoid scheduling sex, I would recommend that. Let it happen organically. Frankie will know when the time is right. It's been okay how things have evolved so far, right? She's respected your need for schedules?"

"Mostly, yes. Love means willing to adapt to change. I've rearranged my schedule four times for her. I'm glad it was four times and not three."

Jillian laughed. "Yeah, God forbid anything happens in threes. You good now?"

"Yes. I'll bake more cinnamon rolls and ask if she got back together with Sam."

"Good luck, and no more tugging on your hair. You won't look half as good as you do now if you're bald."

"Sinead O'Connor and Demi Moore looked good bald."

"True. They both lucked out because they have nice shaped heads. You don't want to take the chance that your head is all lumpy."

"Okay."

I hung up the phone and began pulling the ingredients for cinnamon rolls from my pantry.

†

With the pan in my hand, I knocked four times on Frankie's door. A beautiful smile blossomed on her face when she answered.

"Good morning, Zari. What have you brought me today?" She rubbed her hands together and widened her smile.

"Cinnamon rolls. I didn't have time to make a full brunch because I was eager to see you and ask if you got back together with Sam. She didn't screech out of your driveway yesterday."

"Come on in. How about if we eat these on my back deck? I can fill you in on what happened."

"She brought you roses."

Frankie chuckled. "She did." She took the pan from my hand and kissed me firmly on the mouth. "Oh, Zari, maybe I should have come over late last night. Since I told you not to worry, I had hoped you would trust me. We didn't get back together. The path is clear to date you if that's what you want."

I ruminated over her comment about dating as I followed her inside and waited patiently for her to dish my cinnamon rolls onto two plates. She poured another cup of coffee for me and put in my four creamers and two teaspoons of sugar. After handing me the cup and picking up both plates, she motioned with her head to follow her outside. I pulled open the sliding glass door leading to her deck and sat in the chair on the right that had become the one I always used when I joined her for coffee.

"I thought we were dating already. I know you're not my girlfriend because we haven't had sex yet, but doesn't dating involve spending time together and kissing?" I asked.

"I suppose it does. It's my fault we jumped the gun and moved the timeline for kissing."

"I'm not complaining. Jillian said I shouldn't ask you to schedule sex, but can you tell me how many more dates until we have sex?"

Frankie choked a little on her coffee.

I finished my thought. "Because then I'll know when I can tell my mom I have a girlfriend."

After she recovered and wiped her mouth, she shifted in her chair. "You need the label, don't you?"

I didn't ask her what label. I already knew she was talking about the being-her-girlfriend classification. I nodded. Labels helped me understand complex concepts.

"Zari, I don't want any misunderstandings. I just ended a relationship because she defined being her girlfriend in a manner I wasn't comfortable with. If I'm your girlfriend, neither one of us gets to kiss other women the way we've been kissing each other. That goes for sex, too, when we get to that point in our relationship. Speaking of sex, we don't need to rush into that for you to tell your mom you have a girlfriend. Just so you know, sex is not a prerequisite to an exclusive relationship."

"Those are good rules, but we will have sex, won't we?"

"I certainly hope so. We won't have sex until both of us are ready. I can't tell you how many dates before sex. I'm sure you already discovered that on your own—you know, that there isn't a specific number of dates before sex. It varies by the couple."

"It was confusing. One psychologist said the ideal time was a few dates during the course of a month. We haven't known each other for a month yet. Another site said the average number in a poll of women was nine, but that seemed to apply to men and women. I couldn't find anything on lesbians, other than eighty-six percent of lesbians commit to each other after between one and ten dates. If we count driving lessons as dates because we have dinner together after our lesson, then we've had enough dates to commit. I suppose it makes sense that we can be exclusive before sex because the survey didn't mention sex."

Frankie smiled and wiped her brow. "Whew, glad we got that settled."

"We did?" I wasn't sure what we had settled.

"No sex until we're both ready. It could be tomorrow or in another month," Frankie clarified.

"Okay. I'm glad I won't have to wait more than a month. Thank you for giving me a range to work with. It's not as good as a schedule, but it's the next best thing. Should I wait for you to tell me when you're ready? I'm ready right now."

Frankie frowned. "I don't like being the one who holds all the cards. That doesn't seem fair." The crinkle in her forehead deepened.

"You're worried about us having sex. Why?"

"Um, not everyone clicks. Sometimes it takes a few times for two people to discover what the other person enjoys. I guess I feel a bit of pressure to make your first time an enjoyable experience. It will be your first time, right?"

"Yes. I've watched a lot of videos and read a lot of books. I know what to expect. You're the first woman I've wanted to have sex with. Since I like kissing you, I don't think you have to worry about me enjoying my first time. I'll tell you if something doesn't feel good."

Frankie's smile returned. "You know what? You're right. I shouldn't worry at all. Miscommunication is the root of most breakups, and that's not something we'll ever have to worry about. I adore that about you. It's more than a little refreshing. I'll never have to guess what you're thinking or feeling."

"I'm so happy you're my girlfriend."

This time I initiated the kiss. "Mmm, me too, Zari, me too."

"When do we leave for your favorite place?" I asked.

"Oh, that's right. If it wasn't so far away, I would have suggested we take the bikes. Ugh, after I finish my backyard, I'm going to need to offset all those baked goods with regular exercise. Are you up for some future dates on our bikes?"

"Yes. That would be nice. More bike rides will make it easier on your buttocks. You were out of shape on our last ride."

"So true. Shoveling may get rid of my squishiness, but biking uses different muscles. Not driving has given you a distinct advantage. Give me a few weeks, and hopefully, I'll catch up to your state of health."

†

Even though I'd driven around the neighborhood and Frankie told me I was a perfect student, she said it would be better for her to drive because we had to go on the highway, and motoring through a winding road might be tricky. As we pulled into the parking lot next to the lodge, Frankie told me about the history of Snoqualmie Falls.

"Snoqualmie is a Salish word meaning moon. The Snoqualmie Tribe founded the Falls. Even though the salmon don't run above the Falls, there is an abundance of edible bulbs, roots, and berries. I thought you would love exploring all the plants around the Falls. There's a trail through there." She pointed to the paved walkway surrounded by trees, grass, and other plants I was eager to learn about.

Along the way, she let me stop at every plaque and read. That was something I learned not everyone has the patience for. When the school would take us for a field trip to a museum, I always wanted to read everything on offer, but it slowed down the group, making both the teachers and students frustrated.

Other hikers passed us when they discovered how slow we were walking. When we reached the end of the paved walkway,

I could hear the rush of the Falls. There was a light wind, and I wanted to feel the moisture on my skin.

"Is there a way to get closer?"

Frankie nodded and took my hand. "Come on, we can walk back more quickly, and I'll take you to the lower parking lot. I didn't know if you wanted to be that close, but the Falls are amazing from the trail off of the other parking area."

I was excited to complete my driving lessons so I could buy a car and take trips to places like Snoqualmie Falls. Sundays could become new adventure days. That would work well in my schedule. As we walked to the car to retrieve the food Frankie had packed, I let her know I was agreeable to another schedule change.

"I would be amenable to using Sundays for exploration. We can skip brunch, too. We did that this morning. After I learn to drive, I could research different spots to travel to."

Frankie reached into her back seat and turned to look over her shoulder. I couldn't decipher her expression. It was a little like surprise, but not quite because she was smiling.

Grabbing the basket, she said, "I'd love that. There are so many places I've wanted to go but never got around to exploring before. This state has an amazing number of parks and other scenic trails. We could spend an entire lifetime getting to all of them."

It was a little past lunchtime, but I didn't care, because that meant we could find an open picnic table. As Frankie set down the basket, I said, "I didn't recognize the expression on your face earlier when I said we could change our Sunday schedule."

"Wonder. Amazement. I know you like your schedules to remain constant, and yet here are doing something we hadn't precisely scheduled." She turned her wrist. "And it's way past lunchtime. I'm so sorry about that." Her brow furrowed, and she frowned. "I guess I didn't time this very well. I also didn't make a fancy lunch. Buying everything at the store was a lot easier." She laid out the roasted chicken, potato salad, and a bag of chips.

"That's okay. I like roasted chicken. I can make the potato salad next time."

Frankie wrinkled her nose. "I know. Grocery store potato salad isn't very good. The squirrels and birds probably won't eat it either. Hopefully, the chicken and fruit plate I brought for dessert will be enough. I've also been known to polish off a whole bag of chips by myself. It's not moderation, but when I haven't gone to the grocery store, it works."

"Will I get to meet your family now? My mom and dad will want to meet you."

"Oh, I hadn't considered that. Um, yeah, I suppose," Frankie said. Her voice was hesitant.

"You don't want me to meet your parents?"

"No, no, that isn't it. My father can be…overwhelming. I guess that is the best word to describe him. I'd rather not scare you off before we've begun."

"Does he yell a lot?"

"No. My father is firm sometimes, but he doesn't raise his voice. Penny didn't respond well to that, so that's never been an issue with him. However, he and I have very different views on a lot of things. He's very overprotective. Penny still lives at home with him and my mom. They've never pushed her out of her comfort zone, not even a little bit."

I nodded. "Your father might not approve of you dating someone with autism."

"I don't know, but it doesn't matter because I'm happy spending time with you."

"And being my girlfriend?"

"Yes, and being your girlfriend." She moved closer to me and kissed me. In the open, for everyone to see.

†

On Monday, when I was rolling into my garage after finishing nursery day early, I felt the buzz of my phone in my pocket. The only people who ever called me on my cell phone were Jillian and my mom. I hadn't even given Frankie my cell phone number yet. My dad had insisted I carry a phone in case I needed to call 911 for an emergency.

"Hello," I answered.

"Why didn't you tell me you had a girlfriend? I had to find out from Jillian. I was picking up my new apple tree, thinking I would see you, and she told me you'd already left to go to your driving lesson with your girlfriend. You need to put in your schedule a family dinner so we can meet this young woman."

"Okay. I'll ask Frankie."

"Frankie? That's an odd name for a girl."

"I thought that too since the only Frankie I know is the one who fixes your car, but she said that's her name."

"It must be short for Frances. Still, not a very modern name. Jillian says she's nice."

"She is and very pretty. She's also a good kisser."

"You two are kissing already?"

"Yes, we were kissing before she was officially my girlfriend. A person can date casually and kiss or have sex without being exclusive."

"Are you having sex?" Her voice squeaked at the end.

"No. And we haven't scheduled that either. Although, Frankie gave me a range after I asked her. We'll probably have sex within the next month. I'm ready now, but I don't think she is. She hasn't watched as many movies as I have or read all the books."

"Why don't you ask her if she can join you tomorrow night or Wednesday?"

"Okay. I have to go now. I see Frankie walking over. She usually greets me before we walk to her house and start our lesson. I like that she does that."

As Frankie approached, I could tell she wanted to ask me a question but saw that I had my cell phone to my ear.

"Let me know, honey, which day works for you and Frankie."

"Okay. Bye, Mom."

"I guess I knew you had a phone. I've just never seen you use it, except to put things in your calendar."

I put my bike away and refocused my attention on Frankie. "The only people who have my number are my mom and dad and Jillian. Do you want my phone number?"

"I'd love to have your phone number. Sometimes it's nice to get a text in the middle of the day. It tells a person that someone is thinking of them, even if it's something innocuous like confirming a date or asking if I can pick something up from the store."

"Did Sam text you?"

"Sometimes."

"Do you think of me in the middle of the day?"

"Yeah, all the time."

"Me too. I should get your number."

"Absolutely." She held out her hand. "Give me your phone, and I'll program my number into it. You can call me, and then I'll add your number."

"Okay." I handed her my phone.

While Frankie put in her number, she asked, "So, that was your mom on the phone?"

"She wants me to bring you to a family dinner on Tuesday or Wednesday."

"Oh, already?" Frankie shifted her weight on her feet, and I could tell she was nervous.

"You're nervous."

"Yeah, a little. Meeting someone's parents is a big step." She gave me back my phone. Although I wanted to call her immediately so she could have my number, I decided what we were talking about was too important to become distracted.

"It is?"

"Yes, it signifies that you're very serious about the person you're dating."

"I'm serious about you. We can wait for me to meet your mom and dad if you're not yet serious about me."

Frankie grabbed my hand. "Oh, Zari, if you only knew the whirlwind of emotions I have right now. But, yeah, I'm nervous because of how quickly those feelings have surfaced. I'm afraid I'll hurt you if we don't do this right."

"I've never read about the *right* way to establish a serious relationship. I'm not the only one that can be hurt. I know a lot more than people give me credit for. I know my sculptures are worth a lot of money. Seeking advice from others is not a weakness, especially if you trust them. Putting your trust in someone who doesn't deserve it, that's a bad idea. I haven't done that for a very long time. I didn't know what love was before, but at least one thing I know is that love is taking a risk for someone you trust. Because even if there's a chance I'll get hurt, it's worth it. I know that I love you. You don't have to say it back."

"I'm not sure I even know what love is anymore. I know that I could easily fall in love with you. Maybe I have already. Before I tell you I love you, I want to be one hundred percent sure. It may be prudent to wait to have sex until I'm sure."

"Okay. Will you know that before the month is over? That's the timeframe you gave me before."

"I sure hope so. Are you ready for your lesson?"

"We go on the highway today? Right?"

"Yes. I thought maybe as a celebration, we can have pizza in Roslyn. That's a short distance on the highway, plus some practice on a few smaller roads. Did you read the next section in the book?"

I nodded. "I understand about right of way and stop signs. Can I call you now, so you'll have my phone number?"

Frankie laughed. "Sure."

"Tuesday or Wednesday?" I asked again because I knew I'd get another call during our lesson if I didn't let my mom know which day.

"How about Wednesday?" she answered.

"I'll call my mom before our lesson and pizza."

CHAPTER TWENTY-FOUR

FRANKIE

I wasn't sure what kept me from admitting to Zari I was falling hard for her. I wasn't lying when I told her that meeting the parents was a big deal. It was huge, in my opinion. Something I wasn't sure I was ready for, but we were going there with her mom. I couldn't blame her mom for wanting to meet me.

After I finished college, my protective streak came out with Penny, and I was sure I'd want to meet anyone she was seeing, anyone she called her boyfriend. Or girlfriend. It was hard to tell with Penny. She didn't show a lot of interest in men or women. I think that made my parents happy. I wasn't sure how they would react to Zari. I found her charming, kind, and wonderful. They might have a completely different perspective if they judged her on first impressions, shaded by their own experience with a daughter on the spectrum. I wanted them to see beyond the quirks to the beautiful woman beneath.

I let Zari drive to her parents' house after our lesson to give her additional time behind the wheel. She was a fast learner and hadn't struggled to learn everything. If anything, she was overly cautious. I expected her to be precise. That was reflected in the way she always remembered to adjust the car before moving. And she obeyed every instruction to a T. She never changed the position of her hands from eight and four. She wasn't lazy with a stop sign, like every other driver I knew who made rolling stops when the traffic was light.

Even when another person waved her to go forward, she shook her head and turned to me, stating, "I don't have the right of way. We came to the stop sign at the same time, and that car is on the right." I had to tell her that sometimes people are courteous and when they wave you to go through, it's okay to do that. She nodded, but I could tell she wouldn't ever do that.

Zari pulled into the driveway of a modest house in an older neighborhood. I liked the color of the house. It was a moss green that exuded warmth and comfort. An apple tree sat on the grass, still in a plastic bucket. The landscaping around the house was as pristine as the house itself, and the only thing out of place was the new tree.

"Mom is waiting for me to assist her with her fruit tree. I was going to put something on my calendar, but I wanted to check with you first."

"Why?" I asked because I wasn't sure why she needed to check with me.

"Unless I interrupt my work during sculpture day, or leave earlier from the nursery, helping my mom with the tree will impact our evenings when we usually have dinner together."

I was so touched by how mindful Zari was with what I hoped she considered sacred time with me. She had adapted to a new pattern that we'd established early on. I wondered if she had that penned into her calendar, so I had to ask. I knew she only used her phone until she could transfer the dates and times to her master calendar.

"Zari, is dinner with me on your calendar for every night?"

She nodded. "I can put that in pencil if you want. I have a pen eraser too, but it doesn't work as well as removing pencil."

"I enjoy having dinner with you every night. We never talked about that, did we? It sort of evolved into a pattern."

"Yes, I recognized the pattern. It made logical sense."

"What made logical sense?" I asked.

"The days that you would arrange for food, versus the days that I would cook. I had more time to prepare our meal on sculpture days. I suppose I could have ordered takeout, like you."

I laughed and playfully pushed against her shoulder. "Hey, I cook sometimes."

"I like the takeout foods. I'm not complaining." She grinned. I thought that maybe Zari was learning how to tease back.

"Well, in answer to your question, I'll give you plenty of notice if I can't make our standing dinner dates."

"Okay." Zari unhooked her seat belt and opened the door. After walking around to meet me on the other side, she paused as she looked at me, then took my free hand, and our fingers tangled together. I carried the pie in my other hand, balancing it so the pie wouldn't splat all over the walkway. "My parents will love you as much as me. Don't worry."

218

Before we got to the beautiful wood door, the door flew open, and an older version of Zari smiled at me. Tiny lines appeared at the corners of her eyes, but I couldn't find any gray in her hair, which was almost the exact shade of Zari's. The only difference between the two was her eyes—an expressive kaleidoscope of green, gold, and blue.

"Hello, I'm Gracey. You must be Frankie. I hope you like barbeque. Tom insisted on grilling tonight. I think he wants to impress you." She winked at me. She moved to the side, and Zari led me into the house.

"Um, it's very nice to meet you as well. I brought a pie for dessert."

I wasn't sure if her parents drank adult beverages like wine or beer. I figured pie from the bakery was a safe bet since I hadn't thought to ask Zari about that.

"Oh, that was very thoughtful of you."

As I stepped into their living room, I wondered if Zari's mother had decorated her house because it had the same cozy feeling as Zari's. The furniture was all-natural colors. The pillow accents featured muted shades of blue and green. A tasteful rug with a bamboo design covered part of the glossy wood floor. The house was more compact than Zari's, which gave it an even cozier feel.

"Why don't you girls go outside and say hello to your father while he's grilling his masterpiece. What can I get you to drink?"

"I'll have water, thanks," I answered.

"We have wine and beer if you'd prefer. I like a bit of wine from time to time, and Tom will drink beer."

"I told my mom that you drink wine. Was that a secret?" Zari chimed in.

I laughed. "No, not a secret. Okay, I'll have whatever you're having, Mrs. Woods."

"Gracey, please call me Gracey. And Tom doesn't like to be called Mr. Woods, either. He remembers when his teachers would call him that when he was misbehaving at school. I married a trouble-maker."

We followed Gracey to the backyard, and she introduced me to her husband, who looked up from the grill with twinkling blue eyes. His dark-brown hair was graying at the temples. I could see how the two of them might have graced the homecoming stage as king and queen. No wonder Zari was so naturally beautiful coming from this gene pool.

"Tom, Zari and her, uh…special friend are here."

"I see that." Tom stuck out his hand. "Tom Woods. I'm sure glad you could make it. I've been dying to try out my new grill." He pointed to his massive stainless-steel grill. "A Weber Summit S-660. Gracey thought I was crazy for spending so much on a grill, but wait until you taste the food. A man needs the right tools to make a masterpiece. Isn't that right, Zari? You wouldn't skimp on your sculpting tools, would you?"

I shook his extended hand. "Nice to meet you. Your wife says I shouldn't call you Mr. Woods."

"She's right. Tom, just Tom."

"You girls sit, and I'll bring out the drinks. Zari, do you want sun tea?" Gracey asked.

"Yes, please."

Tom whistled as he turned over whatever he was cooking on the grill. The aroma of seared beef and a kind of tangy-sweet smell wafted in the air. My mouth watered in anticipation.

"That smells heavenly, Tom," I stated once I'd settled in one of the comfortable chairs on the patio. The cushions were thick as I melted into the chair. Everything about their house was cozy and comfortable, including how warm and welcoming they were to me. I relaxed into the evening.

"Wait until you taste it. I try not to brag, but you won't taste anything that'll melt in your mouth more than my brisket or barbeque chicken, if you prefer that. Gracey makes homemade baked beans just like my gramma. Best you'll ever have," Tom bragged.

"Now I know where Zari gets her talent for baking and cooking."

Gracey returned from the kitchen, holding two drinks. "What's this about Zari and cooking?"

Accepting the wine, I answered, "Zari welcomed me to the neighborhood with delicious cookies, and the treats have kept on coming. I swear the brunch she prepared was worthy of being served in the finest New York restaurant."

Gracey arched her eyebrow. "That's new."

I'd just taken a sip of wine when Zari answered, "You can learn any new skill on the Internet, even sex." I choked on my wine.

Gracey didn't miss a beat as she patted my back. "Are you all right, hon? I thought you would be used to Zari by now."

"Um, yes, I am. Zari's direct approach to everything is one of the things I love most about her."

Both Gracey and Tom smiled proudly. And then I realized I'd used the *L* word. What was said could not be unsaid. Would Zari consider that as an admission that I was in love with her? And would she know the distinction between loving someone and being in love? Not that I knew for sure whether there was a difference in this case. As I pondered all of this, I almost missed Gracey's next question.

"Jillian tells us you're a teacher. Where do you teach?"

Tom turned his attention to me, and both sets of eyes focused on my answer.

"I teach at the local elementary school. I'm their one and only special education teacher. Although I prefer the term 'exceptional education teacher.' I like finding different ways of adapting to a variety of exceptional learning styles."

Gracey and Tom both nodded their heads. "Are there any kids on the spectrum?"

"Just one. The school is small, so I have to adapt to all the different learning styles and unique gifts of the various students."

Both Gracey and Tom's smiles widened.

"Frankie's sister is a person with autism. She feels a little guilty for not being there for her as much as she should have while they were in high school. Frankie's ex-girlfriend told me that's why she's dating me, but both Jillian and Frankie said that wasn't true. I believe them over Sam."

"Is everyone ready for some lip-smacking barbeque?" Tom asked.

I was never so grateful to have someone interrupt the conversation. I knew I needed to follow up with Gracey. Tom hadn't reacted to Zari filling in the blanks, but I saw the subtle narrowing of Gracey's eyes.

†

"Frankie, hon, will you give me a hand with the biscuits and beans? Zari hasn't visited in a while. Now I know why. I want to give her a chance to talk with her dad while we're bringing out the rest of the food."

"Um, sure." I set my wine down on the table and followed her into the kitchen through the sliding glass doors.

She had a tight smile on her face. "Frankie, I try not to be too overprotective of Zari. When she first moved out, she would come to dinner every Sunday. After about a year, she wanted to try once a month. Finally, she decided she wanted to try scheduling random dinners. They still had to be at 5:30, but venturing outside the rigid Sunday routine was immense growth. We miss seeing her so regularly but are proud of the progress she's made."

I felt guilty thinking that her mom might believe I kept Zari from spending time with her parents. Before I could say anything to correct any possible misunderstanding, her mother continued to reveal her real concern.

"She's an adult now and has done remarkably well on her own. In most ways, she's capable of taking care of herself. The one area I still worry about is relationships. She has an almost childlike or adolescent view of them. I can tell she's quite enamored with you, which will make it very hard on her if you aren't serious about establishing a relationship. Dating might feel casual to you, but to her, it's a step toward a long and happy future."

"I'd be worried, too, if I was in your shoes. Zari is a lot more astute about relationships and her feelings than I've given her credit for. In her way, she set me straight on that. We haven't officially been dating for long, but the moment I met her, something wonderful happened. I felt such a draw, and it helped me reassess what I want in a relationship. What I deserve. I care a great deal about Zari. She's the kindest, most genuine person I've ever met. Plus, I always get her unadulterated views on everything. There is no subversion with her. That's more than refreshing. It's what I crave. I hope I make her as happy as she makes me."

Gracey nodded. "I know my daughter, and you may not recognize it, but she's deliriously happy. Now, I'll be the mother she needs and get out of the way to let her explore this new chapter in her life. I met Tom in high school and fell madly in love with him. We've been together for thirty years. Most have been good. A few were a little rough. I'm fortunate that he's been my one and only. I never had to deal with heartbreak."

"I have, and it's not a lot of fun."

"The ex-girlfriend?"

I nodded.

"She's completely out of the picture now?"

"Yes, completely."

"And out of your heart?"

"Sam was my first love, and when you love someone, they never fully leave your heart. That isn't a bad thing. I decided to end things and kept to that decision despite Sam wanting to get back together, so you don't need to worry about that. We were not meant to be."

Gracey smiled. "We should return to the party before they think I've murdered you. Zari is surprisingly intuitive and also naïve at the same time."

"She is," I agreed.

"Grab that basket of biscuits and the honey on the counter, and I'll pull the beans from the oven."

†

Although the rest of the evening was more relaxed for me after my heart-to-heart with Zari's mother, Gracey surprised me when she hugged me goodbye. I didn't think she was the hugging type until she reached for Zari next.

"You know the rules, Zari. I get one good hug a day when you visit."

Tom awkwardly patted her back and said, "You know where to get more world-famous barbeque. And bring your friend back. I could tell she appreciated the brisket."

I smiled. "Oh, I did. I really did. Thanks for the leftovers. They'll come in handy when it's my night to cook." I winked at Zari. "Zari is clearly the better cook."

"You come around anytime. Put it on Zari's schedule and let us know. We don't go out too much anymore, so any night is fine." Gracey left the door open as we made our way to the car before I thanked them one last time for their hospitality.

"I'll drive home since it's getting dark. I'd like a more controlled setting before I take you driving in the dark."

"That would mean having a driving lesson after dinner."

"Yes. Can we make that slight schedule change toward the end of our lessons?"

"Okay."

After Zari buckled herself into the passenger's seat, I took a few moments to readjust the mirrors and put on my seat belt before backing out of the driveway. "Your parents are lovely."

"I know it was a ruse when my mom asked you to help her. Did she try to impose rules on you?" Zari asked.

I chuckled. "No, your mom wanted clarification on a few things. Sometimes parents need assurance about intentions."

Zari was silent for a minute and then added, "I don't think anyone can adhere to a rule of never hurting the person you love. I might say or do something that hurts you, and you may need to explain why you're hurt. But I can make sure I never hurt you on purpose."

"Oh, Zari, I don't believe you would ever hurt another person on purpose. And, you're right, I hope I never hurt you, but I might. I trust you will tell me if I do."

"I will."

CHAPTER TWENTY-FIVE

ZARI

I was wondering if we would finish our driving lessons before having sex. Frankie would let me touch her breasts, and she would touch mine, but we never went any further than that. I was watching the calendar, and the end of the month timeframe was coming up on Saturday. It was time to talk to Jillian.

When Jillian came into the nursery to open on Friday, I blurted out, "We haven't had sex yet, and tomorrow will be one month since we talked about not scheduling it."

"Is one month a magical number?"

"No, but she said it could be the next day or a month, and that was one month ago. I would have preferred to know exactly when it would happen, but the next best thing was a timeframe."

"All right. Here's what we're going to do. You're going to plan a romantic evening, and I'm taking you shopping for something different to wear. You can't romance the girl in khakis and a T-shirt."

"If we both leave to go shopping, who will serve the customers?"

"I'll close for a few hours and leave a sign on the door. Family emergency."

"It's not a family emergency," I stated.

"It sure is. You're family, and you need my help to get laid. We're going to go all out tonight. Romantic dinner, candlelight, flowers, and you in a hot outfit."

"Frankie cooks or gets takeout on Fridays."

"Not tonight. Text Frankie right now and say you're taking care of dinner."

I pulled my phone from my side pocket and texted, Jillian is helping me plan a romantic dinner for you tonight. You don't have to cook or call for takeout.

"Let me see what you wrote," Jillian ordered.

I showed her my phone.

"Jeez, Zari. You didn't have to lay it all out. Now there's no surprise."

I heard the buzz of the phone and wanted to read what Frankie texted back. "Can I see?"

Jillian laughed. "I suppose this works for you two."

Great, not having to cook or decide on takeout is a wonderful schedule change. Can't wait.

I'd been experimenting with emojis and sent a smiley emoji with hearts for eyes. Jillian looked over my shoulder as I sent the emoji and shook her head.

"All right, Casanova, what's your preferred style, slinky dress or tailored suit?"

"Which is more comfortable to wear?"

"Suit, I think." Jillian grabbed her chin and tapped her mouth with her index finger. "Hmm, I wonder if a tux would be over the top?" A second later, she answered herself. "Nope, go big or go home. Text her back and tell her that dress is formal tonight."

I pulled up Frankie's contact information and texted, *Jillian said to tell you, dress is formal tonight.*

Intriguing. I might have to dig in the back of my closet, but I'll come up with something. Are we still on for our driving lesson? If so, I'll need to change after the lesson.

I read her response and wondered how to answer. "She's asking me if we still have a driving lesson tonight."

"Hell no. It's essential to prepare everything. Trust me. You'll need the extra two hours to make sure everything is perfect. Text Frankie back and tell her no go on the driving lessons, and she should just come over at five."

No driving lesson tonight. Come over at five instead. Is that okay? I ended with a contemplative emoji.

Very okay

Jillian rubbed her hands together. "If she doesn't melt and lose her clothes after tonight, I can't help you anymore. She'll understand the vibe. You need to take charge after dinner. She wants you, Zari, I can tell. I'll bet the only reason she's holding back is that sometimes you aren't as demonstrative as you need to be. Make the big move, and the rest will come naturally."

✝

Fifteen minutes before five, I tugged on the bow tie to get it perfectly straight. I'd prepared Chateaubriand for two with a homemade béarnaise sauce. The cheesecake was cooling in the refrigerator, and even though I didn't think oysters on the half shell went with the beef dish, Jillian assured me I should serve them. I bought lilies again and used roses to create an aromatic path to the bedroom. It was hard for me to spread the petals on my floor, but Jillian said that was a clear message I wanted tonight to be our special night.

At five minutes until five, I lit the candles on the table. The Cabernet Sauvignon was breathing on the counter. Jillian said I wouldn't appreciate the wine, but that she was sure Frankie would. She was the one who said I needed to open the bottle ahead of time to let it breathe, and I should at least pour a small glass for myself to make a toast.

I was careful not to disturb the rose petals that I'd laid on the floor when I opened my front door after hearing Frankie knock.

Frankie's eyes widened. "Wow! You look, um…great."

Frankie wore a satiny emerald dress that lay flat against her belly. The color complemented both her eyes and tanned arms. I'd never seen anyone so beautiful. Even models on television didn't look as good to me. She'd fixed her hair differently, letting her auburn curls fall across one shoulder.

"You're the most beautiful woman I've ever seen. The color of your dress matches your eyes. I've always liked your eyes. Did you know that only two percent of the world population has green eyes?"

Frankie laughed. "I did know that. Can I come in now, or did you want to gawk some more?" she teased. I now understood when Frankie was teasing me.

"Can I kiss you now, or will I mess up your lipstick?" I asked.

She cupped my jaw and pressed a firm kiss on my lips in answer to my question.

As she followed me deeper into the house, I heard her gasp. "Oh, Zari, everything is beautiful. My mouth is watering. Whatever you've prepared smells heavenly."

I pulled out a chair, and she sat. Her eyes glistened with unshed tears. I didn't think she was unhappy because of what she'd just said, but I asked anyway.

"You're not sad, are you?"

"God, no. Just emotional, because no one has ever gone to this much trouble to create the perfect romantic dinner." She pointed to the beginning of the rose petal path. "You put rose petals on your floor. How does that not drive you nuts?"

"It's a little hard for me. I'm trying not to look at the mess. It's like when I know there's a mess in my studio, I focus on the sculpture instead. Otherwise, I would interrupt my work to clean all the time. I'll clean them after our evening is finished." I picked up the wine on the counter and filled her glass, then poured less into mine.

She tilted her head, and that half-smile I love appeared on her face. "Red wine? Are we having beef?"

"Chateaubriand. But first, I have oysters on the half shell as an appetizer. I know that doesn't go with the main meal or the wine, but Jillian insisted."

"I'll wait to try the wine with the main course. You're trying to seduce me," Frankie stated, then grinned.

"It's been almost a month."

"Yes, it has. Good thing I like raw oysters. You should tell Jillian that was a risk. Not everyone appreciates that particular appetizer."

"Oh, maybe I won't like them."

"You might not, but don't worry, oysters aren't necessarily an aphrodisiac for women, but that tux you're wearing most certainly is."

"Yes, I know. Oysters have a lot of zinc, which is good for the production of sperm. It's the sensuality of the eating experience. The way you sometimes moan when eating my baked goods means I could have baked something and gotten the same response. I made us a cheesecake."

Frankie laughed. "I am so looking forward to dessert."

Retrieving the oysters that I'd stored in the refrigerator, I set them on the table, along with the tiny forks that Jillian had me purchase. Then I turned off the oven. I didn't want the beef to overcook.

The oyster's taste wasn't bad, but I wasn't sure if I liked the texture. I must have made a face because Frankie asked me, "Don't like the oysters, huh?"

"I like the taste. The texture is slimy."

I'd learned to recognize when Frankie was worried, even when her expression was only a fleeting look.

"Is it important that I like oysters for this evening to go well?"

Frankie paused and set down the tiny fork. "I'm not quite sure how to put this." She gathered her breath and continued, "If slimy bothers you, I'm afraid you might not like certain aspects of physical intimacy."

"Oh, you mean like when licking someone causes the person to excrete juices. Are those juices slimy?"

"Maybe not slimy, but certainly slick."

I used my fork to pull another oyster from its shell. "Sometimes, I need to get used to new experiences. I think it will be okay."

Frankie grabbed my hand after I ate the second oyster and set down my tiny fork. "I sure hope so, but it isn't the end of the world if you don't enjoy a particular form of intimacy. There are so many ways to be intimate."

"The Kama Sutra says there are one hundred different sex positions for women."

"Okay, wow! I'm sure I haven't tried them all."

"I will try them with you, and then we can decide on our favorites." I started to enjoy the oysters and reached for my third one as Frankie smiled, then grabbed the last oyster left in the tray.

Popping up to pull the beef out of the oven, I sliced the tender meat and placed it on a platter with the roasted potatoes and asparagus. Stirring the béarnaise sauce I had on a low burner, I transferred that to a gravy bowl and then brought the main course to the table.

Frankie was never shy about digging in and grabbed three pink slices of meat along with several red potatoes and spears of asparagus. She waited while I added food to my plate.

"Do you have a toast you'd like to make, or should I say a few words?" she asked.

"Even though I practiced, I don't think my toast is very good. Maybe you should make the toast."

She raised her glass. "To the best girlfriend a woman could ever hope to have. I adore you and everything you've done to make this evening special." After we both sipped the wine, she added, "Mmm. I'm not an expert, but this is outstanding."

233

I disagreed, but I swallowed what was already in my mouth.

She laughed. "Zari, you know you don't have to drink the wine if you don't like it. That won't change a thing. This evening will still be an amazing night for both of us."

CHAPTER TWENTY-SIX

FRANKIE

I hadn't worked up the courage to tell Zari I loved her yet. The moment I saw her dressed in her tux and the scene she'd laid out before me, every niggling hesitation disappeared. I should have woven that into my toast, but I'd blown the perfect opportunity. I knew where the evening was headed, and if I was honest, I couldn't believe I'd held out for so long. Zari was never tentative with her kisses or touches, and neither was I, but I'd kept everything to above the waist so far. The tingling and need I felt below could wait.

Now I was faced with telling her how I felt while not in the throes of passion, even though, for me, it was hard to separate the rush of feeling from my raw desire for her. I moaned with delight after I let the first bite of creamy cheesecake slide into my mouth. The partly tart, semi-sweet strawberry sauce added the perfect balance to the richness of the dessert.

I pushed the plate away, declaring I was almost too full to move. "I'm not moving from this chair. I'll just live here from now on," I joked.

"I think you're teasing. Since I love you, I want to make love tonight. Do you think after maybe an hour, your food will have digested enough for me to take you to my bedroom?"

I chuckled. "God, I love you. Your directness is so utterly charming. I can never resist you." And there it was, just like that, I'd said it. I needed her to know it wasn't merely an offhanded expression. I did love her. I was in love with her. I grabbed her hands and pulled her along the path of rose petals to her bedroom. "You're not going to want to clean all those petals off the bed right this second, are you?"

"We can't get into the bed with the petals."

I swiped at the delicate petals, and they floated to the floor. "Done, they can join their sisters and brothers lazing about on the floor." I sat at the end of the bed and pulled her next to me. "How about we get undressed and take things slow? I'm sure by the time we hit our stride and get to the main event, my meal will have digested enough to not feel like a beached whale."

"Beached whales are usually due to sickness or injury, but the cause can also be old age, bad navigation, hunting too close to shore or storms. Toothed whales are the most common to find beached."

"Are we going to talk about beached whales or get naked?" I teased.

"Definitely get naked," she answered.

Neither one of us moved as we sat at the end of the bed. I still held Zari's hand, and her thigh was touching mine. I stood, then pulled her to her feet and turned her so I could wrap my arms firmly around her for an embrace that would get us started. The kiss started slow and built quickly to where I was desperate to remove her clothes. I stepped back enough to ask, "Can I undress you first and then you can help me out of this dress. I almost had to develop contortionist skills to pull the zipper up."

"Okay."

Starting with her adorable bow tie, I removed each piece of clothing. She let me unwrap her like a birthday present I was eager to reveal. She surprised me when she moved her hands behind my back and found the zipper. Then she kissed my neck, and my pulse raced. Why would I think that just because this was all new to Zari, she wouldn't be able to drive me crazy or find the right spots to ignite my arousal?

The matching royal blue panties and bra didn't seem to fit with the tux but undeniably showed off her nearly perfect body. Zari was on the slim end of the continuum, but definitely had curves. I moved my hand around to her back to release her breasts, and she followed my lead by unclasping the front of the lacy black bra I chose for the evening. I didn't have perfect matching underwear, but at least they were black.

We stood facing one another in our underwear, having helped each other to remove the rest of our clothes. We'd both taken the extra time to fold our clothes neatly and then place them on the dresser. The unhurried pace was just right for me. I wasn't too self-conscious about my body, even though I wasn't kidding about how full I was, and my protruding belly was proof. I grinned before pushing Zari on the bed. She smiled in return. The more I got to know Zari, the more she would share her unfiltered self, which included laughing or giggling at the strangest moments. That sounds so odd because most people would consider Zari unfiltered all the time, but she wasn't. She was methodical and precise.

"Go right ahead and laugh at my Buddha belly. If you had one, I would laugh at you. Besides, I want to hear you laugh. I love it when you bust out in laughter. It's contagious."

"When I was younger, that would get me in trouble sometimes." She turned her body, put her hand on my belly, laughed, and said, "I like your little round belly."

Looping my finger into the edge of her panties, I announced, "These have to go. They are in the way of our ultimate goal. Complete nakedness."

She giggled and said, "Yours are in the way, too."

I hastened to remove my panties, then helped Zari take hers off. I flung both on the floor, and at last, we faced each other completely naked. She started giggling again. "Our underwear is keeping the rose petals company."

"Zari," I exclaimed. "You just made an intentional joke."

She grinned and moved her hand over my hips and then back to my breasts. She moved closer and began kissing my neck again.

"Mmm…good place to start. My neck is absolutely an erogenous zone," I said.

"I could tell," she responded as she moved down to kiss and lick my breasts before taking one of my nipples in her mouth.

I moaned. "You found another place."

"I like the way you smell."

I squirmed, and my hips had a mind of their own as they lifted to the ceiling, seeking her touch. At the same time, she lavished attention on my breasts, and her hands stroked me with precision. I reached out, desperately seeking the softness of her skin. I could tell she was affected by either my arousal or how my hand firmly traced patterns on her body. Her hips moved in almost the same rhythm as my own.

"God, Zari, who knew you would be so good at this?"

"Can I touch your clitoris now?"

"Yes, please."

I tried to reposition myself, so I could touch her at the same time. She sensed where I wanted to go and obliged me by opening her legs a little wider. I found her center already wet and inviting, and it was almost enough to send me soaring. I knew I wouldn't last long this first time with Zari. When she found my clit and began long strokes, the sensation built quickly. Her hips kept moving, and I took a chance by dipping one finger inside. She seemed to want more, so I added a second.

"Is this okay?" I asked.

"Oh, yes," she answered in a breathiness I'd never heard from her.

Before I could instruct her to go inside, she found my opening and curled her fingers, hitting the exact spot I needed her to stimulate.

"I'm close, Zari, so close. Do you think you can come with me?" I asked.

"Oh…oh…yes, I think I am having an orgasm right now," she declared.

That was all it took for me to fall over the edge. The pulsing against my fingers felt divine as I continued to push in and out while having that perfect feeling of fullness against Zari's finger.

As we lay together wrapped in each other's arms, Zari whispered. "That was one position. We have ninety-nine more to try. How many do you think we should try tonight?"

I burst out laughing. "I think maybe I need a few minutes, and perhaps I can show you one of my favorites."

"Okay." She giggled.

†

When I woke the next morning in Zari's bed, a smile appeared on my face as I stretched my arms above my head. I'd discovered that no matter what challenges we might have, because all couples have difficulties, sex would not be one of them. Satisfaction permeated every corner of my body.

I turned my attention to my sleeping partner, who had her fist curled under her chin, with her beautiful strawberry blonde hair feathered across her pillow as she lay on her side. Overwhelming feelings of love and desire bubbled to the surface, and I was unable to contain them. When her deep blue eyes flickered open, I blurted out, "I'm in love with you."

"I was hoping for that. Even though I know couples have sex without loving each other. I think it's better if you're in love."

"Oh, it is. It definitely is. You know, you're as good a teacher as I am. Maybe instead of various sex positions, you could be persuaded to teach me how to bake?" I chuckled.

"Okay. What do you want to learn to bake?"

I grinned. "Cinnamon rolls?"

"They're easy."

"Says the woman who could be a master baker in addition to a famous artist." And then I remembered Saturdays were her short sculpture days. "Oh, I'm so sorry, you probably have a sculpture to work on today."

"I do, but until last night, I couldn't work out the details. I tried to envision how your face would look."

I covered my face with my hand. "Not another statue of me." I groaned. "I am not one of your more interesting models."

"It's a sculpture of us," she responded.

That piqued my interest. "Can I please see it?"

"I don't like to reveal unfinished works. This one has been hard to finish. I needed to get it just right."

"I understand. But will you let me see it before you unveil it for the rest of the world?"

"It won't be for sale. It's for our new house when we move in together. Two-thirds of couples choose to live together before marriage. Lesbian couples move in more quickly than other couples."

I chuckled. "Well, since we live right next to each other, I don't think there is a need to rush the whole moving in together trope. Has Jillian told you the joke about what a lesbian brings to a first date?"

"Yes, a U-Haul. I can't even drive yet, so you'll have to be the one to bring the U-Haul."

"Was that another joke, Zari? I'm impressed."

Her only response, a wide smile.

"We can talk about serious subjects like moving in together and a timeline for that, but right now, I'm starving. Let's get back to the cinnamon rolls, please."

"When will I meet your family now that we are a proper couple?"

I sighed. "I was hoping to spare you for a little while longer. I didn't want to scare you away. I love my dad, but he can be less receptive to certain notions than your parents. We argue because I don't see my sister in the same way as he does. He doesn't view Penny as a fully functioning adult, and he would go apoplectic if she brought home a girlfriend or boyfriend."

"Why?"

"Overprotectiveness on steroids and perhaps a less enlightened view on so many things. I try to touch base with Penny at least once a week to encourage her to break free from his tight control." I sighed. "I haven't been very successful yet. But you know what? If anyone can alter his views, you're the person for the job. He'll be impressed to meet you, considering he has one of your pieces. Mom will make him behave. She is a force to be reckoned with. She'll think you're lovely. Any progress Penny has had toward independence is because of my mother's efforts to wear Dad down."

"Will you squeeze my hand if I start citing random facts? Then I'll know to stop talking."

"Nope. Never feel like you have to change a thing about yourself to impress others. I love who you are."

"I love who you are, too. No matter how upset you are, you never raise your voice. I've never met anyone else like that. Even Jillian can get loud if she's angry. Sometimes my mom and dad yell at each other, too. I think that is the most special thing about you."

I melted right there in her bed and kissed her. It was only a peck because I wasn't sure I should start anything and continue down the list of Kama Sutra sex positions.

"Jillian advised me to brush my teeth before we kissed in the morning after sex because neither of us would have pleasant breath, but it wasn't as bad as she made it seem."

"No, not bad at all. I'm okay with kissing before brushing if you are."

"I shower first before I brush my teeth, so that would be a long time not to kiss in the morning. I'd rather not wait." She pulled me close again, and this time it wasn't a quick peck.

†

We went along happily for the next couple of weeks. It was an odd sort of domesticity, but that worked for us, and if I was honest, it had been established long before we slept together. However, now we had the benefit of incredible physical intimacy. The fact that Zari always had been an open book, no pretense, added a new level of emotional intimacy and connection that I had never enjoyed in past relationships. In short, I was in bliss and so in love sometimes it scared me. Even though I was clamoring to see her new sculpture, she wouldn't show me until she finished. I was surprised she didn't bring up meeting my parents again. When my mom called after running into Sam, I knew it wasn't fair to keep her out of the loop. She hadn't exactly cozied to Sam, questioning my choice for someone to settle with.

I was putting the finishing touches on the pond by adding plants and fish when I felt the buzz in my pocket. Instead of looking to see who was calling, I simply answered after the third buzz.

"Hello."

"Frankie, why didn't you tell us that you and Sam split? I knew you were having issues when you accepted your father's urge to move out of that crappy neighborhood, and Sam didn't move with you. But you told us you were still together. Now I have to hear from Sam that you are seeing someone new. I never liked Sam, so her snide remark about this new woman did not hit its mark with me. But I do want to meet her. Your father does as well."

"He owns one of her sculptures. Maybe he already met her at the gallery." I'd never asked Zari if she ever went to any of her shows where her art was sold, or if she always remained in the background as that elusive, eccentric artist who never allows the world to see her face.

"Oh, so she must be a very talented artist if your father bought one of her sculptures. What's her name?"

"Zari Woods."

"Oh, yes, the piece you love. It's very nice. But no, your father never met her. Bring her for Sunday dinner." I knew my mom enough to decipher a directive from a suggestion.

"I'll check with her to make sure she's free. She probably is because that's an unscheduled day for her."

"Dinner will be ready by six, come a little early, please?"

I briefly entertained the idea of asking her to change to 5:30, which was our usual dinner time, but with Penny to consider in the equation, I figured Zari was more adaptable. It was only a thirty-minute difference.

"Okay, Mom, I'll call if we can't make it. Otherwise, you can expect us by no later than five."

I was lost in thought as I dug in the dirt, planting the perennials in the beds around the pond. I'd wanted to add a little color and had gone back to Growth Spurts to pick out flowering plants that would pop up every year without me having to buy new plants. I didn't hear Zari arrive before she startled me.

"It looks good. I was worried because you usually meet me in my garage."

I looked up at her. "Sorry, I got distracted and lost track of time, but the honeymoon is not over, I promise," I joked. "My mom called today. She wants us to come for dinner on Sunday. Are you okay with eating a little later than usual?"

"How much later?" she asked.

"Six?"

"That doesn't change dinner time too drastically. Yes, I would very much like to have dinner with your family."

"Why do I feel you're checking boxes on an invisible checklist intended to meet this ultimate goal that amazingly you haven't revealed yet?" I teased.

"Marriage proposals are supposed to be a surprise, but I shouldn't ask until we're at the right point in our relationship."

I coughed to hide my nervousness because the prospect of a proposal was both exhilarating and terrifying at the same time. "There's the Zari I know and love. Someone gave you the wrong data. Proposals should only be a surprise after a couple has thoroughly discussed their vision of marriage, and both people want to take the relationship to that stage without hesitation."

"You don't want to marry me?"

"That's not what I said. But I'd be disingenuous if I didn't say that considering marriage scares the shit out of me, especially before we've ever lived together."

"Okay." Zari lost her smile.

"How about we work through that checklist together? We need to add serious discussions about marriage and our potential future to that list."

Zari remained rigid and stood there, contemplating what I had shared with her. I brushed the dirt off my shorts and set down my hand spade to take her in my arms.

"Zari, I don't want you to misunderstand anything I've said. I have daydreamed about our future together. There are so many other variables, important issues we haven't talked about, such as kids or how we want to spend our golden years. You haven't ventured out much, and I love to travel. We still have so much to learn about each other. I don't want to waste a minute of the exciting phase we're in right now because we're rushing to the next step."

"That makes sense, as long as you still love me. Sometimes people fall out of love."

"Yeah, they do. But in my case, I just keep falling deeper and deeper every day I get to spend with you." I punctuated my declaration with a deep kiss.

Zari's smile returned. "Me too. I should live for today, rather than worry too much about tomorrow."

"Uh-huh. Well said. Besides, I need more time to up my game with you. So far, you've been the one doing most of the romancing. I think it's my turn to woo you."

"I've never had someone woo me. I think I would like that."

"It's something you deserve. As much as I'm nervous about taking you to meet my family, I want them to know how important you are to me."

"I'm looking forward to meeting your family. Will Penny be there?"

Despite calling Penny every week, I hadn't seen my sister since moving into my new house. The joy at the prospect of having time with her must have registered on my face. "Yes, and that part is something I'm very much looking forward to. My mom's great too. I love my father, but he can be opinionated and pushy sometimes, and that is challenging for me."

"If you're worried about me, don't be. As long as your father doesn't raise his voice, I'll be okay. He's not a bully, is he?"

"In some ways, yes. Neither he nor my mom ever took a shining to Sam. He was more obvious with his displeasure. My mom is subtle. I can always tell, but others can't. I'm sure my nervousness is more about how he always gets under my skin. Nothing is ever good enough for him. Where I lived. My chosen occupation. And usually who I date. You may end up being the exception."

"Should I research making a good impression on parents?"

"Why not? It can't hurt. Maybe they'll both appreciate the effort." I laughed.

CHAPTER TWENTY-SEVEN

ZARI

While Frankie drove to her parents' house, I asked her about the other suggestions in the article regarding making a good impression on your girlfriend's parents. One tip was to bring a gift. Since her father bought one of my sculptures, I asked for Frankie's opinion to pick out another one for their home. She said that was too much of a gift, and she was sure the article was referring to a smaller gift like flowers or wine. But I wanted it to be something personal. In the end, she selected the hummingbird sculpture that I'd had so much trouble refining. She thought they both would love it. It was one of my smaller works, and I was happy I'd finally finished this particular piece.

After we loaded the sculpture and pulled out of her driveway, I asked, "What do you think the article means when it says I should be affectionate with you? Does that mean kissing in front of them?"

That must have been the wrong interpretation because Frankie swerved the car as she looked at me and answered, "No, no kissing in front of them. Holding hands is okay."

"I'm glad I asked."

"You have no idea how glad I am that you asked," she answered.

I didn't have very many nice clothes, other than the tuxedo I bought, so when the article said to wear a button-down shirt and nice pair of pants, I asked Frankie to help me pick out something appropriate to wear to dinner. So I thought I had that covered. The other suggestions seemed easy to comply with. I was always polite, and I took note that Frankie called my mom Mrs. Woods at first until my mom asked her to be less formal. I would stick with Mr. and Mrs. Carlson, as the article said.

I decided I liked making jokes with Frankie, so I followed that question with one I already knew the answer to. "I'm supposed to tell them about my interests and hobbies, and also what we enjoy doing together. Should we tell them about us making our way through the one hundred different Kama Sutra lesbian sex positions?"

Frankie swerved again. "Are you trying to get us killed?" She saw the smile on my face. "Funny, Zari, you have to develop a devilish sense of humor, now?" She laughed, and I giggled with her.

"Sorry, but I like it when you laugh, and it's because I've done something on purpose."

Frankie's voice lowered in that tone I now recognized as her *serious* voice. "You know, when I laugh, it's never at your expense. I always find you charming and funny. It's just one of the many things I love about you."

I never tired of her telling me she loved me.

Frankie's shoulders seemed to tense the closer we came to the enormous house at the top of a vista. Her family's home had an ideal view of the cliffs overlooking the Columbia Gorge and rows of grapevines. There weren't any other houses in sight, and I wondered if all the land belonged to her parents.

"This is pretty, but I like the variety of plants and trees where we live. There isn't enough green here other than the grapevines," I stated.

"You may want to keep that opinion to yourself. My father always wanted to own a vineyard, so they moved here after Penny graduated high school. He still has a place close to Seattle where he conducts most of his business, but I think he prefers it out here."

"Is that why you drink wine?"

"Goodness, no. I still don't have the nose or palette to tell a great wine from something my father would deem mediocre."

"If your parents offer wine, will it be rude not to accept? I am supposed to be polite but not get drunk."

"If you don't want a glass of wine, you shouldn't feel obligated to accept one. I want you to be yourself, not a version of what that article says is the perfect girlfriend. Although, I still don't want you to discuss our sex life or kiss me in front of them." Frankie shot me a quick wink.

We made our way up the long, winding driveway that ended in front of a four-car garage. I saw more color around the perimeter of the house and wanted to scrutinize every flower, plant, and bush.

"There are unusual plants in the beds surrounding the house."

"That's my mother's handiwork. She appreciates color. I'm sure she'd love to take you on a tour of her gardens. You should see what she has planted out back."

Frankie put her car in park in front of the garage. She sucked in a sizeable amount of air before turning her body toward me. "Ready?"

I nodded and slipped off my seat belt. Frankie walked around the car and met me, taking my hand in hers. We walked along the path, and I resisted the urge to look more closely at the plants along the edge of the stone walkway.

"This stone would work well in your backyard if you wanted to create a stone patio and pathway to your pond."

"I'm sure it would, but the cost is not something remotely within my budget."

"I have plenty of money. I'm not sure where you want to live after we move in together, but if we choose your house, we should replace the wood deck."

"How about we talk about this later, like after we get home?"

"Okay." I liked how she said home as if it was our place, even though we weren't technically cohabitating. We had spent every night together since my romantic dinner.

We reached the ornate front door, and Frankie breathed deeply before knocking. An attractive woman who could have been Frankie's twin except she had a few extra lines around her eyes, smiled as she opened the door. A tall man with piercing blue eyes joined her. He wasn't smiling.

"Ah, the thrifty daughter has arrived to bless us with her presence. I wish I could call you the prodigal daughter, but I had to use your unfortunate circumstances with Sam to get my way and have you move to a safer neighborhood."

Frankie's jaw tightened, and I saw her grind her teeth. "I told you. I am going to find a way to pay you back. I don't want any strings attached to your gift. I don't want to join your firm because I'm never going to agree to law school."

I squeezed her hand, and I could feel her relax.

The woman, who I assumed was Frankie's mom, glanced at the tall man, and her eyes narrowed to small slits. He didn't say anything else. "You must be Zari. It's so nice to meet you. Come in, come in."

"It is very nice to meet you, Mr. and Mrs. Carlson. The gift I brought is still in the car. Frankie helped me select one of my sculptures that she thought would go well with the décor in your home. The article said I should bring a gift and address you formally. There were other suggestions, like talking about hobbies, but I think that is something that should wait until dinner."

Her mom chuckled. "Well, thank you. That was very thoughtful of you. Frankie mentioned you were a famous artist. Please, come in," she repeated.

"We can get the gift later. Dad, you have one of Zari's sculptures, so I imagine you will appreciate her gift."

Her father lifted an eyebrow. "You're Zari Woods?"

"Yes, Mr. Carlson."

He nodded. "At least my daughter had the sense to become involved with someone more refined than her last girlfriend. I never liked her."

We followed her parents into the enormous tiled entryway. Everything was so pristine. I appreciated that about her parents' house.

"Where's Penny?" Frankie asked.

"She's in the den watching something on the National Geographic channel about big cats. The show will be over in fifteen minutes," Mrs. Carlson answered.

"I'm going to say hello and introduce Zari."

"Come back to the sitting room, and we'll have cocktails before dinner," Mrs. Carlson suggested.

"If I have a cocktail, I can only have one with very little alcohol. I won't make a good impression if I drink too much. I don't drink alcohol too often, but I want to be polite and accept what you are offering," I said.

Her mother chuckled again, and then Frankie turned and added, "A mixed drink that's more on the sweet side would be great. No dry martinis for either of us."

Frankie tugged lightly on my arm, leading me to the set of stairs on the right side of a wide hallway off the central part of the house. As we made our way down the stairs to the den, I asked, "Why not a dry martini?"

"Because if you don't like most wines, you'll hate a dry martini. You would make that face again, and I don't think that would be part of the ten-step plan to impress my parents." Frankie smiled, and I knew she was teasing me.

When we reached the bottom of the stairs, Frankie went straight to the young woman sitting rigidly on the sofa watching a seventy-inch television. A pride of lions was chasing down a zebra. She squeezed her shoulder. "Hey, Penny. When your show is over, I want you to meet my friend."

Penny didn't turn around and said, "Lions are the strongest predator of all the big cats that live in the African Savanna."

"Cheetahs are the fastest animals on the planet. They can reach speeds of up to one hundred kilometers. That's as fast as

I've driven on the highway." I'd seen the same show and was eager to talk with Penny since I knew how much Frankie loved her sister. I thought making a good impression on Penny might be more important than her parents.

Penny turned her head and looked at me. "Yes, that's correct. Are you Zari?"

I nodded. "It's nice to meet you."

She turned around to focus again on the television. "Do you want to watch the show?" Penny asked.

"Okay. I've seen it before, but I can watch the end again." I sat on the far end of the couch, and Frankie squeezed between her sister and me.

Frankie whispered in my ear, "I'll join the 'rents and tell them you're watching the show with Penny, and you'll join us for drinks after the show ends."

"Rents?"

She chuckled and quietly added, "Parents. Sorry, that's slang. By the way, you should avoid using that term. I'm sure that would be considered rude and ruin your chances to make a good impression."

After Frankie left, probably to give a stern warning to her father to be kind to me, Penny and I took turns sharing facts about big cats with each other.

Even though I liked the strawberry daiquiri that Mrs. Carlson made for me, I stuck to just one, so I wouldn't become intoxicated. Frankie was right. I enjoyed this mixed drink.

Mr. Carlson seemed interested in my sculptures and the process for each piece after we brought in the gift. I was glad it was a big hit. Even Penny ran her hands over the sculpture and announced that she liked it.

"Your art has been a very lucrative business for you?" Mr. Carlson asked.

"Yes, I have plenty of money. Money isn't very important to me. My friend, Jillian, and my mom and dad often warn me about people taking advantage of my generosity. But I wonder why would I need to save it and let it sit in a bank versus spend it on people I love. I heard the top ten percent earn nine times as much as the bottom ninety percent. I think if everyone who has a lot of money holds onto it, that makes it harder to sustain a healthy economy because it puts too much pressure on everyone else."

"I see that you have bought into the flawed studies of inequity. Perhaps you should also read the Forbes article that points out those flaws and offers a different set of facts, such as the metric that the rate of extreme global poverty has decreased from ninety percent to ten percent over the last two hundred years." Mr. Carlson sat back in his chair and folded his hands in his lap.

"Thank you. I will look that article up when I get home tonight." I was always interested in learning new things.

"Can we table the political arguments, Dad? I'm getting indigestion," Frankie interjected.

I was confused because I didn't think I was arguing and hoped I hadn't made a poor impression with my statements on income incquities. Frankie squeezed my hand and smiled at me.

Mrs. Carlson seemed surprised that Frankie was teaching me to drive and wanted to know more about that and about how we spent our time together. When Frankie talked about my baking and cooking skills, I said, "You should come to dinner on Sunday. I could cook and bake for you."

Mrs. Carlson glanced at Mr. Carlson, who nodded slightly. "That would be lovely. What time?"

Frankie frowned, and I wondered why. I thought that maybe Penny had a hard time breaking a routine. "Six?" Even though our standard time to eat was 5:30, it hadn't been difficult for me to adjust the time by half an hour.

As we were leaving, I made sure to thank them for the lovely dinner. "It was very nice meeting you. Thank you for having us over for dinner. I really liked the meal."

"We don't get to see Frankie too often. It would be wonderful if you both could join us for Sunday dinner again." Mrs. Carlson hugged Frankie, then patted my arm. I wondered if she thought I wouldn't react well to a hug. I knew that some people on the spectrum did not enjoy hugs, and I wondered if Penny was like that. As long as the pressure was enough, hugs were okay for me.

Her father stood awkwardly in the entryway and added, "Yes, I'd like to hear what Zari thinks about the Forbes article."

"We'll see, Mom." Frankie grabbed my hand and brusquely walked to the car. She seemed in a hurry to leave.

CHAPTER TWENTY-EIGHT

FRANKIE

We'd made it through the family dinner relatively unscathed. Although my father got in a few digs at me, he seemed genuinely enthralled by Zari. I wasn't expecting that.

After making the turn on the highway as we headed home, I turned briefly to Zari to reassure her, in case she worried about the impression she had made on them. "I must say, I don't believe I've ever seen anyone melt my father's icy exterior, but you charmed him. I shouldn't have been surprised. After all, you charmed me within the first hour after you brought cookies."

"I think maybe bringing gifts is the key," Zari responded.

"So, what is next on that checklist of yours?" I joked.

"A serious discussion of what each of us envisions for a future together. You mentioned that as a precursor to moving in together. Should we each make a list of questions that we both need to answer? I thought about the things you wanted to discuss, like having children and traveling. It was hard to think about retirement or how I envision us when we are old and gray because that is so far off, but I've been trying. That's why I knew about the income inequity issue because it came up in my search on how to prepare for retirement. Did you know that sixty-four percent of Americans are not prepared for retirement, and forty-eight percent don't care?"

"That doesn't surprise me at all." And then I blurted out, "I want to have kids. Even if that makes it harder to prepare for retirement, I would want to pay for their college, and that is extremely expensive these days."

"Yes, in the last thirty years, the cost of college has increased 213 percent. But that wouldn't be a problem because I have a lot of money in my balanced portfolio. My accountant assured me I never have to worry about money. My interest earnings and dividends have been more than enough to live on. The money keeps growing because my needs are small. Plus, my sculptures keep selling. We could send our kids to college."

"You would want to have kids?" I asked, almost afraid of the answer. If Zari wasn't able to handle that challenge, because I knew it would be a challenge, I worried about our future.

"With you, yes. I know there will be hard things to overcome, and maybe we would have to explain how our family is a little different from a more traditional family, for more reasons than my autism. I think kids understand more than people give them credit for. Loving a baby that you birthed would be easy because they are a part of you. You could help me show them the kind of love I always felt from my parents.

That's the only thing I worry about. I had a hard time getting a girlfriend. I wouldn't want to mess up loving a child."

"I don't think you would, but you're right, there would be things we'd have to do to make it work. Children are loud and messy. Well, most children are. You probably weren't." I ventured a glance and smiled at Zari. I hadn't even addressed her comment about having enough money. I wondered just how rich Zari was.

"No, I wasn't loud or messy," she confirmed.

"Not that having this conversation isn't important, but I think it is better to have these kinds of discussions over dinner or during our dates. Do you understand this is not a one and done conversation? Zari, we are not going to check this off the list just yet, okay?"

"Okay. So, can we make a list of questions and determine how many discussions are necessary?" Zari asked.

"Yup. I believe that is a very manageable compromise."

"I can do my list tonight."

"I think I might need a little longer to develop my list. I don't want to rush this important stage."

"How much longer?"

"Can you give me a week? We can reveal our lists next Sunday at dinner."

"Did you want your parents and sister to weigh in on the answers?"

"Hell no." And then it dawned on me that my parents were supposed to join us for dinner on Sunday because Zari had extended the invitation that my mother eagerly accepted. "Shit, that's right. You invited my family for dinner, which, by the way, is one of those things we have to talk about. I'm not mad, but maybe in the future, we should talk about stuff like that before extending an invitation."

"Okay. Can you write the specific question related to what you mean by stuff like that?"

I chuckled. "Check. I will add relationships with the in-laws to my list."

"We can go over our lists on the following Monday," she suggested.

I feared Zari would want to rush things and push through all the questions in one sitting. "Since the list of questions is a guide for topics to discuss on our dates, how about we set another rule of not discussing more than two questions on each date?" Initially, I was going to suggest three, but then I remembered Zari hated odd numbers, and slowing everything down wasn't a bad thing.

"That is very efficient. I like that rule."

I grinned at her. "I thought you might."

"Perhaps we can share the full lists on Monday and then set a schedule. Then I could prepare for the discussion. Important topics require preparation for me. I have to think through the issue to answer honestly, like after I considered whether I saw myself having children."

I thought that if Zari and I did ever decide to marry, we might be the most prepared couple to take that big step due to our systematic approach to getting to know one another.

†

The schedule we agreed upon comprised of two questions a week to discuss after dinners on Monday because Sundays had evolved to family night, which had not affected our ability to have an adventure earlier in the day. Upping my game meant planning elaborate adventures that I thought Zari would enjoy. Sometimes we would go to my parents' house, other times to her parents' house. Sundays, where we hosted the dinner, were my favorite because Zari would prepare a feast for everyone. In the beginning, it seemed as though my father had a hard time mingling with Zari's parents. The one thing they had in common was their experiences raising a daughter on the spectrum. That bond ended up loosening my father enough to have him consider perspectives previously foreign to him. Zari had a way of educating him that wasn't offensive, and as a result, my strained relationship with him lost its sharp edges.

Although Zari now had a car, she rarely used it, preferring to bike whenever possible. I started following her lead as the only way to keep from gaining too much weight. Before we would have our Sunday family dinners, we would use one of our vehicles to travel to whatever place I had picked out to visit. Leaving early in the morning was never a hardship for either of us because, in our first round of questions, we learned that both of us were early risers.

I was looking forward to the final two questions that we both decided to save until the very end. The area where I felt there was an imbalance was financial, even though I had never asked how much money Zari had in the bank. Although we hadn't argued yet, all couples, no matter who they were, had rough spots, and it was essential to talk about how to handle those when the eventuality of that came to pass.

As we sat on my couch with our pie, I started the Monday discussion.

"I feel a little uneasy asking you how much money you have. You have such a laissez-faire perspective on money, so I am assuming it's massive. And that brings me to my other discomfort—the obvious inequity between the two of us related to financial resources. How we handle finances is a big concern of mine. I don't like feeling unbalanced. I'm proud of being a teacher, but teachers don't generate a lot of income. I had a hard time accepting my father's gift of the massive down payment on the house. Because the down payment was so large, I can handle the mortgage payments. Barely, I might add." I sighed after finishing the mini-speech I'd agonized over.

"I read that money is the top reason that leads to a couple fighting. It sounded like that was because of not having enough, but maybe there was a lot more to it. I'm glad this was one of your questions so I could think about this. The recommendation was to work out a budget. The last time I looked, which was yesterday to prepare for this conversation, I had $11,657,450.62 in my long-term accounts. My financial advisor manages those funds. My accountant manages my house account, which has $106,945.26. I have immediate access to that money for groceries and day-to-day living expenses."

"Holy shit." I whistled. I felt a little sick to my stomach. I knew Zari was well off, but I hadn't imagined, not in a million years, how financially set she was.

"I thought that maybe the best way to do things is to have a joint household account proportional to our resources. We could have a monthly amount automatically deposited into that account. What do you think about that idea?"

I laid my head back on the couch. "I think I need a little time to process this new piece of information."

"I want to share everything with you, including my money. I hope we will get married someday, and at that point, I don't want us to have separate accounts. I don't like that idea. I don't like the idea of a prenuptial agreement, either."

I was curious about why Zari was opposed to an agreement that seemed right up her alley because of her need to have everything defined and scheduled. "Why?"

"I am already way too robotic in relationships. I wanted at least one aspect, granted a big one, to not be so dispassionate. Prenuptials are like a business arrangement. I don't like that."

I smiled because, in bed, Zari was very passionate. "Oh, I would say there is another aspect of our relationship that is plenty passionate."

"Thank you," she replied.

"This is important to you?"

She nodded.

"I suppose I need to get over my hang-ups. I've saved a measly five thousand and change. My annual salary is less than sixty thousand. Given the figures you just shared, my proportion to the household fund would be a pittance. How about I contribute what I currently spend each month?"

Zari's head nodded vigorously as she exclaimed, "Yes. Does that mean we can live together now?"

I smiled. "I think so, after we address the last question and open a joint household account. Although, we might have a hard time deciding which home we'll live in. I know it's selfish, but I enjoy hanging out in my new backyard. We put all that work into it, but I'm comfortable in your home, too. There's also Cleopatra to consider. She doesn't like it when we ignore her. Both houses have their special touches."

"I've been thinking about the last question and where we might live. I thought maybe we should both keep our houses and put a second set of clothes and grooming kits in each house.

Then we can stay in both houses based on who makes dinner. Will Cleopatra mind if we shuffle her between our houses?"

I chuckled. "Practical and efficient. I like it. Cleopatra won't care as long as she receives her nightly round of adoration. She's used to you now. What about Sundays when we go to the in-laws?" I grinned.

"My bed is more comfortable. We can stay at my house on Sunday. It makes sense because, on some Sundays, I cook."

"Deal. Now, what about the final question?"

"I had a lot of challenges with relationships when I was younger. It helped when I went to a therapist. Jillian and my parents were great at giving me advice, but they aren't professionals. I figure that if we have a rough spot, we could agree to couples counseling. I read that too many couples give up rather than work through the issues. I never want to give up. I'm not afraid of hard work. I love you and would have a tough time adjusting to a new girlfriend. You're nearly perfect."

I felt tears prick my eyes. Zari was incapable of lying, and the fact that she'd declared I was nearly perfect was about the best compliment she could have given me. Even more astounding was how she wanted to approach the inevitable challenges we would face. She would not bail the instant trouble hit, and that meant the world to me.

"Zari, you're not nearly perfect, you *are* perfect. At least perfect for me."

"Why are you crying? Did I say something wrong? Was telling you you're nearly perfect, instead of perfect, the wrong thing to say? Or do you think there is something wrong with seeing a counselor?"

"These are happy tears, Zari. Sorry, I know that's a little confusing to you. I'm over the moon about your answer to the final question because I know it takes hard work from both people in a relationship to make it endure the test of time. Sometimes getting help from a professional is exactly the right choice. That might not be needed, but I'm glad you're willing. I love you, too. This will be the easiest transition to taking that next step that I believe is humanly possible. No need for a U-Haul. Whew." I mock wiped my brow.

I knew Zari needed a specific timeframe for marriage, but that was one thing I didn't believe should be scheduled. I wanted romance. I wanted a proposal to be more organic and less planned.

CHAPTER TWENTY-NINE

ZARI

When I met Frankie, I was searching for a girlfriend. That had been very elusive for me, and I had wondered if I'd ever find someone who could deal with my autism. I'm happy it didn't take me twenty or thirty years. We've been living together for a year now, and all the research I've done leads me to believe that I should ask Frankie to take the next step.

When we first decided to live together after answering the forty questions, I brought up marriage. I tried to get Frankie to give me a timeframe, but she wouldn't answer me. On the first Monday of each month, I would ask her about marriage. One time I asked about the tradition of getting permission from her father. She made it clear she wasn't a prize heifer, and I better not even think about going to her father to ask him for his permission to propose to her. She kept saying we should see how living together worked before we talked about marriage.

I should have added the question, *How much time should a couple live together before getting engaged*, to the original list, but then that would have resulted in an odd number of questions. I don't like odd numbers. Forty was perfect because it was a multiple of four, my favorite number.

On Wednesday, I asked Jillian if she knew why Frankie was reluctant to give me a time frame on our next step, and she said that Frankie had confided to her about what she envisioned for a proposal. It was the one thing she didn't want to be scheduled, even though she told Jillian she was madly in love with me and didn't see that changing. Jillian said that for once, I should plan an unscheduled night because Frankie needed it to be a surprise. So, I asked Jillian and Patty to go ring shopping with me because they both have spent enough time around Frankie to know what she might like.

On my own, I thought of recreating the night I served Chateaubriand and wore my tux. She seemed to like how I'd planned that romantic evening. I needed to make a few small changes because we lived together, and she would arrive home from work earlier than 5:30. I knew she would want to change her work clothes since I would already have on my tux. I drew up a bath for her and put rose petals on the floor leading to the tub. Frankie liked taking baths.

When she walked in the door, she called out to me, "Zari, what is that wonderful smell?"

I greeted her, and her eyes widened. "Wow, did I forget a special date or something? You look amazing. I haven't seen your tux since…" Her blush was lovely.

"The rose petals lead to the bath because dinner won't be ready for another hour. I thought maybe you'd want to take a bath and change into a nice dress."

"I think the dress I wore that night is at my house. Give me a few minutes to run over and retrieve it."

"I already brought it over. It's on the bed."

She pulled me into her arms and kissed me. "You spoil me. I love it. Almost as much as I love you."

†

Frankie appeared in the kitchen ten minutes before dinner. I loved it when Frankie dressed up.

"Thank you for being on time. You look so beautiful."

The smile on Frankie's face blossomed, and I could tell she was happy. She remembered that first romantic dinner when I set the Chateaubriand on the table.

"Oh, my goodness, will this be a repeat of that night?" Her last three words almost came out in a whisper.

"No, I have a different question than if you want to make love."

She quirked her eyebrow. "Okay, what's your question?"

"We have to wait until dessert."

She chuckled. "I suppose you have everything planned."

"Yes, but not scheduled. I didn't put this in my calendar because Jillian said I shouldn't do that. It has to be a surprise."

"Surprises aren't exactly your speed. Now I'm extremely intrigued."

"After dinner," I replied firmly.

Frankie groaned after her last bite and said, "I'm too full to move. We're going to have to redo our living arrangements. I've decided to live right here from now on."

Just like on that first night I made a special meal, I knew she was joking. "You can't be too full. I made cheesecake again."

"Okay, I think I can make room for one or two or ten bites." She grinned.

I dished up the cheesecake and put the diamond ring on her plate. When I placed the dessert in front of her, her eyes widened. Then she slapped her hand over her mouth. Tears leaked from her eyes. I knew that sometimes she cried a little when she was happy and not sad, so I pushed forward with my plan.

I got down on one knee in front of her. "It's been one year since we moved in together, even though we live in both houses, and that isn't quite like how other couples do it. According to my research, that's enough time to get engaged. So, Frankie, will you please marry me?"

She cupped my face and brought our lips together. "I thought you'd never ask." She laughed and then said, "Yes, I would love to. Go get your calendar because a wedding date is definitely something we need to schedule."

"Okay. Just for clarification, I don't need to ask if we're having sex tonight, do I?"

"Definitely not, that is a given. I love you, Zari Woods."

"I know. Because you wouldn't have agreed to marry me if you didn't, and, if I didn't love you, I wouldn't have asked. I already have a wedding gift for you. It took me an entire year to finish my sculpture. It's a marble sculpture of us making love. I finished the clay model right after the first time we made love."

"Is that why you haven't allowed me in your studio?" she asked.

I nodded. "Sorry, I know that when we decided to live together, I should have allowed you free access to every part of this house, but I knew I wanted to wait until we got engaged."

I grabbed Frankie's hand and led her to my studio. When I removed the cloth covering the sculpture, she gasped.

"Oh, Zari, you've captured the emotion of love amid passion so perfectly. I'm almost sad that no one will ever see this amazing work of yours. This sculpture is for our eyes only, right?"

"Yes, it's titled, *Sculpting Her Heart*. When I described this to Jillian, she thought that was a great name."

"It is." Frankie ran her hand over the smooth marble, and when I saw the tears at the corners of her eyes, I knew for sure they were more happy tears without having to ask her.

"Should we go looking for a new house now? I don't think that people live in two houses after they get married, and we'll need to find a place to put this sculpture where others won't see it."

"I suppose that is the next thing on your list. Do I need to give you a timeline for that?"

"Yes, please, and also one for when we'll have kids."

Frankie groaned. "We are not going to schedule kids. Unless we adopt, it doesn't work like that. The best you can hope for is a date to make an appointment with a fertility specialist. And before you ask, not before we've been married for at least two years, but not greater than five years because I don't want my eggs to shrivel up and die, or whatever they do when a woman gets older."

"Okay. I can work with ranges."

Frankie pulled me into an embrace. "God, I love you."

"I'm glad you moved next door. I only wanted a girlfriend, and now I'll have a wife."

"Yes, you will."

ABOUT ANNETTE MORI

Annette is an award-winning author, published by Affinity Rainbow Publications, who lives in the beautiful Pacific Northwest with her wife and their five furry kids. With twenty-two published novels, three Lesfic Bard Awards, and one Goldie Award for her fourth novel, *Locked Inside*, she finally feels like a real author. Annette is as much a reader as a writer and is always looking for the next lesfic novel to queue up. She came up with the *One Fan at a Time* tagline, because it rolled off the tongue much better than One Reader at a Time. After pondering who she was at her core, she feels it was all about connecting to each reader on a personal level. Annette would be the first to admit she doesn't do well with the masses. If someone picks up her book and it touches them, she believes she has achieved what she wants with her writing by reaching each reader. It is who she is at her core. Drop her a line, she loves to hear from readers.

Email: annettemori0859@gmail.com.
Sign up for her mailing list: http://eepurl.com/cS7nr9

Check out her blog: Everyday Occurrences: https://annettemori0859.wordpress.com/
Visit the Affinity Rainbow Publications website for her books and many other outstanding authors: www.affinityrainbowpublications.com

OTHER AFFINITY BOOKS

Soul on Fire by Ali Spooner
A perfect summer ends with danger on the Appalachian Trail for Whit, Mitch and Brad. Once safely home, the relationship between Eli and Whit continues to strengthen as the boys return home and they grow as a couple. Eli falls deeper in love with Whit and North Carolina as the trees come alive with autumn color. The first Christmas at Cast Iron Farm is celebrated with Eli's family as a new chapter in all of their lives begins.

The Boss's Daughter by Samantha Hicks
Vivian Westfall, CFO of *Bridger Holdings*, meets her boss's estranged daughter, Lauren, when a disturbance at the company spring party piques her interest. Lauren is clearly drunk and making a fool of herself. To prevent embarrassment, Vivian forces Lauren away from the party. They have angry words, and

things take an unexpected turn when Lauren kisses her. Months later Lauren pitches a proposal to her father to loan her the funds to start her own health club. Her father reluctantly agrees with a caveat; Vivian must go with her to Scotland to keep an eye on the money. It doesn't take long for the sparks to fly in all emotional directions. When Gregory Bridger finds out about their relationship, he does everything in his power to break them apart. Trust is at the heart of this love story, a fragile emotion that without it, things can and do fall apart.

The Ghost of East Texas by Ali Spooner
Agent Blair Cooper and her partner, psychic Tally Rainwater (Terminal Event), are back in a gripping new murder mystery investigation. When the serial killer Casper Caruso, known as The Ghost of East Texas, was sent to death row, Agent Blair Cooper was adamant that there were more victims of his killing spree. As his execution day approaches, Casper reaches out to Blair. If she agrees to a face-to-face meeting, he will give the whereabouts of 10 additional bodies left in his wake. Blair and Tally must piece together the clues to bring closure for some of the victim's families. However, when you bargain with the devil, there is always a price to be paid.

Terminal Event by Ali Spooner
Tally Rainwater was born with the gift of second sight, something she never understood. A near-fatal accident, at age twelve, makes her visions clearer, but not the reason for them. As she matures, Lisa, a spirit, enters her visions to guide her in using her gift, but still not the reason why. Can Tally and Blair's budding romance survive the possibility? Read this intense murder mystery romance and find out.

The Star Child by Ali Spooner

Eli and Whit are enjoying their life together on the mountain when Whit is called into action for a secret mission at the Pentagon. While she is gone, the Cast Iron Farm comes to life, literally, when Eli discovers a mysterious cave that has a connection to Whit's past. Younger brother Brad joins the gang. When Whit returns, she plans an Appalachian Trail adventure with Brad and Mitch. Join Eli and family as their adventure at Cast Iron Farm continues.

My Dear Vet by JM Dragon

Ava Lawrence, a research veterinarian, is thrown in the deep end when her uncle asks her to cover his country practice while he has a vacation of a lifetime. How could she refuse? His team shouldn't be any different than the crew at her parents' practice, oh, was she so wrong. What she now has to work with is a sassy nurse, an obnoxious receptionist, and an animal whisperer, or so it seems. Ava finds herself embroiled in taking care of animals in the area and local issues outside her experience, making her question her sanity. Throw in chickens, cats, dogs, and a donkey named Theo, along with various other animals. This turns out to be Ava's unexpected adventure with far reaching romantic benefits.

One Shot at Love by Annette Mori

Blair returns to her hometown after the death of her sister. Always an activist, she vows to use her voice to advocate for better gun control. She meets Maribel, an irresistible, sexy woman who proves to be an enigma to Blair. Maribel can't help approaching the weeping woman and learning the origin of

Blair's grief, Maribel thinks she is the last person who should form a friendship with Blair. Ultimately, the allure is too much for Maribel, but how long can she keep her secret and continue to nurture their burgeoning feelings for one another. A committed left-wing social activist could never fall for the poster child of the NRA. Unless taking that one shot at love matters more than anything else.

The Mountain Whispers by Ali Spooner
Arriving home and discovering the betrayal by her best friend and lover, Eli Fortner leaves to run off her anger and hurt. A chance stop at a convenience store and the purchase of lottery tickets sends Eli's life into a whirlwind of change. Able to now pursue her dreams, Eli heads off to see what else fate has in store for her.

Whit Brewer, Eli's neighbor, is everything Eli never knew she needed and wanted. But can she let go of the betrayal long enough to let Whit in? Thirteen black cats, a baby goat, and Cruz, her furry best friend, join Eli on her adventure, new life, and the possibility of real love.

Charlie by Erin O'Reilly
At fourteen, Hannah Garvin met 'the one,' Charlene Gaines, and her life was never the same. They were inseparable and spent every moment they could together. One day, Charlie left without a word and again, Hannah's life took a dramatic change. Hannah vowed to never fall in love again. When she meets Mick, a new arrival to the small Texas panhandle town near her family's farm, her heart remembers what being in love was like, and yearns for more. Will Hannah let the memory of

Charlie go so she can start a new life with Mick? Or will her heart betray her and hold on to her love for Charlie?

Misha's Promise by Renee MacKenzie
Misha Wyatt has settled into a peaceful existence as a healer in Karst, New America. When an airplane crashes in the meadow outside of Karst, Misha hurries to help the pilot. Misha is not expecting the pilot to be alive…or so beautiful. Will her uncontrollable desire to keep the pilot safe be her downfall? Can *they* survive their journey? The last book in the Karst series brings our characters to their physical and emotional limits. Don't miss the culmination of this exciting series!

Heart Strings Attached by Ali Spooner & Annette Mori
Socialite Remy has her world shaken. Bartender Chancy has her orderly life turned around. A mutually beneficial business agreement between Remy and Chancy turns into undeniable attraction. Will the two ignore culture norms to explore their intense desire for each other?

The Panty Thief by Annette Mori
Someone is stealing panties, but who? And why? Joey Hartford is a fourth-year medical student who insists she doesn't have time for a relationship. A new tenant in her apartment building is proving too tempting to ignore. Sabrina is in her final year of her doctoral program and focused on completing her dissertation. Meeting Joey is dangerous for so many reasons. Add a suicidal ex-girlfriend who suddenly reappears in Sabrina's life and Joey's jealous friend-with-benefits, and things get complicated quickly.

Country Living **by Jen Silver**
Peri Sanderson achieves her dream of moving from London to a cottage in the English countryside with her wife, Karla. Peri sees their future as pastoral while chatting with the locals in a quaint village pub. Sexy urbanite, Karla, has other ideas. Secrets are everywhere. Peri quickly senses something not quite right among her rural neighbours and also with Karla. Temptation, betrayal, and intrigue combine to change the lives of both women beyond anything they could have imagined.

Before the Light **by Samantha Hicks**
One year after her long-time partner Meredith's abduction and their subsequent break-up, Kathleen Bowden-Scott's life is spiralling out of control. She meets Bethany Jones and despite an instant attraction Kathleen shies away. In this fast-paced, romantic suspense, lies are exposed and hearts unite as Kathleen and Beth fight for their future.

Wanted for Christmas **by JM Dragon**
Belle Farrow knew what she wanted for Christmas–work. She had little to offer but a minor degree in cookery and household management. Certainly not enough for a decent chef or housekeeper position. Then she saw an advert in the local newspaper. Wanted: Housekeeper/cook/nanny for the period of Christmas until the New Year. This is Christmas. Perhaps Santa reads the ad column too and pushes a little spirit of the season to that request.

Affinity
Rainbow Publications

eBooks, Print, Free eBooks

Visit our website for more publications available online.

www.affinityrainbowpublications.com

Published by Affinity Rainbow Publications
A Division of Affinity eBook Press NZ LTD
Canterbury, New Zealand

Registered Company 2517228

www.ingramcontent.com/pod-product-compliance
Lightning Source LLC
Chambersburg PA
CBHW051532260626
47170CB00003B/897